DAN

by

VALERIE SAXON

CHIMERA

Dangerous Inheritance published in 2006 by
Chimera Publishing Ltd
PO Box 152
Waterlooville
Hants
PO8 9FS

Printed and bound in Great Britain by
Cox & Wyman, Reading.

DANGEROUS INHERITANCE

Valerie Saxon

While Leah was thus engaged she felt her hands being taken and forced behind her back, and before she could do anything at this intrusion she heard the clanking of metal. Her heart sank with dread upon sight of the manacles in the hands of the judge's manservant, but he had no qualms as he snapped them onto her wrists, and she wondered how often he had done the judge's dirty work, he seemed so adept at his job.

'I see Jarvis is readying you for your discipline.'

Leah turned as the judge entered the antechamber, her lips ready to plead with him, to beg him to spare her, her limbs trembling with fear.

Chapter One

Leah Brown frowned into the cheval mirror in her bedchamber, touching her naked curves uneasily. Her pink-tipped breasts blushed and swelled in her hand. Her fingers swept over her creamy stomach and down to the pretty blonde nether-curls that hid her pulsing sex. A shiver ran through her as her awakened senses made her body course with feeling. Rose, the cook, said she had blossomed into a lovely young woman, but she was beginning to think there was something wrong with her. Wherever she went the male gender followed her with their eyes. Just the day before a handsome Cavalier had been castigated by his lady for staring at her.

Even her father, Dr Thaddeus Brown, was acting strangely and she was beginning to think that all men had taken leave of their senses. She was saying as much to her maid, Jane, a little later, as she helped her with her toilette.

'It defies explanation,' she vowed. 'Papa is acting so out of character.'

Leah's frown deepened and Jane giggled. 'If the wind changes you'll stay like that!'

Leah frowned into the hot water Jane had poured from the pitcher into the bowl on the nightstand. 'Do you think he's found me a suitor? After all, I am of age.'

'What makes you think such a thing?'

'He persists in trying to hide letters from me and he keeps giving me thoughtful looks.' Leah paid special attention to her toilette that morning, as if in doing so it would rid her of her bad imaginings.

'The doctor's tired,' Jane excused. 'He does far too much.'

Feeling slightly better Leah dried herself in a soft towel, and allowed her maid to dress her in a lace-trimmed chemise that she pulled carefully over her blonde head. This was followed by a green gown with a low round neck that was softened with more lace. The skirt was separated into panniers in order to show off the paler petticoats. Green silk stockings were rolled over her slim legs, fastened by lace garters at the knee. Jane helped her slip her feet into high-heeled, shiny shoes, which were pointed at the toe and squared off at the tip. Her blonde hair was brushed until it shone and the natural curls twirled deftly into ringlets.

'You don't realise how fortunate you are to have such good hair,' Jane remarked with a warm smile. 'Most ladies have to suffer agonies to gain a little kink. You have your mother's looks, there's no doubt about it. But beware, my love, there are those who will be jealous of such pure beauty and perhaps try to harm you.' She gave a resigned sigh. 'And of course there will be men who will try to take advantage of you. I will protect you as much as I can, but you must be aware of these dangers.'

Leah gave a wicked smile, thinking of their cook's version of such events. 'Rose often boasts about her assignations. She says her thighs are often sore from the attentions of her beau and that her breasts smart from the pressure of his fingers.'

Jane's mouth tightened into a disapproving line. 'Rose has flights of fancy. Do not listen to her meanderings.'

Leah suppressed a giggle; Jane had been taught manners by her own good mother – who had been the daughter of Lord Foxborough – and spoke like a lady. Jane and Rose often clashed over the girl's ripe language and bawdy stories, though Leah often listened to the tales of Rose's sensual liaisons with fascination. Just that morning she had gone into the kitchen to find Rose complaining about her sore rump.

'It's my latest love,' she'd explained with a wry smile. 'He likes to smack my arse before he spends his seed in my cunny. Turns him on, see. Says my arse wobbles like a junket and fare sets him up for the day. Mind you, I likes it too.'

6

Leah had felt extremely strange afterwards; wicked feelings encompassed her, and her secret place began throbbing interminably. She had been obliged to touch herself there; explore her sex, and pay special attention to the nub that lie in her cleft. When the intoxication of climax began she rubbed until the last wave of ecstasy washed over her and she was left with a wonderful sense of wellbeing.

Just yesterday Rose had taken great pride in describing a similar act in great detail. 'My Harry likes to tease my nubbin with his tongue,' she'd boasted. 'Makes me come over and over again, he does.'

The thought of a man with his head between her thighs made Leah blush and tingle all over. Of course, she never related any of this to Jane, who would have gone to her father and insisted that Rose be dismissed on the spot.

Jane glanced out of the window. 'The streets are filling up, we'll be late for market and all the best will be gone.'

'There will be aplenty left, do not fret,' Leah soothed, as Jane threaded a green ribbon through her curls.

They slipped tall iron patens over their shoes before they left, for it had been raining all night and they needed to lift their petticoats from the filthy gutters. Martin, the houseboy, took them most of the way in the cart, for he had errands to run for the doctor. But they needed to walk through the last of the narrow streets that would lead them to market. Dogs and children tumbled in and out of the rubbish, and people rushed by intent on going about their daily lives, many holding nosegays or pomanders to their noses to avoid breathing in the fetid smell.

An obese gentleman passed in a Sedan chair, his servants red-faced and straining to bear his weight; the man quite unaware of the trouble he was causing them. Jane and Leah suppressed their merriment as the gentleman urged the poor men on, and he glowered at them.

Leah trod carefully on her tall patens over the uneven cobbles, her blonde ringlets bobbing in unison, radiating like gold in the sunshine; thinking how different things were now that Oliver Cromwell, who had ruled in Whitehall Palace as Lord Protector, was dead.

Luckily his sour-faced son's rule was brief and Charles II had finally claimed his throne. Few mourned the passing of the strict regime of Parliamentarian rule. England had become a sombre place where women hid their charms beneath drab colours and gaiety was frowned upon. Now places of entertainment were reopened and style had returned with the Royalists from the brilliant Court of Louis XIV.

London seemed to ring with new life as Leah passed through its streets, breathing its heady excitement. Its music lulled her, wrapped her in its embrace as milkmaids, coalmen, tinkers and a dozen others hawked their goods. Shouts of 'cherry ripe' and 'fine strawberries' rose to meet the tiled roofs, smoking chimneys, and the spires of the many churches dominating the skyline.

She passed an alleyway and stopped dead in her tracks to see a whore plying her trade. She was cosying up to a well-dressed gentleman, showing him her massive breasts that flopped out of her dirt-spattered dress, the nipples large and pendulous. He grabbed them, breathing hoarsely, slavering over them as if they were the king's gold.

She obligingly hitched up her skirt. 'That's the way, me darling. Suck me titties. Sarah fair pines for yer cock, I does. Come in this here hay cart and we can do it for as long as yer like.'

The man shoved one hand between her legs, expelling his breath loudly. 'Phwoar, you're as hot as Hades!'

Leah knew she should pass by quickly, but the unexpected scene fascinated her. Although she had attended a few births with her father, and listened with great intent when the servants talked about such things, she was an innocent with a thirst for knowledge.

Sarah spread her ample girth on the hay, throwing up her skirts to reveal grimy legs as thick as tree trunks, and a bush as black as night. 'See how ready for yer I am,' she said,

8

pointing at her pink cleft, the lips of which were prominent enough to make Leah blush. 'Come on, me love, don't be shy.'

The man needed little persuading, the front of his breeches bulged and Leah's eyes widened. Fiddling with his clothes he shovelled out a cock as big as the coalman's horses and, climbing on the cart, slid between the meaty legs. Leah tried to smother her maidenly cries as he proceeded to ram it inside Sarah's cunny.

Sarah had no such qualms; from the moment he entered her she began shouting her delight until the alleyway echoed with the sound. The man grunted just as loudly, ramming his tool home, riding her as eagerly as any beast of the field, his breeches around his knees, his skinny bottom bobbing fiercely in his lust.

Leah's sex pulsed and her breasts pressed against the material of her gown. She wrapped her arms around her waist, wondering what it must feel like to have a man do such things to her. Sarah was definitely enjoying herself.

She jumped as the man began to make the most awful sound, and her jaw dropped as she wondered whether he was crying out in pain or ecstasy. Sarah was urging him on, crying out with him, and he seemed to finish in a great surge of energy that ended with him lying on top of her, panting.

Sarah patted him fondly. 'That's it, me beauty. Take yer rest, but don't be too long, there's more waiting for the same and there's no time to dawdle.'

Jane, who had been busy buying fish, hurried up behind Leah and she was obliged to turn away, laughter bubbling in her throat. Jane caught sight of the sated pair, and with a distressed cry took Leah's arm and hurried her away from the bawdy scene, praying the girl did not have her mother's sensual appetite, for Elizabeth had been a trial at times.

'What about visiting The Exchange on the morrow?' Jane asked loudly, trying to distract Leah's thoughts away from the unsavoury sights of the city. ''Tis time we did some serious shopping.'

9

But Leah was not listening; a stall of pretty falderals caught her eye, and forgetting the whore and her customer she paused to examine the wares. A sudden breeze lifted her curls, sent the contents of a tray of ribbons she was perusing flying skyward, streaming in gay profusion past wood framed buildings. Leah's green eyes shone with glee and she giggled as she, her servant Jane, and the distressed hawker, chased the brightly coloured streamers, tottering awkwardly on their tall patens.

Apprentices ceased their shouts of 'what do yer lack?' and joined in the chase, stopping traffic, causing chaos in the crowded thoroughfare. Shouts and curses joined the cries of the hawkers, drowning out descriptions of their assorted wares. A fine gentleman stepped from his coach, his fist swiping angrily at the air, incensed by the delay, only to be quietened by the contents of a slop pail thrown from a nearby window.

Leah giggled louder, and taking pity on the hawker purchased the ribbons she had rescued, and catching Jane by the hand slipped away from the confusion.

Dolly the flower seller was on her usual corner, and Leah dug deep into her purse, knowing the poor woman had no husband and a large family to support. She purchased a fine posy and was rewarded with a toothless smile.

'God bless yer, me dear.'

Leah and Jane walked on and Leah purchased some rosy-red apples, and just as she was placing the fruit in the basket a tow-haired youth pushed into her and everything tumbled from her fingers. She and Jane bent together to rescue the items, but another pair of hands beat them to it.

Leah watched the dark head and wide shoulders curiously, the strong brown fingers that dexterously plucked her possessions from the street. When the basket was full he stood up, dwarfing her. Dark eyes scanned her avidly, sensual lips parted to expose strong white teeth as he handed her the shopping. 'Thank you, sir,' she said shyly.

As Jane chased a recalcitrant apple he doffed his wide-brimmed hat, the bright plume fanning in the breeze. 'My pleasure, mistress. 'Tis not often one has the chance to help such a beauty as yourself.'

Feeling a blush rise to her cheeks beneath the constant perusal of those dark eyes, Leah dropped her head meekly. He slid a finger beneath her chin, and raising it stole a kiss.

'Fair exchange, I think,' he said with a broad grin, before bowing and striding away.

Gideon Tempest could not resist turning and staring over his shoulder in rapt admiration at the dainty, golden-haired wench who lent such beauty to the summer's day. He was captured by the oval sweetness of her face, the large green eyes, framed by sweeping dark lashes, despite the glorious light hair; the pretty red lips that would make a man kill for the promise of one lingering kiss.

His cock was swollen in his breeches and he knew he would be obliged to find a willing lass in a tavern to ease his discomfort. There was one pretty piece he had in mind in the *White Swan*; her mouth was like velvet and her purse tight enough to please any man.

So occupied was he with his thoughts a dray cart almost ambled into him, the drayman sleepily letting his horses take him on his usual route unhindered. Noticing the cart just in time Gideon cursed and swerved to avoid contact, and in his haste his feet slipped on the greasy cobbles and he fell headlong into the filthy street.

The drayman, now wide awake, brought his cart to a halt and hurried to assist Gideon, who had risen from the ground and was busy brushing dirt and cabbage leaves from his coat and breeches, righting the plume on his hat. He cast around for the vision, who had by now disappeared in the crushing throng of humanity, and in his frustration he took his wrath out on the unfortunate despoiler of his day.

Leah, quite unaware of the havoc she had left behind, walked on, her pulses racing, her eyes misty; her first proper

11

kiss, and he so handsome! She rearranged her skirts and patted her hair. 'Impudent rascal!'

Jane ran up to her holding up empty palms. 'I'm afraid the apple was run over by a cart.'

Leah smiled dreamily. 'Don't worry.' A god had just kissed her; the fate of an apple was no longer of interest.

They completed their final purchases and wound their way homeward. 'What a handsome man,' Jane murmured, still thinking about their encounter with the dark stranger. 'He's the kind I warned you about. On the surface he is charm itself, but beneath his codpiece his tool is stirred by your beauty. And a man heated with passion is a dangerous one.'

Leah laughed. 'Rubbish! He was kindness itself.' But she recalled his kiss and blushed; glad Jane had been occupied chasing the fruit.

'I saw the look in his eyes and you would do well to…' Jane was about to expand on the matter, but instead rolled her eyes in distaste and held her handkerchief to her face.

Leah chuckled and wrinkled her dainty nose; the prevailing wind was carrying the stench of the tanneries below the city walls, on the slopes between Ludgate and Newgate, towards them. She pushed her nose into her posy, thankful Jane had been silenced. But memories of the tall, personable young man kept intruding on her thoughts, so forcing the mental pictures away she glanced hastily in the watch-menders window. She would have to hurry; she wanted to make sure that Rose had everything ready for her father's lunch.

When they arrived home Rose was eager to relate her latest forebodings. She was a great one for prophecies. 'I had dreams about yer last night, mistress,' she told Leah importantly. 'You will have three suitors. Two will bring yer evil. The one with the smell of the sea about him is the only one to be trusted.' She smiled slyly. 'He is handsome, too.'

Jane gave her a look of disgust. 'Piffle!'

Rose was quite upset by the remark. 'No, 'tis the truth, you mark my words. It's in the blood, you see, me being the

seventh child of a seventh child. The dream was a warning.'
Pushing a hand inside her woollen frock she pulled out a
piece of string bearing a rabbit's foot. 'This here talisman
keeps me from evil. Would yer be wanting me to get you
one, mistress?'

Jane shook her head dismissively. 'Of course she doesn't,
you silly goose. Get on with the cooking.'

Ignoring Jane, Rose bobbed a curtsy at Leah.
'Everything's in hand. 'Twill be ready when the doctor
returns.'

'Thank you, Rose.' Leah nodded her appreciation. 'Papa
will have a fine hunger on him when he gets home.'

Leaving Jane to put the shopping away she started for her
bedchamber in order to tidy herself, wondering about Rose's
dream. Her foot was on the first stair when the front door
knocked, and knowing that Jane was busy and the houseboy
Martin was on an errand, she hurried to answer it.

Percy Darlington, one of her father's patients and a
regular visitor of late, stood sparkling on the doorstep. It was
the first description that came to mind, and on second sight
she decided it was apt. The sun bounced off his blonde wig
so that he appeared to be wearing a halo, and illuminated his
bright blue silk coat and breeches. His gold buttons dazzled
her and she blinked rapidly and shifted her gaze to the fine
coach and six behind him.

The bays snorted impatiently, stomping their hooves on
the cobblestones and tossing their manes proudly. Although
she was quite unaware of the fact, the carriage was the last
of the finery left to the Darlington's, thanks to the excesses
of his father, Sir Barnaby. Leah glanced uncertainly at the
young lord, her eyebrows raised questioningly.

'May I come in?'

She tried to think of an excuse to refuse his entry; he had
been paying far too much attention to her and his advances
were not welcome. But knowing it would be bad manners to
leave him on the doorstep she stood aside reluctantly,
hoping it would not be a long visit, for the foppish Percy

irked her. He shut the door, a triumphant smirk on his face, and they were squashed in the small dark passageway. Leah tried to sidestep her way into the sitting room, but Percy pressed against her eagerly.

'Excuse me,' she said stiffly. 'It seems we are a little pushed for space.' But her words made little headway, for Percy suddenly pressed his mouth on hers. It was hot and dry and she panicked, pushing against him with all her strength.

'Don't be coy, give us a kiss,' he urged, his buttons cutting into her flesh, his hands sneaking around her waist and roughly dragging her to him.

'Sir,' she began, aghast at his temerity. 'Take your hands off me at once! I don't know what you're thinking.'

'Come, wench, be nice to me.' His breath was sour with ale and his voice was urgent. He blew the curls away from her neck and kissed the fair flesh.

She tried again to push him away, noting that although the dandy had paid attention to every minute detail of his dress, his nostrils were devilishly hairy, and nervous tension made her want to giggle. 'Please, Percy,' she said more firmly. 'Be sensible and unhand me.'

'Please, Percy,' he mocked grimly. 'Damn you, woman. I could be in the *Jolly Pig* right now plunging between Annie Riggs's sweet thighs, but I chose to come to you. So open your legs for me, sweeting,' he demanded, trying to prise her thighs apart.

She blanched. 'I think you'd better leave!' Her green eyes blazed as she pulled back from his touch. 'And don't come back till you're sober!'

'I must have you,' he intoned more urgently, his voice hoarse.

'I insist this stops right now!' Leah gasped fearfully.

'Not possible,' he crowed. 'Feel this.' Taking her hand he squeezed it against the front of his breeches, and she gave a small scream at the hardness of him.

'How dare you?' she squealed, but she was wasting her

breath for his sap was up. She struggled against him as he held her wrists, cringing as he squeezed her breasts through her gown, his knee inferring itself between her legs.

His lips were on her throat, and the more she struggled the rougher he became. His breathing was hot and heavy and his hands roamed lower, as he took his cock from his breeches and placed it in one of her now freed hands. Her cries were muffled in his questing mouth, and before she could stop him he spurted his seed into her hand, leaning heavily against her.

Distressed and angry she pushed him away, swiping at the mess on her gown in disgust. 'Get out of here!' she cried, tears of shame pooling in her eyes.

Percy leered down at her. 'You'll get used to it. I intend servicing you regularly.'

'I'll tell my father,' she threatened. 'See how brave you are with a man.'

Her words seemed to sober him. He caught her wrist cruelly and she thought her bones would be crushed. 'Not a good idea,' he snarled. 'Do you think the fine ladies he tends would still allow Dr Brown near them when they learn his daughter is whore to half of his patients?'

A despairing sob escaped her. 'But I'm not,' she denied vehemently. 'You know I'm not.'

'Aye, but 'tis easy to put word about. And when the rumourmongers have their day your father will be ruined.' He grabbed her face cruelly between thumb and fingers. 'You're mine. The sooner you admit it the better.' He tucked his wilting cock away and tidied his person. 'I shall call for you on the morrow. We can visit Vauxhall with its pleasant music and cosy arbours. A good fuck will soon make you see what you've been missing. Until tomorrow, Mistress Brown.'

When the door was shut firmly behind him she fled up the stairs, and pouring some water from the jug washed her hands in the basin on the nightstand. She hated Percy Darlington with a vengeance, but she could not allow him to

15

shame her or her father in such a way. She had no option but to dance to his tune.

Tibbs the house cat scratched at the door, and still shaking from Percy's abuse she let him in. He brushed against her skirts, purring loudly, as she tried to unfasten the back of her gown without success, and in her distress and anger tore at it repeatedly until it gave and she threw it into a corner. No matter how well washed and repaired it was she would never wear it again. She didn't want to be reminded of the way he had forced her to hold his manhood, or the way he had spilled his seed in her hand as though she was a street whore.

Slipping a shawl over her chemise she sat heavily on the bed, her aching head resting on the soft pillows. Tibbs jumped up beside her and she smoothed his silky coat, burying her face in the sweet familiarity of his fur. His purring went some way to calming her, though she could not forget that she was to see Percy again. She didn't know how she'd be able to cool his ardour; she had little experience of these things.

Returning home from his rounds, Dr Thaddeus Brown eased himself into his favourite chair and rang for Martin to bring his customary glass of sack. He loosened his cravat and unbuttoned his coat before reaching into his bureau for a letter. His kindly face was thoughtful, his white brows set in a deep frown. His eyes roamed the shabby but cosy room with a deep sigh; if his rich patients spent less money on falderals, gambling and wine, they would be able to pay him his dues and he would be far more affluent than he was.

By the time Martin brought his refreshment and positioned the glass by his elbow he was deeply engrossed in the letter, his brown periwig slightly askew. He read and reread between long sips of wine, and then sighing deeply returned the pages to his bureau.

His thoughts winged back to the night two years before when he had met the writer of the letter, William Penrose, in

16

the ale house. His speech had been that of a gentleman, and as they conversed Thaddeus learned that he was in dire straits. The more they talked the more he had liked the man. He was the youngest son of a Cornish squire sent out into the world to make his fortune, and he was determined to prosper. He had spoken of the vistas opening up to him in the New World, and his spirit of adventure captured Thaddeus's imagination.

He had invited him back to his home, given him bed and board for a few weeks. William in turn had taken a fancy to Leah, and begged Thaddeus to keep him in mind as a suitor. He would make his fortune and send for her, he promised it on his oath. Thaddeus had smiled paternally, but he never expected to hear from him again. But William surprised him by corresponding as regularly as the distance and vagaries of the mail would allow. He had done everything promised and settled in the Caribbean on a luscious plantation in Barbados. The gods had blessed him a thousand fold, but he could not forget the lovely Leah and urged Thaddeus to send her to him to be his bride.

He absently lit his pipe. The sooner he sent her away the better. That young whelp Percy Darlington had been sniffing after her of late, and there was more to that than met the eye. What would Darlington want with a poor physician's daughter? The whole family was corrupt, but he knew nothing of Leah's inheritance, he would stake his life on it.

He grimaced at the memory of Percy's family changing sides in the war to suit their own purposes, flattering Cromwell to line their purses. But when the monarchy was restored they soon forgot their Parliamentarian leanings and began to fawn over the king. 'Aye,' he muttered, 'Percy Darlington's a layabout who spends his time in Shoe Lane throwing his money away on cockfights and whoring. He'd break her heart given half the chance.'

Thaddeus sighed, he didn't have much time; the pains in his chest were getting worse. He didn't mind, he was ready to join his Elizabeth, but first he would have to follow the

17

terms of Leah's grandfather's will and find her a husband. He called for Martin. 'Fetch Mistress Leah to me, lad.'

'Straightaway, doctor, sir.'

Leah took a deep breath when Martin tapped on her door and told her Dr Brown wanted to see her. She made her way quickly downstairs, a sweet smile lighting her face.

'Papa,' she said with surprise. 'I didn't hear you come in. You look tired. I'll see how Rose is doing in the kitchen.'

Her instinct was to flee from her father lest he somehow suspect she had been sullied by Percy. She hadn't been a willing party to the act, but she still felt guilty, felt she should have been able to put a stop to his urgent fumbling. Afterwards, in her bedchamber, she had surveyed her spoilt gown and her anger turned into longing, her insides surging with a strange desire. She didn't understand the workings of her body. How was it she ached to be fondled in her private place now, when she hated Percy Darlington's touch earlier?

With great wickedness she had imagined him rubbing his erect penis against her, imagined him inserting his leg between her thighs, following that with his hand. Her pulses quickened and the little nub Percy had touched with his knee throbbed in such an outrageous manner she was obliged to tend to it with her own finger. At the same time she was forced to stroke her nipples with her other hand, first one then the other.

There had been such a fever of need in her she barely knew the creature she'd become. Her finger flew so fast across her nubbin her wrist ached afterwards, but it brought her such delight, such relief it was worth it. Though she was still embarrassed by the images in her head she was also ashamed, for she knew her father would be appalled that his angel had had such wicked thoughts.

'Sit down, Leah,' Thaddeus replied quietly, pointing to the footstool beside him. 'I have something of import to discuss with you.'

She smiled despite the gravity of his words. 'What is it?

You seem preoccupied.'

Thaddeus filled his lungs. 'I will get straight to the point, daughter. It's time you were married and I have decided upon your husband.'

She gasped in amazement; she had been right all along. 'No, papa, I've no wish to marry.'

'My decision is irrevocable,' he said more firmly. 'You will recall William Penrose who went from us to make his fortune in the Caribbean?'

Leah nodded; her father had acquainted her with the news.

'He has asked for your hand and I've accepted.'

Her eyes widened in horror. 'No! How could you expect me to leave you – my home, everything I love to go to a stranger?'

'William is a good man who loves you. A strong man, who made his way in a strange land where others have failed.'

The blood drained from her face. She longed to tell him that William had taken every opportunity whilst there to seduce her, but she knew he would be appalled, or even wonder if she was making excuses so she wouldn't have to go to the ends of the earth to be married. Her lips pursed stubbornly.

Thaddeus viewed her impatiently. 'Has it ever occurred to you how difficult it's been bringing up a daughter with just the help of a servant?' Her chin trembled. 'But I've tried to do my duty by you.' He sighed. 'Now I am tired and ready to hand your welfare over to a husband. William will look after you well. I will be satisfied with no one else.'

Leah choked on a sob. 'How could I have been so blind? I am sorry, papa, I will do as you ask.'

His face was grim. 'I will begin the arrangements as soon as possible.' He sighed tiredly. 'There are other things to discuss but I am weary, we will talk again. Leave me now,' he said, hastily removing his eyes from the stricken girl, his voice gruff with emotion. 'I will rest.'

With a strangled sob Leah ran from the room, and

Thaddeus leaned back in his chair clutching his chest, his face gaunt.

Leah ran up the stairs and threw herself on her bed, sobbing her anguish into the pillow. She remembered William Penrose well enough. He was not displeasing to the eye, but his manners left a lot to be desired. He had been the perfect gentleman when her father was around, but as soon as she was alone he would make a beeline for her and mutter amoral suggestions.

And his hands had a habit of wandering when they were conversing about the smallest matters. At times they strayed to her waist, where his thumbs would insinuate themselves at the side of her pert breasts, stroking in a teasing manner. And he often rubbed against her, squeezing her into tight corners where she would blush and stammer until released.

She recalled how his mouth would go slack and his hands would tremble. In her innocence it took her a while to realise that these happenings were far from accidental. When she did she would shake him off with great indignation, but he would act as though perfectly innocent of any crimes towards her.

Her flesh crawled when she remembered one particular evening. She had retired after her father had been called out on an emergency, and was drifting off to sleep when she heard the latch being opened on her bedroom door.

She peaked out from under the covers expecting to see Jane, but a larger, stronger hand than hers held the candle that lit the darkness, and the flames illuminated male features. William's eyes were red from the drink he had consumed in the tavern that evening, his rubbery lips loose. He staggered across the room towards her and she gave a small scream of fear.

'Save your strength,' he scorned. 'Doctor Brown has been called away and Jane has gone with him to give a hand with a birthing. Rose has sneaked out to meet one of her men friends.' He grinned. 'She looks ripe for a good seeing to.

20

That woman certainly likes her cunny being plugged. She gave me a run for my money, I can tell you.'

She had been disgusted. 'You mean you and Rose…?' She was quite unable to put a name to what they did, and dropped her eyes in embarrassment.

'Oh yes,' he purred. 'We had a good frolic in the kitchen after supper. It was an appetiser for what you and I are about to do together.'

'Go away. Martin will come if I scream,' she warned.

He laughed loudly. 'Martin has partaken some of the doctor's sack and is snoring his sweet head off. So you see, my pretty, you are all mine. Come, mistress,' he leered, 'lower your covers and let me see the beauty of the body you hide beneath your virtuous gowns.'

He took a step towards her, his hand trembling with lust, the candle sending ghostly figures to writhe on the walls. 'It's just you and me now.' His mouth broke into a frightening grimace. 'You can give up all pretence. I know you're playing games with me. You're every bit as keen on sex as the bawds on Fleet Alley. You give flirtatious looks from under those long lashes and when I take the bate you turn all coy. Well, no more. We'll play my games tonight.'

Leah knew she had to save herself somehow, so without a second's pause she reached for the candlestick on her night table and aimed it right at him. His movements were slowed from the drink and the candlestick caught him on the shoulder, and still keeping hold of his candle he grabbed his injured person, shock dulling his eyes.

Leah followed the candlestick with her chamber pot and it smashed by his feet, its contents splashing over him.

'God's teeth!' he growled. 'She's turned into a mad woman.'

'If you really want to see how mad I can be,' she cried, 'take another step closer and you'll find out.' Her words were brave but she trembled with fear. Although William had been slowed by her well aimed missile, she knew she had sharpened his temper.

21

'Brave words, when I have the upper hand.' His teeth glinted wickedly in the candlelight and he stepped forward, grabbing her night-rail, exposing her young breasts that rose and fell rapidly with each breath she took. His fingers shook as he set the candle on the night table and, holding her firmly with one hand, caressed a rose-tipped peak with the other. 'Perfection...' he drawled.

Trembling, Leah cast around her for protection but she had run out of ammunition. Her heart sank but her determination was as strong as ever. She reached beneath her pillow. 'One step nearer and my knife will find its way into your heart, William Penrose.'

He stopped then, swaying drunkenly where he stood, his eyes darting uncertainly to the arm that was half hidden beneath the pillow, then back again to her unflinching gaze. 'You'd do it too, wouldn't you?'

'To save my honour I would.' Her chin jutted forward to add conviction to her words, but her hands trembled. What if he called her bluff and found out that she had nought but a handkerchief beneath the white linen on her bed?

But she didn't have to wonder for long, for there was the sound of voices and the street door opening and shutting. 'If my father finds you here he'll kill you!' she hissed, praying he would scamper back to the guest chamber like the rat he was. Dr Brown had not been in the best of health and Leah didn't want him worried by the likes of William Penrose. 'And there's no welcome left in this house for you,' she added bravely as he made for the door, leaving her to sink back on her pillows where she said a silent prayer for her deliverance.

The following morning, to her delight, Penrose was gone and her father explained that he had found a friend willing to stake him on his adventures. Had she known then that she was to follow in his wake her smiles would not have been so wide.

22

Chapter Two

Leah could not bear to leave her room at all for the rest of the day, and when a troubled Jane brought her a tray she left it untouched. Along with the food had been a letter from William. In it he spoke of his love for her and of his plans for them for the future. If she hadn't been so miserable she would have laughed at his gall.

She felt suddenly stifled and badly in need of air, so not wanting to alert anyone she shrugged into a cloak and pulled the hood over her curls, for stormy clouds had been building all afternoon and now it was raining.

Slipping out through the front door into the street she hurried over the cobbles, oblivious to anything but the cold emptiness inside her. Folk glanced curiously at the graceful figure winding her lonely way through the city – where was her chaperone, her protector?

If the truth were known Leah had never been lonelier in her entire life. Her birth had killed her mother, robbed her father of his wife, and made her a burden. She had never looked at things in that light before; was she totally devoid of feeling? Shame coloured her cheeks, lent a false brightness to her eyes. She must have been such a trial. No wonder papa was ready to relegate her to the Caribbean as soon as possible.

Her tears mixed with the rain on her face, disguising the fact that she was heartbroken. Well, she would cause him no more trouble. She would go to William Penrose with good grace, at least outwardly, although her own feelings on the matter would never change.

It was almost dusk and lanes turned and twisted one into the other like a maze, but Leah walked on unseeing, thinking only of what lay ahead in that new land across the sea, of the intimacies she would be expected to share with a depraved stranger.

Raised voices broke into her thoughts, the sound of

children crying and the restless snorting of horses from the stables of a nearby inn. A lone horseman trotted by, rising in his saddle to view her dainty form better. She flushed crimson and darted down an alley, his hearty laughter echoing after her.

The streets were even narrower now, houses with overhanging upper storeys making dark passageways. She could smell the river and realised she had wandered much further than intended. She hoped papa had not noticed her absence; she was not allowed to wander around the city on her own.

A dark shape lurched from a doorway and she swerved to avoid it, hurrying on, unsure of her bearings. Her father's warnings of thieves and murderers, river pirates and procurers who robbed decent women off the street to use in their brothels, screamed in her head. She remembered Temperance Jones, the baker's son taken by a press gang and not heard of since, the way his mother mourned him as though he was already dead, and she shivered.

Two bawds sniggered as she passed, grabbing jealously at her fine cloak. 'Who's this, then?' said one. 'Lady bleeding muck, I suppose. I hopes you ain't thinkin' of taking over our alley. We got good pickings, but there ain't enough for three.'

'What man 'ud want a skinny rat like that when there's tits around like mine,' said the other, proudly weighing her breasts in her hands.

'Aye,' her friend agreed slyly. 'And I bet she don't know how to suck a cock till it squirts fine spunk in yer mouth.'

Leah managed to pull free and hurried away, her breath rasping in her throat, her heart fluttering in her breast like a caged bird.

She could see the wharves now, ships anchored alongside. A dark mist caused by the sea coal used for fuelling the fires on this chilly summer evening mingled with the dusk, enveloped the paraphernalia on the wharf in a cloak of mystery, snaked down her throat and chest making her cough.

A babble of voices, loud and raucous, assailed her from a nearby tavern, and she hid in a doorway as the inmates spewed forth and ambled by.

She waited until they were out of sight before continuing her journey, glad they had not noticed her. But as she dared venture from the safety of the doorway the tavern door reopened and she was illuminated in the light of the lanterns. Two men emerged, and before she had time to draw back into the shadows they spotted her.

'What have we 'ere, Ned?' said one, closing in on her, his breath warm and fetid. 'A pretty piece to be sure.'

His companion, taller and of a broader build, towered over the diminutive Leah and grabbed at a silken curl that peeped from beneath her hood. 'Hair like spun gold, Jem.'

Leah tried to pull away but his hold on her hair was far too firm, and she gasped as he tore off her hood to stare in wonder at her golden ringlets.

'Just look at this, Ned,' the other fellow drawled, fingering the cloth of her red cloak. 'She be a fine lady.'

'Unhand me at once!' Leah demanded, her voice sounding fragile even to her own ears.

'Now that ain't very friendly.' Ned fondled her hair and she cringed from the mucky fingers.

'Yer wanna' be nice to us, wench,' Jem wheedled, mentally adding the cost of the material she wore. 'Your family'd be only too pleased to give us a fortune for yer, I'll be bound.'

'That's right,' agreed Ned. 'And you wouldn't want us to spoil yer pretty face first, would yer?' He dropped his hand from Leah's curls and attempted to unfasten her cloak, but stricken with terror she fought his every move until he was forced to pin her arms over her head with one hand while exploring with the other.

Her resistance was negligible in comparison to their strength, and they taunted her unmercifully. She was reminded of Tibbs, and how he toyed with mice.

'My father won't pay a farthing piece to either of you,' she snapped, trying to keep her voice steady. 'He's not a wealthy man.' How could she explain to these ruffians that she and Jane made her clothes from material obtained cheaply from a grateful merchant who owed his life to her father's skill?

'So yer takes us for fools, eh, wench?' Jem growled. 'He'll pay all right. And before he does we'll each take some pleasure from yer. What say you, Ned?'

'Aye, soon as we gets back to my place.' His hands were spanning her trim waist in wonder, snaking over her buttocks, his face red with excitement. 'How's about a little kiss first?'

Leah squirmed her head away in disgust, and bringing up one daintily shod foot kicked hard at his shins. 'Leave me alone, you stinking oaf!' She took a deep breath and screamed at the top of her voice, but nothing happened, no one came. Everyone was keen to stay out of the rain and busy with their own business that night; they had no time for her. As if to prove the point the laughter and slurred voices in the tavern rose and someone broke into song, a bawdy ditty that brought much glee.

Jem grimaced, rubbing his painful shin against his other leg, his fingers like a vice around her wrists. 'Fiery little wench, ain't yer? Scream as loud as yer like, they'll think you're a witless bawd taken too much gin.' He eyed her in admiration. 'Mayhap I'll take her in that doorway, Ned. My blood's up.'

He began to fiddle with his breeches and Jem began to drag her towards the dark alcove that had once been her refuge. But the awful truth of her dilemma gave Leah added strength. She would not be attacked and raped by these two louts! So she bit down hard on the man's fingers and pushed him with all her might. He gave an anguished cry and tottered backwards into Ned.

Caught completely unaware they fought to regain their balance, giving Leah precious time, and she shot off down

26

the street as quickly as her long skirts would allow, twisting and turning as lanes and alleyways led off one another like rabbit warrens.

Minutes later, her lungs bursting for air, she paused to take a breath, panting heavily. Her sides ached and her feet were sore; her dainty shoes were not made for such ill usage. She had forgotten her patens and they were full of the filth from the gutters. She gazed around. She was alone and she had thrown off her pursuers.

Candles glowing in a nearby window illuminated the hem of her gown, torn on a projecting nail during her flight. She bit her lip in vexation, praying her father would not witness her return, for she proved to be a sorry sight. Leaning against a wall she silently gave thanks for her blessed release from danger. As soon as she regained her strength she would find a link boy to light her through the dark streets and return home with all haste.

But unfortunately her feelings of security were proven to be false, and the sound of running feet interrupted her newfound calm. Then a voice she would remember until her dying day tore through the darkness.

'There she is, Ned. Quick, grab 'er!'

Leah's mouth opened in a silent scream, she turned to run but the one called Ned grabbed and held her fast.

'Run from us, would yer? I'll show yer what happens to wenches who don't do what they're told.' He cuffed her on the jaw and shook her so roughly her teeth knocked together. Leah sank to her knees almost senseless from the shaking. He forced her upright, her head spun and her jaw throbbed.

Jen grabbed the limp girl, angry at having his lust interrupted. 'I'll have yer yet, wench,' he promised, dragging her closer, forcing his foul mouth down on her soft lips.

'It ain't safe,' Ned cautioned. 'Let's go back to mine.'

'Like bloody hell we will!' Jem spat. 'I'll have her here and now.'

27

Ned eyed him with disdain. 'Can't yer wait? You're nothing but an alley cat!'

The two men turned on each other, bandying oaths, and Leah was almost pulled in two by the warring pair. 'Unhand me,' she begged raggedly.

They pulled apart and Jem dragged her into the shadows, and as he bore down on her she let out a terrified scream, closing her eyes at the pure lust in his face.

'You need a good beating first to quiet yer down,' he decreed angrily, upending her, pulling her skirts up and away from her curvy bottom.

Leah stopped struggling; she was dizzy and weak now as he held her like a rag doll, his hands coming into contact with her soft, sweet smelling skin. He circled one cheek first, his breathing agitated, then the other, grunting his pleasure.

Then he slapped hard, catching both cheeks at once, admiring the way they bounced at his prowess. The man was strong, the power of his hands crushing the breath from her body, her crying and pleas for mercy falling on deaf ears.

He took great pleasure in spanking her and her bottom stung unbearably. If he wasn't holding her with one meaty paw she knew she would have fallen to the wet and dirty street, where she would have stayed bereft of all strength.

His hand slapped nearer her sex, catching it at the same time as her cheeks, and though it stung mightily a pleasing fire like she had never felt before shot through her core.

She perked up, and her bottom surged a little higher in order to receive more pleasure from Jem's palm. He was getting into a steady rhythm now and Leah began to pant as his palm came in contact with her cunny time and time again. A sticky fluid seeped from her entrance, coating his fingers.

A loud grunting noise alerted her to the fact that Ned was standing beside them, his penis in his hand as he masturbated, his eyes on the slapping hand of his friend and Leah's quivering bottom and dewy sex. This served to excite

28

her all the more and her beaten buttocks lifted towards the punishing hand that both hurt and delighted her, then with one last slap she gasped and tensed as her climax ripped through her in a wave of ecstasy.

'Me thinks yer ain't as innocent as we thought,' Jem chuckled, clawing at his clothes, releasing his penis. 'I think you're more than ready for my thick meat, little tease.'

Sight of the huge male member brought another scream to echo through the streets, and she closed her eyes against the sight. She was near swooning, her every attempt to escape foiled by his massive strength, when an alien sound alerted her to another presence and her eyes flew open just in time to see Jem being thrown off her to the filthy street.

A tall, muscular stranger surveyed her tormentors, his cloak flapping in the brisk breeze that whistled off the Thames so that he resembled a huge bat. 'I'll teach you to waylay helpless women,' he roared, his sword waving menacingly, but a distressed cry from Leah forestalled him. Her world was slowly closing in on her and he rushed to catch her just as she fell.

Leah moaned; her head ached so. She opened her eyes, only to close them tightly against the glare of candlelight, but her second attempt was more successful and she peered around in confusion. She was not in her own room – why? Where was she? She lay in a strange room in a velvet hung bed. Shadows played on the walls and a fire flickered in the hearth. Somewhere a door clicked open, footsteps came nearer.

'Ah, so you are awake. How do you feel?'

The voice was deep and smooth and she glanced up curiously. The man was over six feet tall; even taller than the king! The thought came of its own volition and she viewed the stranger guardedly, something stirring in her foggy brain.

He moved into the circle of light and she could see him clearer. Wavy hair was his own, dark and lustrous. Broad shoulders tapered down to lean hips and long legs. His face was unquestionably handsome, and somewhere in her head something snapped into place.

It was he, the man she had met in the marketplace. Had it only been that morning? It was inconceivable, but her whole life had been turned upside down in just a few hours. When she had first seen this stranger she'd been carefree, and now she could not be more miserable.

'How are you feeling?'

She dazedly watched his sensual lips move. 'A little ill used.' She recalled the rough handling and the spanking she'd received from the ruffians in the streets near the river, and her eyes filled with tears at the shame. Her bottom stung and was so uncomfortable she wanted nothing more than to turn on her stomach and bare her cheeks, feel the air on them. She should have stayed at home and played the dutiful daughter, not gone roaming the city on her own.

He reached out to brush aside a stray curl from her brow and she felt a charge, almost like lightning striking as his fingertips touched her.

He obviously felt a similar reaction, for he was momentarily stunned. He paced in front of the fireplace and she noticed he had a slight limp. 'I'm Gideon Tempest,' he said quietly. 'Be assured you are quite safe in the home of a friend of mine, Lady Roseanna Roebuck. To ease your mind, if you should pull that rope,' he pointed to a bell-pull by the bed, 'a maidservant will hasten to do your bidding.'

He smiled, and despite her discomfort she smiled back. How well she remembered that face despite glimpsing it just the once. It was strong and lean and very brown, his eyes dark wells, his nose straight, his smile bewitching above a deeply dimpled chin.

'I believe we are briefly acquainted,' Gideon remarked with a flash of good humour. 'We met in the marketplace this morning, but I doubt you will remember; it was so crowded.'

A blush swept over her features. How could she not

remember him? 'I am deeply grateful to you, sir, for without your intervention I would have been...' Her words trailed off and she dropped her lashes in embarrassment. Had he seen what they were doing to her? If so she would surely die of shame.

But then she cheered a little; it had been far too dark in the doorway, surely he had seen nothing of her naked bottom. She heated, recalling the strong hand that spanked her naked cheeks, the sound of Jem's roused groans, and the sight of Ned masturbating beside them. The erotic feelings this had given her, the pleasure she felt at the beating. What was happening to her? Why had she enjoyed being debased by those two ruffians? Her eyes darted to Gideon's face. 'You seem to be forever coming to my rescue.'

'Those rogues should have been thrown into Newgate!' he growled. ''Tis unfortunate you fainted; I'd have taken great pleasure in impaling them on the end of my sword. As it was they fled like rats when I came to your assistance.'

She winced as she shifted her position in the bed and he looked concerned. 'You're in pain.' He tugged the bell-pull and a maid entered. 'Violet, see if Doctor Fitzherbert has arrived yet. May I know your name?' he asked, moving nearer to the bed.

'Leah Brown.'

'Leah Brown,' he repeated, and his eyes seemed to caress her in the candlelight. She blushed, but the briskness of his next sentence made her wonder if she had been mistaken. 'Now if you'll tell me where I might find your guardian I'll put his mind at rest.'

Leah gave a cry of despair. 'Papa! He'll be ill with worry. I stepped out without telling anyone.'

'An unwise action,' he said sternly. 'But it explains why you were wandering around without an escort.' She dropped her head in shame. 'Your address,' he reminded in a gentler tone. She told him and with one last glance at her he made to take his leave. As he strode to the door it opened and a short, stocky individual of middle age in a brown periwig entered.

31

Gideon was pleased to see him. 'Ah, Fitz,' he began, his words lost in the crackling of the fire in the hearth. They spoke in low tones and Leah knew they were discussing her foolishness. When Gideon took his leave she felt completely bereft, but the doctor's twinkling eyes soon put her at ease.

His examination was brief and thorough; though she was glad he had no knowledge of the cruel red marks on her sore rear. While she looked on dubiously he pulled a phial from his portmanteau.

'You're extremely lucky.' He poured out a good measure of the strangely coloured medicine. 'Drink this, it will relieve your pain and help you sleep.'

She drank the medication; glad it did not taste as unpleasant as it looked.

Dr Fitzherbert viewed her kindly. 'Try to get some sleep; you've been through a great ordeal.'

Leah closed her eyes, thinking how nice he looked when he smiled; the skin around his eyes crinkled up just as her father's did. With that comforting thought she drifted into a deep slumber.

But her dreams were not as soothing as she would have liked. From the darkness of the night came frightening shadows in male form that reached out for her, stripping her of her clothes, hands invading her body, voices rough, voices she recognised clearly as being that of Ned and Jem, their words vile.

'Leah... Leah Brown,' they muttered darkly. 'We've come for you. You'll never escape us. We need to touch you, to fill you with our seed. We're going to have you this time and nothing can stop us.'

'No,' she cried. 'Go, leave me in peace.'

But the fingers held her firmly to the bed and the limbs of the shadows entwined with her limbs, their unsubstantial arms and legs wrapping around her like damp fog. She twisted and turned, trying to escape their questing fingers, but they were stronger than she thought and held her fast, their dampness sinking into her bones until they ached.

But the aching was soon quenched by a fire that rose from within as the shadows slowly slid over her breasts, flicking at her skin like devils' spawn, teasing her nipples into hard buds. She cried out at their invasion, but her cries were no longer pleas of release. This time she urged them to do as they wished; to have their way with her until she was sated.

The shadows crept over her stomach, caressing that delicate area, swirling over the satin of her flesh and down to the nest of golden hair that hid her treasures. They swirled down into her labia, teasing, caressing, and hissing into her ear, 'We're going to fuck you, Leah, eat your cunny and spank you till you scream for mercy.'

Leah shuddered. 'Yes, oh yes.'

'Saints alive! Hush lady, hush. You're having a bad dream. Hush now.'

Leah slowly surfaced from her nightmare to find herself in comforting arms. 'Violet, it's you,' she said, calming a little. 'I've had such an awful dream. There were shadows and they were trying to ravish me.' Leah relaxed as Violet nursed her gently, whispering soothing words in her ear. The maid kissed her hair and forehead.

'There, mistress, do not fear, Violet is here now. I'll look after yer.'

The night-rail had worked its way up her legs, almost up to her waist, and Violet surveyed the golden curls that hid Leah's womanhood with delight. Her night attire was damp from her recent struggle with her dream assailants, and Violet clicked her tongue. 'There, sweet mistress, let Violet take this damp gown from your person. I'll warm yer with my body for the fire is slowly dying and you'll catch cold.'

Leah, still groggy from Dr Fitzherbert's medication, laid back passively as Violet stripped her of her clothing. Then the maid removed her own clothes and slid into the bed beside her. She smelled so sweet Leah vaguely wondered if she had used some of her mistress's perfume, and worried that she'd be punished for it.

But soon all worries left her mind as the soft female body

lent its warmth, and she sighed with pleasure as Violet's hands rubbed some heat back into her. She skimmed her arms and smoothed over her proud breasts, which perked up beneath her fingers.

'There now, beautiful mistress,' Violet breathed. 'Warm me as I warm you. Let us breathe life into one another as only us girls know how.'

Leah realised that Violet's breasts were nudging her own, the dusky nipples proud like spring buds. She gazed in wonder at Violet's body as it covered hers, the slim curves of the girl pleasing against her own.

Violet kissed her forehead, drifted her tongue around Leah's ear and she gave a little cry of elation. Then for a brief moment the girl looked longingly into her eyes, her brown orbs soft and gentle. Her lips were as red as berries and twice as alluring. She slowly placed her mouth on Leah's and the gentle persuasion of those sweet lips awoke such a longing in her she was lost in wonder. Her cunny stirred as her breasts met Violets, as their nipples kissed as passionately as did their mouths. Soon the girl was busy sucking her nipples and Leah felt her insides melt and her cunny ache with need.

Violet made a path of kisses down her stomach, curled her fingers into the golden triangle, and lent her lips to the pouting lips of her labia. She tongued her from her perineum to her clitoris and back again as Leah writhed on the bed, sighing with pleasure.

Then the sweet lips were back on her own, as warm and soft as she remembered, but this time they tasted of her own juices and the knowledge was most pleasing. Violet reached for Leah's hand and positioned it on her breast. Leah caressed it, and though smaller than her own it brought her immense pleasure. She was completely awestruck by her fascination with the other female's body, by the feelings it gave her. She had never been aroused by another female before.

She stroked the nipple and smiled with pleasure when it

became hard in her hand. Then she became more curious and her hand wandered to the dark curls at the apex of Violet's legs. Her fingers slowly delved and she was met with a damp warmth and a hard little bud that she knew beat with as much longing as her own.

Violet paid her the same compliment and they were stroking each other, gently at first, building to a quicker stroke as their libidos became more urgent, more insistent to be satisfied. When Leah reached her crisis it was a revelation; she'd never had another person do that for her. The pleasure made her shudder with emotion and release, and then radiate with so much happiness she thought she would explode.

Violet kissed her gently, and slid from the bed with a smile that warmed Leah for the rest of the night.

The following morning Jane brought Leah some clothes, but she was overcome with a headache and was obliged to lay abed for most of the day.

Come evening she felt better and slipped into a fresh chemise and her favourite blue gown, which clung to her waist and showed off her creamy bosom to perfection. The evening sun slanted through the sitting room windows, turned the handsome brocade curtains to a richer gold. Leah glanced around in appreciation; she had never seen anything so grand as this palace that stood on the southern side of the Strand. Rich carpets adorned the floor and the furnishings were gold and green velvet, the wood finely carved.

Banks of sweet smelling blooms ran down to the sparkling Thames, and she had stood on the steps leading to the water earlier, soaking in the heady beauty, until a ribald remark made by a sculling waterman sent her rushing back to the house.

She viewed the portrait of the dark-haired woman over the mantel curiously; according to Violet this was her absent hostess. If the portrait did her justice she was surely one of the loveliest women in England.

35

The sound of the door opening alerted Leah to the presence of Gideon Tempest, and she turned.

'The doctor tells me you are almost recovered from your ordeal, Mistress Brown.'

His eyes caressed her and Leah's hand fluttered self-consciously to her cheek. If anything he appeared even handsomer this evening. 'I am deeply indebted to you, sir. You probably saved my life.'

'From what you said in your sleep I don't doubt it.'

'My... my sleep,' she stammered. The thought of this man watching her while she slept brought a deep blush to her cheeks.

'I came to your chamber on my return, but you were asleep, muttering something about being kidnapped, so I sent Violet to soothe you.'

Leah's blush deepened. She was glad he had no idea of how well Violet did her job. 'That's very kind of you.'

His face was stern. 'Those knaves would have ransomed you off to your father, but once the money was paid over I doubt they'd have let you live to identify them. But they would have used you well by then and you'd have welcomed death.'

Her face flamed. 'I was foolish.'

He captured her chin with his fingers and looked deep into her eyes. 'The thought of you coming to any harm disturbs me more than I can say.'

Leah was overcome by his sweet breath, by the overwhelming nearness of him, and suddenly she was in his arms and his lips were on hers, not briefly as they were in the marketplace, but passionately, and she knew she should have fainted clean away had he not held her so tightly.

Violet had given her some female love in the dark hours of the night, but she knew that her true persuasions lay with the likes of the handsome Gideon Tempest.

'Leah, Leah,' he whispered into her hair. 'You have bewitched me like no other.'

'And you me, sir,' she said shyly, loving the smell of

36

sandalwood and clean male that enveloped him. Her pulses raced and she wondered what lay beneath his codpiece. Was he as big as Sarah's partner had been? Were his thoughts running along the same lines as her own, perhaps thinking of the female secrets beneath her gown? She knew that if he touched her in any of these forbidden places she would be undone, for she could not resist him. His hips ground towards her and she was able to feel the hardness of him, the male tool that she knew was ready to thrust inside her softness. Her insides melted and she could feel her delta moistening.

She looked into his eyes, eyes that were a tobacco-brown in the daylight, soft and luminous, just like those of a puppy. And when his lips met hers again she knew she was completely lost in a world where nothing existed except the two of them.

His hands moulded her bottom through her gown, pulled her even nearer, as though getting her used to the steel of his shaft. But then the door pushed open and they broke apart guiltily.

A dark-haired woman flounced towards them, her red taffeta gown bouncing over yellow petticoats, her bodice fashionably low. There was no modest whisk to hide her sumptuous bosom, bare almost to the nipples – Lady Roseanna Roebuck dressed to thrill. A patch was stuck alluringly above one white breast and she flung her head back dramatically and pierced Gideon with bright blue eyes.

'I understand we have a visitor.'

Her tone was so cold Leah almost recoiled. She was left feeling flustered and bereft without his arms to hold her and she steadied herself on a nearby chair, trying to maintain her equilibrium.

Gideon explained the circumstances that surrounded Leah's presence, his gaze resting on her regretfully.

Roseanna's countenance broke into a cynical smile. 'Captain Tempest is renowned for coming to the rescue of fair maidens.'

Leah was impressed; she hadn't known he was a sea captain.

Roseanna turned to Gideon. 'I believe you are needed at Deptford, captain. I intercepted a messenger.' She flashed a stiff smile. 'Don't trouble about Mistress Brown; I shall see she reaches no harm.'

With great reluctance Gideon bowed and left them, his wide smile making Leah's heart beat faster.

Roseanna Roebuck surveyed her coldly. 'I don't know what game you're playing,' she hissed, 'but I won't have a filthy trull like you take my man, is that clear?'

The woman's perfume pervaded the room and Leah turned her head as the strength of it upset her stomach. 'Your man?'

Lady Roebuck laughed nastily. 'Oh, I know women like you and it's obvious that your petticoats burned with lust from the moment you set eyes on him. But the captain's mine, do you here?'

'I believe you are under a misconception,' Leah said stiffly.

'Don't use that innocent tone with me! What whorehouse, pray tell, did you crawl out of? Make no mistake; I've seen the likes of you lying on your back in the gutter while some drunken sot paid a few pence to stick his cock in you.'

Leah's face was ashen with the shock of her words; never had she heard a lady speak so before! 'Whorehouse?'

Lady Roebuck's face was eaten up with hate and she glared at Leah. 'No decent woman wanders around the streets alone at dusk. You might fool him, but not me. Captain Tempest is a gentleman, and easily persuaded by soft eyes that fill with tears and pretty lips that lie with each word they spout.'

Leah was appalled at the woman's insinuations. She forced her head up. 'You go too far! My father is Doctor Thaddeus Brown, an eminent physician. I admit it was foolish to venture out alone but I have paid for my foolishness.'

The older woman twitched at the folds of her gown thoughtfully. 'Doctor Thaddeus Brown, eh?'

'That's right.' Roseanna seemed impressed, but Leah just wanted to get away from the unpleasant personage. 'I am grateful for your hospitality,' she said wearily, 'but if you'll be good enough to find me a coach I shall be on my way.'

Roseanna gulped. 'Forgive me, Mistress Brown,' she said, wringing her hands. 'I must beg your pardon, but I was under the impression you were a ne-er do well. I was misled. Servants are sometimes careless with words. I shall see that the creature is punished.'

Leah was taken aback by the reversal of her mood and distressed that a servant would be punished for giving Lady Roebuck the wrong information about her. 'Please,' she said softly, 'be lenient. I am sure it was a mistake and there is no harm done.'

Roseanna sighed her compliance. 'Very well. It seems the captain has rescued a saint. You are far kinder than I would be in the same situation.'

'I hope you never fall into such danger.'

Roseanna smiled winningly. 'Please, won't you dine with me? Mayhap a pleasant meal will make up for my silly behaviour. Cedric will drive you home after we have supped.' Leah was about to refuse but the woman touched her arm. 'Please,' she said in a wheedling voice she knew she could not resist.

Leah nodded her acceptance and was truly surprised to find that the lady was indeed a fine dinner companion. She was beautiful and a great raconteur; it was little wonder the captain loved her. But did he, she wondered idly? Rose had said that men took their ease wherever they could find it. On the other hand, there had been a mighty surge of feeling between her and the captain; was that the beginning of love?

Roseanna talked about him in great length, her smile wide. 'Gideon captains a merchant ship. He ran into a bad storm on his return from the West Indies. But apart from a little damage to his ship and a slight leg wound, he escaped virtually unharmed.'

Leah returned the smile. 'That accounts for the limp.'

Roseanna nodded and led her into the dining room. The meal was succulent; they dined on fine lobsters and delicious, damson plum tarts. Roseanna spoke about the manners at court and the romantic liaisons of the lords and ladies.

Leah was glowing with excitement; Jane and Rose would be agog when she related her adventure to them. She was about to render her thanks for the lady's kind hospitality when a great dizziness overcame her.

Roseanna smiled smugly. 'Are you not feeling well, Mistress Brown? I hope the wine did not upset your delicate constitution.'

Leah held her spinning head. 'No, I… I'm feeling quite ill.' She saw the glee on her hostess's face and her stomach roiled. 'You have poisoned me!'

Roseanna rose from her seat at the table and rang for the servants, her face a mask of evil. 'Fear not,' she said blithely. ''Tis not a poison, just a light draught that will keep you quiet until my men can dispose of you in some place where you can't get your claws into Gideon. You see, Leah Brown, it has taken me a long time to wind him in, so I will not have a whore like you stealing him away from me.'

Leah tried to stand but her head span and she fell to the floor as Roseanna's laughter echoed in her ears. She saw the men who came for her through a hazy mist. A piece of hemp sacking was thrown over her, and they picked her up and carried her through the garden she had admired just hours before. She was quite unable to smell the odour of flowers through the suffocating cloth, only the muffled song of the birds found its way into her dark world.

The man carrying her over his shoulder was breathing heavily, and she knew he was the corpulent gardener she had seen once or twice that day. The other man was a stranger, no doubt one of the under-servants Roseanna used for her dirty work.

There were cheery shouts in the distance; probably the voices of people being carried by watermen on the river. She wondered if they knew how lucky they were to be hale and hearty, and most of all free.

She was roughly thrown into a wherry, moored at the landing stage at the bottom of the garden.

She wanted to reason with them, to beg for mercy, but her head was spinning and she felt dreadfully sick. Whatever Roseanna Roebuck had given her it had upset her badly. The foul smell of unwashed bodies sickened her all the more and she fought against the nausea. The hard boards beneath her flesh made her already injured body yearn for some softer resting place; and the fear of what they were going to do with her made her whirling head spin faster.

For a few moments the sacking was tugged down to her feet and she was able to see the sparkling Thames, the gaiety of the people in multi-coloured garments that travelled that waterway.

There were many wherrys and lighters abroad that evening and her heart soared; there was help out there should she call for it. But she was too weak, and when a dirty rag was stuffed into her mouth she heaved against it. She thought she would choke, but she calmed and another filthy piece of cloth was wound around her mouth and tied at the back of her head. Her hands and feet were tied also, so she was quite unable to escape even if the drug wore off.

'That's it, John,' said the gardener, dusting his palms off. 'She's trussed like a bird for the cooking pot.'

'Why do old Roebuck want such a fine looking wench taken away?' his companion in crime asked curiously, his eyes skimming Leah's heaving bosom as she lay completely indisposed at the bottom of the boat.

The gardener studied her with narrowed eyes. 'Who knows? But she's a fine looking filly, all right. I'd like a turn on her, that's for sure.'

John grinned, and lifting her skirts gasped at the shapely legs that lay beneath. 'There's yer reason, Joe. Roebuck's a jealous besom and, according to Violet, the handsome captain only had eyes for this one.'

The gardener nodded. 'Aye, yer could be right. Took her a few years to land that fish it did. He weren't interested when her husband was alive, though she tried hard enough to get him to fuck her.'

'That's the truth,' agreed the other. 'Though she had her arse plugged by plenty more, I can tell yer. I recall Violet saying that she walked into the mistress's bedchamber to find the stable lad between her legs, licking her cunny like there was no tomorrow. And her a-screaming and carrying on and playing with her own nipples, she was, like she didn't have a care in the world. And her poor sick husband downstairs in the parlour.'

'None of them aristocrats got any shame. They reckon 'tis the same up at the palace. All them duchesses and the like going round with painted faces. Aye, they're all light skirts! They say the king's got secret passageways so's he can sneak round without anyone knowing.'

'There ain't no reason why we can't have as much fun as the gentry,' John said thoughtfully. 'Come the dusk we can drag her under some of them bushes over yonder and do what we wants with her.'

The front of John's breeches surged and he held the bulge with one hand. 'I can't wait till dark. Let's cover her up with the sack and take her there now, my dick's fair aching for the taste of those sweet lips.'

The gardener looked around warily, and Leah's eyes watered with fear. Here she was tied up like an animal, lying on hard, damp boards in a stinking boat on the Thames, and she was soon to be abused even further. If only Captain Tempest was there to save her again. But he was at the docks seeing to his own business, she could expect no help from that quarter.

Water lapped at the sides of the little rowing boat, licking higher when other craft passed by, and Leah stared miserably at the sky. She could see nothing now but that, and the two men who had nothing but evil intent towards her.

The gardener's hands groped, massaging her knee, pushing his stout fingers between her thighs and up further to the shining 'V' of her nether hair. It curled prettily around her sex and the man drew a huge breath.

'I bet you ain't seen anything prettier than that little cunny.'

'I surely never have,' John breathed, his lips running with spittle as his tongue dipped in and out of his mouth in excitement.

Leah felt the warm air on her cleft, on her labia lips and, despite her fear, she was disgusted to find that between that and the drooling perusal of the two rogues she was beginning to feel aroused. Her sex ached with need and her nipples pushed at the material of her gown.

The gardener was playing with the pretty blonde curls, delving into the damp pink folds that lay beneath. John was breathing unsteadily, the spittle dripping off his whiskered chin. His hand held on tightly to the bulge in his breeches, and Leah glanced from one to another wondering what they would do to her; appalled as her body answered the plundering fingers by secreting its sticky dew.

John grunted and pulled her skirts up even higher. 'Let's take a look at that pretty arse, Joe. I swear I'd give a king's ransom to see it.'

When Leah was turned a little and her skirts hauled up to expose her rump John blinked in surprise. 'There's more to this than we thought. See the red marks on her cheeks? Looks like some cove beat her.'

Joe felt the blotches on her bottom warily. 'Mayhap you're right.'

John was almost bursting through his breeches. ''Tain't none of our doing. We can still play with the chit. Let's get on with it before Roebuck comes to spoil our fun.'

Leah's insides roiled, it was just like the night Jem and Ned snatched her off the street, but this time Captain

Tempest was not around to save her. She was completely at their mercy!

Chapter Three

But John was too late. A sharp retort, that deflated his cock as swiftly as it had risen, rang out loudly behind them.

'You're taking long enough to contain the rubbish I gave you.'

Leah knew that voice only too well; Lady Roseanna Roebuck was on the warpath again, making sure her well thought out plans were put into action. The two men flushed as guilt coloured their complexions.

'Just finishing up here, me lady,' said Joe, dragging the sack back over Leah's body.

'That's right, me lady,' muttered John, sketching a low bow to the heavily perfumed lady.

Roseanna peered into the wherry to see the small bump covered in sacking that was the drugged Leah. 'Very well. You can take your leave and come back after dark. I'll give you my instructions then.'

The servants faded quietly away; they had no wish to risk Roseanna's wrath, her temper was renowned in the household – she had given many a servant a good slapping. And if that did not suffice she made sure they were whipped too.

'Are you enjoying yourself, Leah Brown?' she asked with a wicked smile. 'Although you cannot speak I am aware that you can hear me. So listen well. After dark you will be taken from here and dropped off at a place where you can do me no more harm. I will not have my life disrupted by a snivelling little chit like you.'

Roseanna tugged at the ringlets that caused her maid so much trouble – for the lady's hair was as straight as a poker – winding one around a finger. 'If you are wondering how I became aware of your schemes to steal Gideon away,' she said with a snigger, 'beware the look in your eyes, for I saw your regard for him shining out of them like a beacon. You gave yourself away, Leah Brown.'

Leah needed a drink. Her throat was dry and she wanted to sneeze. The dust and the strong oily smell of the sacking had risen up her nose, giving her much discomfort. And though her cheeks were wet from the tears that ran down her face she vowed to stay strong. She would not allow this witch to get the better of her. One way or another she would escape.

She recalled the conversation between Joe and John; they had bemoaned Roseanna's disgraceful behaviour with the other male servants and the way she tried to make Gideon fall in love with her, in spite of the fact she'd had a husband then. What a wicked woman she was; along with most of the court, or so it seemed.

But then Thaddeus often spoke in a derogatory tone of the carryings on at court, especially after the king's mistress had left her husband. 'All the better to get at the king,' he'd remarked caustically. 'The congress of a man and a woman should be something for the marriage bed. The fine people of the court seem to think it is naught but a sport. 'Tis a disgrace.'

Thaddeus was wise; she wished she had as much wisdom. It would have saved her from her present predicament.

Roseanna carried on talking, her hands all the while fiddling with her gown, twitching it off her shoulders, as was the fashion, pulling her bodice lower, smiling at some of the people of consequence that had ventured out that day on the river.

'And may I say what a splendid lover Gideon is,' Roseanna went on, playing with the fine ribbons that were threaded through her dark hair. 'The best I've had.' She smirked. 'I'm not a shy or bashful person, Leah Brown, and I like my men lusty so they can fuck me long and hard. And Gideon gives the best fuck ever.' Leah heard a brittle laugh.

'Poor you, that you will never be able to be loved by the best.'

With a swish of her skirts Roseanna dismissed the presence of the pathetic little figure curled up in the wherry at the bottom of her garden and sashayed up the path, plucking a bright red rose from a bush and inhaling its fragrance as she went.

Leah didn't know what the time was; she listened to the sounds of the river, all the while wishing she was able to free herself.

After a while her head stopped aching and she was less nauseous. But it brought her little relief, for her limbs were beginning to cramp and she recoiled at the pain. And as if that wasn't enough to put up with she heard small feet scuttling in the boat, heard strange squeaking noises. Something ran over her leg and deep in her throat she let out a tiny scream that no one could hear.

The perspiration began to pour from her brow; she hated rats. So strong was her fear that she shivered and shook from head to foot. She wriggled hard and the little wherry swayed alarmingly as she prayed the vermin would go. She wondered what her poor papa would be thinking. He would be so worried.

She lay there on the wooden planks of the rowing boat, the sacking hiding her from the rest of the world, determined to survive this nightmare, but so frightened she hoped her heart would not give out before nightfall. If it did at least she would be free of the unwanted attentions of Roseanna Roebuck's servants and the murky death she was sure they planned for her in the river.

It was unthinkable, but because of the drug in her system Leah fell asleep. When she awoke it was with the greatest thirst ever. The rats were still scuttling around her, but now there were no tiny rays of light trying to push through the dusty sacking. It was night and she knew that John and Joe would soon come for her.

A rat nibbled at her skirts and she screamed her

46

ineffectual scream deep in her throat. She heard voices and the sound of feet coming along the garden path; twigs snapped and the footsteps were heavy. They had come for her! The gag in her mouth hid her moans of distress and she tried to huddle into a smaller figure as the footsteps came nearer.

The sack was pulled from her, the dirty rag removed from her eyes and she blinked against the glare of a lantern. 'There you are, my sweet,' Joe cooed. ''Tis a shame we had to leave yer when we did. But never fear, we'll soon warm that pretty little minge of yours.'

She was able to see his large frame bending over her, and John's slightly smaller shape behind him.

'Aye,' John agreed. 'My cock's been ready for yer all day.'

Huge hands momentarily hid the light of the lantern as Joe bent down to lift her from the boat. The rats scuttled away, the men kicking out at the vermin as they disappeared into the river. She felt herself being hauled upwards, saw the lantern throw Joe's large nose into relief, his knobbly chin. She wriggled and kicked, determined not to make it easy for them, but she received a sharp slap on the rump for her trouble.

'We're going to lay yer down on that soft patch of grass over yonder,' he explained. 'Better on the old knees. And then, my pretty, you'll feel the best meat between your thighs you've ever had.'

'Mayhap she's a virgin,' John whispered, scared lest someone hear their words and interrupt their pleasure again.

'No,' Joe whispered back. 'She's far too bonny.'

They laid her on the grass. Leah fought against her bindings but she was held fast. Her wrists and ankles hurt from the chafing of her restraints and she tried to alert them to the fact that she needed to answer a call of nature.

'Stop fussing girly; won't get yer nowhere! Untie her legs,' Joe ordered. 'Let's get into that sweet flower. Cor blimey, it's like I've died and gone to heaven!' he said as

47

her legs were untied and he laid the lantern beneath a bush and parted her thighs.

'But what if she be a virgin?' insisted John.

'Are yer?' Joe nudged her shoulder and Leah nodded, her eyes huge in the moonlight.

John chuckled excitedly. 'I ain't never had a virgin. What's it like, Joe?'

'Oh, but it's the best feeling in the world. The cunny's tighter then; ain't been stretched, see. It sheaths yer like a satin glove.'

John looked at her worriedly. 'I dunno. If she be a virgin they'll know and we'll be in for it when they find out what we done.'

John heaved a huge sigh of disappointment. 'I never thought of that. Roebuck nary misses a trick. And the cove this one's destined for'll surely tell all if we should break her in.'

'I bet he's a'licking his kisser right now waiting for that honour. Lucky bastard!'

Leah's ears pricked up. So she wasn't to be drowned, after all. They were going to take her to some stranger who was about to deflower her! She didn't know what was worse.

The pressure in her bladder became almost unbearable and she tried once more to alert them to the fact; wriggling and nodding her head towards her middle.

'Looks like she needs to piss.'

'I think you're right. She been trapped in that boat a goodly time. Is that right, girly? Do yer need to piss?'

Leah nodded fervently, and they released her hands and pointed to a patch of grass a few yards away. 'Squat there. One inch further and you'll feel the sting of my stick,' John threatened, raising a nobbly branch he had at hand, ready to use if he should meet trouble on that dark night.

Leah smote them with her green gaze. 'Pray allow me some dignity,' she grated through dry lips.

'Do as you're told or piss yerself. Makes no odds to us,' Joe replied with a shrug.

With her head held high she retired to the place she had been designated, and lifting her petticoats out of the way, squatted. The men watched her with lascivious smiles, and Leah wished she had a sword to brandish. She would teach them a lesson they would never forget.

When finished she quickly looked around, ready for flight, but the men were ready for her.

'Oh no yer don't,' John spat gruffly, cuffing her across her ear. 'We ain't the fools yer take us for.'

She was dragged roughly to her original position and thrown onto the grass on her back. Her ear stung and she bit back tears of pain and anger. Next chance she got she would be off. She was far quicker and much fleeter of foot than the two brutes. And when she did escape she would bring the wrath of God down on them, and her ladyship Roseanna Roebuck!

A sour smell assailed her as Joe lowered the flap in his breeches and tugged out his swollen member. 'Open your mouth, girly. Seems like I'll have to be satisfied with that.'

Leah recoiled from the rancid odour and coughed as the dryness of her mouth and throat began to irritate, so Joe was obliged to reach inside his shirt for a small flask, which he held to her lips.

She drank deeply, even though unused to the strong spirits he had stolen from Roebuck's liquor cabinet. The drink made a fiery path down her throat and she coughed again, but this time she felt a little better. It did funny things to her head, warmed her stomach, and when Joe put his fingers into her furrow her nubbin surged.

'She might be a virgin,' he averred with a chuckle, 'but she's ripe for fucking, believe me. I ain't met a more willing wench. Feel her, John. Her cunny's fair flooding.'

John placed his fingers eagerly into her channel and exclaimed at her wetness. The fingers that were now coated in her sticky emissions he stuck into his mouth and licked carefully. 'Virgin juice,' he mused happily. 'At least I've tasted a virgin.'

49

Joe grunted and prodded the head of his penis at her lips. 'Come on, girly, open wide.'

Leah almost choked on the huge phallus he proffered. It tasted foul; no doubt it was in need of a good wash like the rest of him, and she gagged at the taste of urine that invaded her mouth, the feel of the wiry hair that surrounded it tickling her chin.

'That's it,' he encouraged. 'Suck old Joe's dick and you'll know what to do when this fancy fellow we're taking you to asks you to do it to him.'

She had heard many stories from Rose about sex, but it was as though she'd been here before. Although she was full of disgust and fear she instantly seemed to know how to suck his cock, how to tease it with her lips, how to lick around the glans. He pushed and pushed and though the back of her throat was straining to accommodate the oaf, somewhere deep inside she knew she would do it.

It was the strangest thing; she hated him, hated what he was making her do, and yet she surged with something akin to animal passion. And though she had never felt it before, she recognised it in herself.

John was between her thighs, licking her juices like his life depended on it. Every few licks he muttered, 'Virgin juice. Virgin juice,' his slack lips dripping into her furrow, his tongue frigging her nubbin.

Leah's thighs heated, her stomach and the urgency of her needs overwhelmed her. She needed John to keep licking her, needed him to keep tonguing her nubbin so that the wicked feeling upon her could be drawn to a satisfactory conclusion.

As Joe shot his load into her mouth so she shuddered into her climax, straining to get every last bit of pleasure from that stiff tongue. As she and Joe groaned their pleasure so John worked his fist up and down the staff he had removed from his breeches, and shortly after he too gave a groan and fell back on his heels, sated.

Joe shook his head in admiration. 'She gives better head

than old Meg down the *Fleet*. She's a natural. I envy the cove that's waiting for her this night.'

Leah blushed. 'Won't you untie my hands?' she asked shyly, her throat and mouth lubricated both by Joe's brandy and his spunk. 'My wrists are sore from the chafing rope.' And if her hands were free she would be more able to escape.

He laughed dryly. 'What do yer take us for, yer silly bitch? If you escape we're done for. You must have guessed by now what her ladyship will do to us if we foul up.'

After feeding his manhood back into his breeches he retied her wrists and feet, and her spirits sank. Before they gagged her again she spoke quickly. 'Where are you taking me?' She was in the most precarious position of her young life.

'To a quiet part of the river where we'll be met,' he explained, slinging her over his shoulder and taking her back to the wherry, John reluctantly dragging behind.

'Who is he, this man?' she asked nervously. 'You keep mentioning him, but who is he?'

'Mistress didn't say. But I gets the idea she knows him pretty well. Seemed to be mighty pleased by the fact, too. Sent a runner to let him know we was coming.'

Before she could utter another sound she was tipped into the bottom of the wherry and gagged again. Her wrists throbbed and so did her ankles, and the cloth in her mouth was as foul as she remembered.

She heard more footsteps coming down the path. They were lighter this time and she guessed her ladyship was coming to make sure she left her land and her life forever.

'So, Leah Brown,' said Roseanna's educated voice, 'you have learned that you are wasting your time here. Let the experience bode you well.'

Leah felt the wherry tilt as one of the men came aboard, heard the oars being dropped in the water, and they moved away from the landing stage and out into the river. She imagined this was how it must feel to be in hell. She could

51

see nothing, and hear nothing but the gentle lap of the oars as they skimmed the water, and the heavy breathing of the oarsman.

The night had turned humid but it was cold on the hard boards, and as the chill settled on her she began to shiver uncontrollably. She had no idea where they were about to land, but prayed it would be soon or she would surely take a fever.

In spite of her invidious position she was almost asleep when the boat came in to land, and she was immediately alerted to the fact that they were just marking time.

After a few minutes she heard a shout and the sound of scurrying feet. The man in the wherry, who sounded like Joe, had a conversation with the strangers, but she was unable to make out what they said because they spoke in whispers.

But she felt herself being lifted and slung over a shoulder. She was carried quite apace before being placed on another hard floor. She was able to hear the whinny of horses and the men speaking in undertones. Finally she heard a door slam and the ground beneath her began to move.

It was then she realised she was in a coach, but where it was taking her was a complete mystery. She was beginning to feel sick with worry and from the constant motion. The driver seemed to take pleasure in driving over every pothole he could find, and she was flung about in the bowels of the vehicle until she was sure all her bones were broken and her skin covered in bruises.

After what seemed like an eternity the coach rolled to a stop. There were faceless voices again. The door was opened and she was untied and dragged out. When the rags were removed from her eyes she was able to see that she was at the door of a grand house. She tried to take a step forward but her limbs were so lifeless she collapsed, and was hauled to her feet and carried in through the elegant entrance.

The inside of the house proved to be far shabbier than she

expected, and she shivered at the rundown feel of the place. A door was opened and she was carried into a large room with threadbare carpets and furniture, and dropped in an undignified heap on the floor in front of the fireplace.

When alone she strove to sit up, feeling her injured person with shaking fingers. There was not a part of her that was not sore, and she vowed that as soon as she got some strength back in her limbs she would take flight.

The door opened and she heard someone enter, and reached for a fire iron from the mucky grate so she could defend herself, but her gaoler was fast and snatched it from her hand, dragging her to her feet.

'I admire your spirit, mistress. But shall we dispense with violence? I am far too tired to play games.'

She knew that voice! Her aching head reeled and she faced him with violent intent. 'Percy Darlington! It was you all along. How dare you put me through that hell?'

He untied her, and when her dainty fists beat his chest he recoiled in surprise. 'A man will do anything for the woman he loves.'

Leah stamped her foot in anger. 'I have been kidnapped, tied up, abused and generally mistreated, and you have the cheek to stand there and tell me you love me?'

He directed her to sit on the settle by the grate, and she dropped to the shabby surface with a sigh of disbelief.

'When Lady Roebuck sent me a message to say she had you in her house and that you were ready to give in to any demands I might make, I was deeply indebted to the woman.'

There was no fire in the grate and she supposed it was because the night was so warm, but the warmth did not penetrate the room, and Leah shivered. 'You didn't stop to think what was happening to me?' She was appalled by his behaviour.

He sat beside her, his pale eyes skimming her heaving bosom, bare nearly to the nipples, her gown having been torn during her ordeal. 'I had confided my love for you to the sweet lady, and when I received her message I could only think of my good fortune.'

Leah followed his lecherous gaze, and deeply embarrassed at her state of dishabille, held the torn material together. 'Good fortune? I do not call being kidnapped and brought unwillingly to a strange house good fortune!'

Percy took her hands and the material of her gown fell away, exposing her near-naked breasts. 'You are not sitting where I am,' he drawled.

She pulled away from him and ran to the door. 'I shall leave at once. Order your coachman to take me home.' She tried to turn the handle but the door wouldn't give. She inhaled impatiently. 'Percy, the door is locked.'

He smiled languidly. 'Of course it is. I cannot allow my little bird to flee the nest so quickly.'

As she thought of a scathing reply the door handle turned ineffectually and the door rapped. 'Percy, let me in at once!'

Percy paled. 'Mama?'

At the sound of the woman's voice Leah's spirits soared. Lady Darlington was but a breath away, she would be saved!

Percy quickly unlocked the door and the lady flounced in, her skirts bouncing around her portly form. 'Mistress Leah Brown, how lovely to see you again.' She seemed to be quite unfazed by the fact that her son was entertaining a lady at such a late hour, or that the lady was in such a tattered state as to worry most normal mothers.

In spite of her sore limbs Leah bobbed a curtsey. 'My sentiments would be the same, my lady,' she said stiffly. 'But I have been brought here against my will and am much aggrieved.'

She explained what had happened to her, from unwisely leaving her home alone, to being set upon by ruffians, and then to her sorry treatment by Lady Roebuck.'

Lady Phyllida Darlington dusted her gown with her fingers. 'I know, dear. But I am sure you will forgive our little ploy. After all, my only concern is to see you and my son happy.'

Confusion gave way to anger and Leah faced her, eyes blazing. 'How dare you treat me so?'

Phyllida clicked her tongue. 'Now, now, my dear, is that a way to speak to your future mother-in-law?'

Leah felt faint, it was all too much. These people were beyond reason. 'I insist on being taken home at once. You cannot hold me here against my will!'

Phyllida smiled nastily. 'There is nothing to stop us. You see, Mistress Brown, no one knows where you are except Lady Roebuck, and she is glad to be rid of you.' As Leah's skin flushed crimson with rage Phyllida turned to Percy, waving her fan daintily.

'I think it time this young lady was taught a lesson, Percy. Don't you agree?'

Percy grinned eagerly. 'Indeed, mama. I do indeed.' While Phyllida stood blocking the door with her huge bulk, so Percy gathered a curved cane from a corner of the room. 'I believe you're due to learn who is master here, Mistress Brown.'

Before she had chance to fight back he had her sprawled over a chair, her skirts folded back, her lovely legs and bottom gleaming in the candlelight. His breathing was shallow. 'Oh, Leah, you're so beautiful.' His hands roamed over her fair cheeks shakily, and she fearfully noted the bulge in his breeches.

'Seems to me that the wench has already been chastised,' Phyllida remarked coldly, upon sight of the red marks that striped the creamy flesh. 'Not to worry, she is far too ready with her temper. She needs cooling off.'

Percy giggled, and with a deep breath arced the cane in the air and brought it down viciously across Leah's soft bottom. She screamed. 'Oh, my lady, please have mercy. I am not a scullery maid or a street woman to be treated so shabbily. I demand to be taken back to my father.'

'You demand?' Phyllida laughed dryly. 'You are in no position to make any demands, Mistress Brown. Percy, cane away.'

The next stroke of the cruel weapon landed full on both cheeks and Leah screamed more loudly. Surely someone in the house would take pity and help her. But no one came and Percy, egged on by his mother, brought the cane down on her sweet bottom time and time again.

Leah's screams became weaker, her body sagging helplessly over the chair as the brute beat her. She had never felt so much agony. She was tortured until her cheeks throbbed with hot pain. It ate into her very being with a fury that was quite alien to her. Even the ruffians down by the river had not hurt her like this.

She was able to see Phyllida's expression, her face flushed, her eyes shining. A man appeared and looked over her shoulder to watch the action in that cold, heartless chamber.

Without taking her eyes off Leah's abused bottom Phyllida nestled her ample form against the man, who was her junior by many years. His arms snuck around her, taking her heavy breasts, weighing them lustily in his palms. She sighed happily and rubbed herself against his groin.

'Darling George, how good of you to share in the discipline of our little Leah Brown.'

'My pleasure, me lady,' the man said in a coarse voice, and Leah realised he must be a servant. 'She's sure got a fine arse on her,' he said approvingly, lifting the lady's skirts to reveal her belly and the untidy mop of straggly curls at the apex of her ample thighs. His fingers began stroking the lady's clitoris and she sighed with pleasure.

'Is her arse better than mine?' she asked.

He kissed her neck, one hand down her bodice squeezing her nipple, his other keeping up a steady rhythm on her clit. 'No way,' he soothed, his gaze fixed on the bouncing bottom of Percy's victim, fascinated at the way the red weals made a pattern on the lovely flesh. 'When I slap yer arse it dimples like no other. And yer cunny smiles wider than any other woman I've met.'

Phyllida was pacified. 'Oh, George, you are adorable. Frig me harder, that's it,' she sighed, as his finger flew over her clit.

Though Leah was fair fainting away by now, she was still very much aware of the debauchery going on in front of her eyes, and amazed that Percy was completely unconcerned by his mother being pleasured by one of the servants.

He gave one last swipe of the cane and Leah became aware of a new sensation permeating the pain. It was as though her insides were alight with desire, her whole being alive with the need to be pleasured. Rose had mentioned that some people believed that pleasure came from pain, but she had never believed it until now.

Percy dipped a finger in her furrow, and when coated with her secretions he began to insinuate the digit into the small hole of her bottom. Leah cried out in horror, but as it burrowed its way inside her private passage it began to feel quite pleasant. He began kissing her neck, squeezing her breast, his finger sliding in and out of her bottom hole.

Leah realised that Lady Darlington had vanished behind the settle with her servant, and she was able to hear her cries of delight as George serviced her. While her thoughts were thus occupied Percy opened his breeches and covered his cock-head in her juices, and when it butted at her anus she anxiously bit her lip. She was stretched cruelly as it pushed inside her, and as she thought she would split in two so her sphincter relaxed and even seemed to welcome the intrusion.

Somewhere a place in her brain registered the disgraceful acts taking place in Dunstan House, but she ceased to let it be a burden for she was quite unable to prevent it happening. The only thing to do was to go with the flow, and as Percy began stroking her nubbin she knew it was for the best.

Chapter Four

The walls were damp in the cheerless room she woke up in the following morning. The sun shone through the window, but the walls were far too thick for the warmth to penetrate and the embers in the grate were fast dying. Her first action on waking had been to try the door, but it was securely locked.

Memories of the previous day assuaged her and her body flushed with embarrassment. She had been used cruelly by all and sundry, and consequently learnt that some of the aristocracy were indeed as perverse as her papa had led her believe. Her body ached from its misuse, and the delicate flesh of her bottom was raw with pain.

That one day would change and reform her life forever was almost unbelievable. She miserably mulled it over. It had begun quite well, had fulfilled its promise when she met Captain Tempest. Her heart melted when she thought of the handsome sea captain. How she wished he knew where she was now. Would he come to her rescue once again? Roseanna Roebuck swore she had seen the admiration for her shining out from his eyes – was it really so?

She gave a mirthless laugh; she would never see the handsome captain again. Roseanna would be sure to lie to him as skilfully as only she knew how, and the captain would easily be assuaged by her teasing lips, by the promise in the sky-blue eyes, the curves of her womanly figure.

Leah lie on her stomach with her chemise pulled up to her waist so that the air could get to her wounded buttocks. Why was her life so complicated? She had run away from one dilemma only to meet another, and here she was the prisoner of Percy Darlington and his insufferable mother. But this time there would be no escape. No one knew where she was except for the hateful Roseanna Roebuck, and she would keep her whereabouts a secret whatever happened.

Her spirits sank lower by the second. Her poor papa·would

be out of his mind with worry. What use did Percy think kidnapping her would do? Surely he realised it made her loath him all the more. She was in the midst of a hornets' nest, and her brain could not grasp the fact that there was no way out.

The door of the bedchamber was unlocked and Leah looked up fearfully to see Percy's mother come in, her fat jowls wobbling as she walked. A girl followed with a tray, presumably breakfast, she thought listlessly, pulling her chemise down so that she looked more respectable.

Phyllida had the girl place the tray on the bed, and sat her ample girth in a chair. 'I've come for a chat, my dear. I think we started off on the wrong foot yesterday.'

'What else did you expect?' Leah snapped. 'I was kidnapped and treated like the lowest whore.'

'Come now,' Phyllida soothed, pointing to the tray. 'Take some small beer and a little sustenance. It will help send the megrims away.' She stuck her podgy fist into a tray of sugared almonds and greedily stuffed her mouth full, wiping her sticky hands in the folds of her ruby gown. 'I can see why my son is so besotted with you, Mistress Brown. You're very beautiful. You would be a favourite at court; Charles has an eye for a pretty face and a shapely figure.'

The woman regarded her keenly, and Leah suddenly realised what the poor blacks must feel like at auction. Her papa had told her a little about slave trading and his opinion of the buying and selling of humans, but until now she had not given it much thought.

While Phyllida stuffed her fat face with sweetmeats Leah drank a little small beer, her appetite deserting her, wondering why she was there. Surely Percy would be wiser to seek someone with a handsome dowry. The house must have been very grand at one time, but now the rugs were threadbare, the furniture of the same condition and there were marks on the walls where once, she was sure, had hung treasured paintings.

'Percy bid me tell you of his adoration. Won't you give

him a chance? A place in your affections?'

Leah was aghast at the woman's suggestion. 'After the perversions that took place last night?'

'You are young, unsophisticated. We were showing you how much fun can be had, that's all. If you want to be a real woman you must learn many new tricks. My Percy is used to the best in life and as his true love you must be ready to appease his appetite.'

'Pray desist from patronising me, Lady Darlington. Youthful I may be, but I was brought up to know right from wrong.' Leah watched the woman wipe her podgy fingers in the folds of her gown and knew she was wasting her breath.

'When you have been here a little while you will learn that having a tumble with a servant relieves the boredom of everyday life. We must inject a little fun now and again. What would the world be like if everyone was as po-faced as you are led to believe? Why, before I was married I had lain with every good-looking servant in my father's household.'

Leah sniffed her disgust. 'I cannot agree with your morals, Lady Darlington.'

Phyllida gave a little chuckle. 'You are a virgin, child. I know that Percy gave you some excitement last night but you are without real knowledge of the carnal delights. When you have a man in your cunny, his stiff weapon throbbing between your thighs, you will know what I am talking about. Why, when I see a handsome fellow my insides melt and my nubbin throbs with such need I have to have him.' She patted her fat, wrinkled face. 'You may think me far too aged for young blood. But I was once as lovely as your good self and had many admirers.' She gave Leah a triumphant look. 'When you are past your best you will find, as I do, that you can still enjoy firm flesh if you have enough coin.'

Leah blushed. 'I think you should know that my father betrothed me to a planter in Barbados.'

'Betrothed?' Phyllida's composure slipped a little, but she swiftly regained her equilibrium. 'Don't lie to me, Mistress

60

Brown. It won't get you anywhere. Seems to me the sooner Percy gets you with child the better. You can be married quietly and no one will be the wiser.'

Leah paled. 'My father will have something to say about that.'

'I think not.' Phyllida sighed theatrically. 'We have heard that your poor father had a strange turn whilst dealing with a patient. I am afraid he is dead.'

Leah's heart lurched. 'Papa? Papa is dead?'

'I'm afraid so, my dear. I thought he looked a little off colour when he attended the earl a sennight ago. But then we all have to die someday. At least you have friends to help you over your grief. And I know my Percy will do all he can to make you feel better.'

But Leah was far too overcome with misery to hear her, and Phyllida was obliged to call the maid, Daisy, back to tend to her while she rustled out of the dank chamber to seek out some more sweetmeats before finding Charles – sad news always lifted her libido.

Leah stayed in her state of abject shock for two weeks, while Daisy tended her, worrying over her like a mother with her babe. But Leah was too heartbroken to eat and naught but a little soup and small beer passed her lips.

'I fear you are fading away to nothing,' Phyllida complained on one of her visits. 'A man likes curves, you must begin to eat. You and Percy will be wed as soon as possible; it will give you something else to think about.'

Her words roused the grieving girl. 'I have been promised to another.'

'Fiddlesticks!' Phyllida was quite out of patience with the chit. 'Your father is no longer with us; you can marry whomever you wish.'

Leah lifted her chin defiantly. 'I will marry the man of my father's choosing.' Lady Darlington opened her mouth intent on argument, but Leah held up her hand. 'Please, there's no more to be said on the subject. The matter is closed. If you

61

will order me a carriage I will be about my business. This farce has gone on long enough.'

She dragged her weak body from the bed and began to don her tattered gown. It was time she pulled herself together. Papa would be distressed to see her so. He liked women with spirit and had no patience with milk sops.

Phyllida's lips set in a thin line. 'Very well, if that's your attitude, so be it. But I am sure you will soon change your mind, Mistress Brown. We will not put up with temper tantrums and stubborn ways in this house.'

With an evil smirk she rang the bell-pull, and within minutes they were joined by a huge manservant. Leah was speechless, fazed by both his size and threatening demeanour. His hands were as big as shovels, and he was forced to duck when he lumbered in through the doorway.

Taking a deep breath, sounding braver than she felt, Leah said, 'Would you please see that a carriage is brought round. I am leaving.'

The manservant stared implacably ahead, and Phyllida laughed. 'You are wasting your breath. Thomas will take orders from no one but family.' Turning to him she commanded, 'Take our guest to her other apartments, Thomas, and make sure she's made comfortable.'

Leah clenched her fists angrily; she'd had enough of this family and their orders, so she dodged around the servant and onto the landing. 'Help me someone!' she called. 'I'm being kept here against my wishes!'

But no one took notice of the plaintive cry and she got no further, for Thomas strode after her and snatched her arms in a grip of steel.

Alerted by the scuffle on the landing, Percy appeared. 'Leah, you are such a trial. Will you not learn? You cannot escape. I aim to marry you and that's all there is to it. Now go with Thomas quietly or he will be obliged to use force, and I prefer to have a wife with comely features.'

Leah hit out at him, catching him unawares, and he yelped like a sulking child and clutched a hand to his red cheek.

'You'll be sorry for that, you little alley cat!' he swore as his mother went to his rescue, kissing his cheek and muttering dark oaths about the ungrateful Leah Brown.

Leah flung him a look of pure hatred as Thomas exerted pressure on her arms, but before he snapped her limbs she allowed him to lead her peaceably down the curving staircase. Daisy lit a candelabrum to light their way, and took the lead.

Leah gritted her teeth angrily; it was like a pageant, everything had obviously been planned and orchestrated in advance. 'Where are you taking me?' she demanded when led through an old door, the hinges of which creaked abominably, and down some steep stone steps into the bowels of the house.

'To your boudoir, me lady,' Thomas said with a sly chuckle.

There was a long passageway which they traversed swiftly, for it was much colder down here and Leah shivered in her flimsy gown, wishing she had pretended to be more cooperative. When they reached a huge wooden door Thomas took a large key from his pocket and proceeded to turn the lock. The door swung inwards with much creaking.

'Your bedchamber, me lady,' Thomas said with a sweep of his arm, pushing Leah cruelly to the floor.

She gaped at the empty cellar. 'You can't expect me to sleep here, there's no bed!'

'Would you like me to keep you company?' he asked with a grin, squatting beside her, insinuating his fingers through the tear in her gown and up to the apex of her thighs. 'I'd keep you warm.' He pinched between her legs and Leah let out a cry of pain.

'Unhand me, you oaf!'

Daisy was cowering in the doorway, the candelabrum seemingly overlarge in her dainty hands. 'Give her a candle, Thomas,' she said urgently. 'You can't leave her here in the dark.'

'Serves her right! See how high and mighty she feels after

spending the night here.' He beckoned to a piece of sacking. 'Your bed, me lady. I hope you find it soft enough for your little arse.'

With an evil laugh he pushed Daisy through the door and it creaked shut behind them, leaving Leah alone in the dark, soulless place. She rubbed her hands together to try to warm them, refusing to let the threatening tears fall. This was a fine mess. How was she supposed to escape from the bowels of the earth?

But she knew her papa was watching over her, and she would be brave for him. She trembled in the cold, knowing it would be wise to keep her mind and hands busy to retain her sanity in that hellish cellar. She took up the sacking, and feeling pieces of loose thread, began to undo the rough material.

Her thoughts turned to Captain Tempest, as they often had of late, and in her mind's eye she saw him rescuing her from her predicament. He would break the door down and, vanquishing her aggressors and saving her from that awful chamber, take her home to be bathed and gowned respectfully. Then he would take her on a carriage ride, his eyes for her alone. The sun would be shining, they would ride through Hide Park and she would watch the other fine carriages with delight. It would be a colourful scene as the *beau monde* took the air in the park, the gentlemen in their flowered, silk waistcoats, and the ladies in their silk and satin gowns, each one seemingly lovelier than the last. Many of the ladies would sport face patches and she imagined them now, most in the first flush of their youth, firm-fleshed and gleaming like graceful swans in the sun. The young men, their backs straight, their wigs elaborately curled, would preen proudly, brilliant as peacocks, ready to catch an eager young eye.

Her daydreams went on and in her mind's eye she could see them skating together on the ice of the Thames, at the ice fair that was held every winter when the river was frozen, twirling and laughing gaily. She imagined herself in all sorts of airy spaces with the handsome captain; it was the only way she knew to keep her mind off the evil of her prison. She painted pretty pictures in her head for hours, her thirst quenched by imaginary cool liquid, her hunger assuaged with the finest imaginary food. But the charming pictures in Leah's mind vanished with the scuttling sounds around her. She screamed – she was to be overrun with rats again! What had she done to deserve such a fate?

But as the sounds increased another sound, louder than the rest, alerted her to the fact that someone was scraping a key in the door, turning it. The door creaked open and the little maid stood in the frame of the doorway illuminated by a small candle.

'Daisy,' Leah cried, never so glad to see anyone in her entire life, 'what are you doing here?'

'In all conscience I couldn't see you rot in this place. I waited until Thomas drank himself into a stupor, as he always does after supper, and stole the key from him.'

Leah hugged her. 'Oh, dear friend, how can I thank you?'

Daisy looked uneasily behind her. 'By hurrying, mistress. Lady Darlington is busy cavorting with George. They will soon be as drunk as Thomas, and Lord Percy is out.'

She led her out and along the cold passageway, then up the stone steps that led to the rest of the house.

'Will you come with me, Daisy?' she whispered, lest they were overheard. 'You will be most welcome at my home, and you will like it there, I promise.'

'Daisy's face flushed in the candlelight. 'Thank you, my lady,' she said with a soft smile, 'but I cannot leave my James. He is the kitchen porter and the love of my life. 'Tis fated that we stay together.'

'But what if they blame you for my escape?' she whispered fearfully. 'I shall never forgive myself should you be punished because of me.'

'There is no need to worry,' Daisy reassured. 'George's fingers will be working on the mistress's nubbin right now, and she wouldn't care if the house fell down around her as long as she was able to have his cock up her cunny. And Thomas will wake up happy, with his key back on the large ring of keys he carries. When they find you're gone they'll believe he was too drunk to lock you in properly, 'cos he'd already put away a fair bit of ale before the mistress called him.'

The strain eased from Leah's features. 'You're such a clever girl and wasted in this household.'

Daisy led her through the house. 'The stable lad owes my James a favour and has promised to leave a mount ready for you in the stables.'

Leah clutched at her hand. 'Why would you do this for me?'

'Your father, the good doctor, saved my brother's life, and I shall always be indebted to him.'

A lump of gratitude formed in Leah's throat and she squeezed Daisy's arm, the candle flickering from a draught, making the house seem alive with evil. Then the sound of someone hurrying towards them forced them to scuttle up the stairs to hide behind the banisters like frightened mice.

Then they heard Lady Darlington shouting out in a drunken voice for Daisy. It boomed down the hallway and Daisy clicked her tongue angrily.

'What's gone wrong? She never calls for anyone when she has George in her bedchamber.' She pointed down the stairs. 'At the bottom, go straight on, turn left and left again and you'll be at the side door. Go safely, my lady.'

Leah gave her a swift hug. 'Thank you, Daisy. I won't forget you and your kindness.'

Lady Darlington's voice boomed out once more and Daisy gave a quick smile and hurried off, taking the candle in order to light her way. Leah followed the banister, for it was so dark she could no longer see her way. She seemed to miss the opening that was the stairs and wondered if she had gone in the wrong direction in her confusion and fear, and she was soon hopelessly lost in the maze of passageways.

She paused as voices came to her through an open

doorway, and trying not to make a sound she shrank back against the wall.

'She remains as stubborn as ever, mama.'

'You will win her over, Percy, have no fear,' slurred his mother.

Leah's hand went to her mouth in dismay; Daisy's plans had all gone awry. No one was where they were supposed to be. What if she should be found out? With her heart thudding in her breast she clung desperately to the wall, listening to the voices inside the room.

'Mayhap I should continue courting the merchant's daughter; she is far easier to charm.'

'Forget the merchant's daughter,' Phyllida said firmly. 'Leah Brown is a much better prize.'

'I don't know, mama. She is the most troublesome wench.'

'Then stronger measures will be called for. But she will not relish spending another night in the cellar with the rats. Mark me well, for she will be meek and mild on the morrow.'

Leah gulped at the ominous note in Phyllida's voice, but she almost cried out as Percy gave a low chuckle.

'Mayhap you are right. And the merchant's daughter is as plain as a pikestaff. I would much rather have Leah Brown in my bed.' His voice strengthened with resolve. 'I cannot wait any longer. Have Thomas bring her to my room. Tonight I will show the lovely Leah Brown who is boss. She will be glad of my name when her belly bulges with child.'

There was a short pause and Leah's heart beat rapidly in her breast. Percy was planning on possessing her that very night! She must hurry to be free of the house before the hue and cry went up. She was about to tiptoe past the door, but then he spoke again.

'What happens if they will not allow her to claim her inheritance when we are married?'

Leah went cold. Inheritance? What inheritance? She heard a derisive snort come from the countess.

67

'Thaddeus Brown cannot speak out from the grave, and my lawyers will make short work of any obstacles put in the way of the girl's fortune. Fear not, I have been planning your marriage ever since I heard Leah Brown's grandfather discussing his will with my papa, and I'll let nothing to stand in its way.'

Leah almost toppled a large plant in her hurry to run from that awful place, and steadied it with shaking hands. So she was to inherit her grandfather's money; that was the reason Percy Darlington was so eager to marry her. She moved quietly along the corridor, trying to halt the shaking threatening to overtake her entire body. But then she heard footsteps, saw a light flickering, hastily turned the nearest door handle and practically fell into the room.

She shut the door behind her and leaned against the solidity of the wood, her breath coming hard and fast. The room was empty. She was safe, at least for the time being. But then a noise in one corner set flames to that myth and, as he stood up from the chair in which he was sitting, Leah looked into the faded blue eyes of Sir Barnaby Darlington.

'Clara, my pretty, where have you been?' he said, dropping a book he was holding, putting a hand out to her.

''Tis Leah Brown, my lord,' she said timidly. She had not seen him in a long while. He had been a patient of her father's and apparently quite ill.

'Leah, how pretty,' he returned. 'Come Leah, sit over here and talk to me.'

Two large chairs sat in front of the empty hearth and Leah perched nervously on the front edge of one, quite unsure of Sir Barnaby's part in her kidnap. All she remembered was that he had always been kindness itself to her, and she decided to ask for his help. She could not imagine that he would side with his slut of a wife or his wayward son.

The earl made himself comfortable in the other chair, his nightcap bobbing as he studied her closely and nodded his approval. Percy favoured his father, she decided, but the earl must have been far more handsome in his youth.

'I'm so glad you returned,' he said, giving her a slightly reproving glance. 'I've missed you so.'

Thinking his sight was failing and that he had mistaken her for another, Leah repeated, 'I am Leah Brown, my lord. I must apologise for invading your privacy, but you see I've been held captive here. Your son wants me for his bride because of my inheritance, but I am betrothed to another.'

He looked at her vaguely. 'Hmm. Captive, you say?'

'Yes, my lord. And I want nothing more than to go home.'

'Of course, my dear,' he said pleasantly, and Leah sighed with relief. It was as she thought; Percy and his mother had obviously made their dastardly plans without the knowledge of the head of the household.

'Thank you, sir,' she said gratefully. 'I really cannot marry Percy. I do not love him.'

He gave her a blank look. 'Percy? Who is Percy?'

Leah watched his puzzled face with rising consternation. What was wrong with him? 'Are you all right, Sir Barnaby?'

He smiled. 'All right? Of course I am. You always make me feel good, Clara. Or did you say Janie?' His eyes lit up. 'I remember her so well, breasts as white as goats milk and a cunny as black as night.' His rheumy eyes stared at her critically. 'What colour's your cunny, young lady? Lift your skirts and let me see!'

Leah blushed to the roots of her hair. 'Sir Barnaby, you disgust me!'

'Disgust?' he said gaily. 'Yes, let's do something disgusting. I remember when we all had a tumble at Jake Durham's birthday party. We had two girls each; with the sweetest peachy cheeks you've ever seen. Trouble is, when we all got down to it – you know, with me doing it to Janie, right up her arse, and Annie and Pearl doing it to each other, licking each other's juicy little cunnies like you wouldn't believe, and Jake fucking Caroline's mouth – well, the bed just collapsed.

'But that didn't stop us,' he chuckled. 'No indeed. If anything it added to the excitement. We changed partners a few times too. Why, I wouldn't be surprised if Jake and I didn't land up fucking each other's arses, we were so drunk!' He lent towards her, a lewd twinkle in his eye. 'But you were always my favourite, Janie. You were such a dirty girl.'

'So, its Janie tonight, is it, sir?'

Leah looked round in dismay. Grinning down at them from the doorway was Thomas, red-faced and smelling of ale. 'Sir Barnaby's going to set me free,' she said, getting shakily to her feet.

Thomas laughed harshly. 'Goin' to let her go, are yer, sir? And you not had yer pleasure yet.'

Sir Barnaby surveyed him crossly, like a child about to be deprived of a favourite toy. 'No, Thomas, of course not. She's come to have fun.' He stood and walked purposefully to the four-poster bed, and rubbed his hands gleefully. 'Let's see what this pretty piece is like between the sheets, shall we?'

Leah glanced numbly from the eager baronet who wanted to bed her, to the large guffawing servant at the door. If only she could wake up from this nightmare!

'Want to go back to yer cellar?' Thomas asked mockingly. 'Or would you rather lie with Sir Barnaby?' He laughed loudly at her flushed face. 'Never did have gout, did his lordship. 'Twas just a rumour put round to avoid scandal. He's mad as a hatter. Thought you'd found an ally, eh?' This brought more raucous laughter to his lips, and tears to his eyes.

'Betsy, Betsy full and fair, pull up your skirts and show me your hair,' Sir Barnaby sang rudely, playing with the bed hangings. Then he stopped and grinned at Leah. 'Ah, sweet Betsy, you're the one who liked to smack my bottom while somebody did it up your arse. Come on, Betsy. Thomas, get the cane!'

Leah was frozen to the spot. What had she gotten herself into? 'T-Thomas,' she said through stiff lips, 'take me back to the cellar.'

70

But Thomas was already reaching under the bed for the cane. 'Can't do that, mistress. His lordship wants to play, and when his lordship wants to play, we all play.'

Leah looked from the surly servant to the dissipated baronet, and suddenly felt nauseous.

'Don't just stand there.' Thomas began to walk around her, his red face and bull-like neck becoming redder in his excitement. 'Lift yer skirts. Let Thomas see yer virgin arse.' He giggled and Leah reeled at the smell of the drink on his breath. 'Although from what I hear that's already been plundered. All the better; the young whelp's made room for a proper man.'

As she watched Sir Barnaby started singing again, then raising his night robe, baring his skinny buttocks, he bent over the bed. 'Come on, Betsy, let the dog see the rabbit.'

Leah almost threw up at the sight of the bandy shanks Percy's father exposed to her gaze. 'I'm sorry, I can't,' she said firmly. 'I want no part of this.'

Sir Barnaby looked as if he would cry. 'If you won't do it,' he said spitefully, 'I'll have Thomas cane you instead.'

Leah's bottom stung at the mere suggestion of being beaten again, so she slowly nodded. 'Very well.'

Thomas handed the cane to her. 'He likes his balls stroked first.'

'No,' she began fearfully, but when Thomas bore down on her she turned to the old roué and, reaching out ruefully, touched the sad seed sacs that hung low between his scrawny thighs. He moaned happily and she began to stroke them as instructed, biting her lip to prevent herself from feeling nauseous again.

'Oh Betsy, Betsy,' he sighed, 'there's not a maid in all the land who can touch my balls like you.'

He turned his head as though waiting for a reply, so she said, 'Thank you, sir.'

Her reply seemed to satisfy him for he smiled and turned away, so she dutifully stroked some more, praying his limp little cock would not rise, and just as she was tiring of his disgusting game he banged down on the quilt. 'Now. Do it now!'

'Give him a few hard blows to keep him happy,' Thomas ordered, 'and then I'm goin' to stick my cock right up yer arse, Percy or no Percy. Then you can tell me who fucks the best, that weak little cocksucker or a real man.'

Leah's eyes darted to the door and Thomas raised his eyebrows. 'Go on, run for it and I'll bring yer back and give you the finest caning ever!'

With a deep sigh Leah glanced from Sir Barnaby's bony backside to the cane, and realising she had no choice in the matter, swept the cane down against his bottom. He screamed and then begged for more. She hit him once, twice, three times, and each time he begged her to do it again. So she did, surprised at the power she had over him. It was an extraordinary feeling, one she could soon learn to relish.

Thomas watched with a gaping mouth, his admiration for the captive turned dominant evident as his manhood began to tent his breeches. He touched it tenderly, loving the way Leah's shoulders squared up to her task, the way she aimed one blow after another in a different place on the skinny rump, so that red weals crisscrossed the parchment-like skin.

She was a handsome wench, and he longed to be there on that bed with the earl, feeling her cane dance over his rump as cleverly as it did over the baronets. Then the longing overcame him and he dropped his breeches and lay beside his master, looking up at Leah pleadingly.

She was awestruck by the turn of events. Thomas had threatened to bugger her when all he really wanted was to be submissive. A small smile danced on her lips. It must be difficult for a brute like he was; everyone expected him to be dominant but all he needed was to be punished.

After giving him two strokes of the cane she found it quite easy to alternate them – striking the baronet and then Thomas. After a few blows she actually warmed to her subject. One skinny pair of half-moons and one sturdy pair, both longing for her to strike as hard as she could, both panting and groaning like naughty little schoolboys.

Oh, but it was so good to finally have the power to do to them what others had done to her. To treat them like objects of shame – like simpering, worthless creatures. That they enjoyed it was hard to realise, but they did. Each bite of the cane was a heavenly embrace to the two men on the bed, and she had complete control.

'Wha's going on?' Phyllida's drunken tones resonated around the room and Leah dropped the cane in shock.

Thomas immediately got to his feet, his glazed eyes suddenly focusing, falling over his breeches, stumbling about as he tried to pull them back up his legs. 'Sir Barnaby ordered me to do it, me lady,' he said quickly 'Had to agree, you know how worked up he gets when he's thwarted.'

Leah kicked the cane under the bed and stepped back, wondering if the fact that she was beating them had actually registered with the inebriated lady.

Phyllida found some ale on her husband's nightstand and began to guzzle it. 'Nat'rally,' she replied, struggling to hold herself upright. 'Wha'ever he wants. Glad one of us's all right. My Georgie's down with a bad cold and there's no one elsh to play with.' She got caught in the tangle of her long skirts and toppled over, landing on the bed with the mad baronet. He took one look at her and grinned.

'Ah, Betsy, there you are. Lift your skirts, my beauty; I'm going to plug your arse!'

Lady Darlington tittered as he began to fiddle with her skirts, and Leah hid a wry smile. No doubt they would both be surprised in the morning to learn that they had slept with their spouse. It must be a rare occasion in this family.

Thomas had managed to sort his clothing and was glowering at her. 'Let's get you back to the cellar before she realises what's happened. She won't remember anything come mornin'.'

Leah turned fearfully; her control over them had not lasted long. 'Won't you let me go?' she asked with a pleading look, but his reply was to grab her arms and manhandle her back down to the cellar.

'Breathe a word of what happened this night and you're done for,' he threatened her nastily.

Leah lay on the sacking on the rough cold floor, listening for the sounds that would tell her that she was not completely alone. And the rodents soon made their presence known, so that she was obliged to bang the floor to try to keep them at bay. But she had to admit that she preferred their company to that of the snivelling Percy Darlington, and fearing that he would come for her at any second she did not get a wink of sleep that night, even though she longed for sweet dreams of her handsome captain.

Chapter Five

As Leah had languished in the home of the Darlington's thinking of her handsome saviour, so Gideon was at the door of her home. He had been wondering how she fared, and ever the gentleman, come to enquire after her health.

But to his abject horror there was a death wreath on the door and the drapes were closed – as was the custom when there was a death in the family. The maidservant to whom he'd spoken that first time opened the portal to him, her face a portrait of misery.

'I am sorry for your loss, Mistress Jane,' he said, his voice suddenly hoarse. 'But I am come to enquire about the health of the mistress of the house.'

Jane's grey eyes filled and she rubbed the already red-rimmed orbs. 'I am sorry, sir,' she said sorrowfully. 'We have not seen Mistress Leah since the night she set out and found herself in dire straits by the river. I had thought you might know something.'

Gideon's lean face paled. 'I fear not. Have you spoken to

74

Lady Roebuck?'

Jane nodded. 'Indeed, but the lady could throw no light on my mistress's movements after she left there.' She wrung the handkerchief in her hand. 'We have been trying to contact her to tell her of her father's demise.'

Gideon swept his plumed hat from his head and made a bow. 'I am mortified to know of the trouble that has darkened your door, mistress. But be assured that I shall follow up the mystery of Mistress Brown's disappearance and not be satisfied until I find an answer.'

Jane's gratitude was obvious in the way her face dimpled up at him with relief. 'It is good that there is someone willing to pursue the matter, for it's a conundrum, and I must admit that I fear greatly for my beautiful lady.'

'I will do all I can,' he promised, his brow set in a puzzled frown as he hurried to hire a coach to take him to the Lady Roebuck's. He would go to the heart of the matter, for it was in that elegant house on the Strand he had last left Leah Brown, thinking her safe and sound.

The mansion sat in the sunshine, in manicured grounds, well away from the hustle and bustle of the rest of London. When Gideon paid the coachman and pounded on the door of the lady's abode it was to be answered by the stately butler, who showed him out into the garden where the regal Lady Roebuck was taking the air.

Her face lit with several emotions when she saw him, ending with a cold glare that she fixed relentlessly on his person, and Gideon knew he was in for a hard time. He had absented himself from her company since meeting Leah. From his first sight of the golden-haired wench he was struck by her beauty. There had been a presence about her that wormed its way under his skin. It had not happened to him before; although he was not a stranger to the charms of the fairer sex he had always kept his head and his heart completely separate – until now.

'I wonder you have the gall to show your face!' Roseanna stormed, flouncing towards him in a pink gown, the panniers

75

pulled back to show rose petticoats, her sumptuous bosom, as usual, bare almost to the nipples. A patch was stuck alluringly on one creamy breast, and she flung her head back dramatically and pierced him with her bright blue eyes.

'I am not here to bandy words with you,' he replied calmly, 'but to see if you know the whereabouts of the lady I brought to this house for shelter a sennight ago.'

'Don't you think you owe me an explanation?' she snapped furiously, ignoring his mention of Leah.

'I have no need,' he replied indolently.

His dark eyes flicked over her with disinterest and Roseanna fumed all the more; there had been a time, not so long since, when her charms had driven him mad with desire. 'So, you have no qualms about your treatment of me?' she derided. 'I have seen nothing of you since the night I dined with your waif off the streets.'

'The lady was not from the streets, as you well know,' he interjected angrily. There was no way he would listen to snide remarks about his golden lady.

Realising she was not putting him in the best of moods and longing to rest in his strong arms, she batted her eyelashes at him. 'Of course. Forgive me. I am merely peeved by your absence.' She bent over to smell a flower, knowing that in doing so she was allowing him full access to the view the creamy globes of which she was inordinately proud.

Gideon took the bait, for he had already decided to put her in better humour. His gaze lingered on her curvaceous flesh hungrily; he wanted information and Roseanna was always ready to talk when she lie abed after being sexually satisfied. She was a sensuous woman, one who always needed a man at hand to bend to her will. Let her believe he was responding to her, that he was as malleable as a willow that swayed easily in the wind.

Plucking a bloom from a rosebush he offered it to her. 'As you should be. I have been busy looking for crew to man my ship when she is ready. It is not an easy task, as you may

76

well recall me remarking on before.'

Her lips, every bit as red as the rose she held, lifted into a smile. 'Then you are forgiven,' she said sweetly. 'Though I should not be so compassionate. Had you thought to send me a message I would not have been quite so upset.'

Gideon took her hand and touched his lips to the pink-tipped fingers tenderly. 'Guilty as charged, milady.'

Roseanna's bosom strained against her stays and Gideon gave a sly smile, knowing well the signs of a woman's aroused body. Sometimes it was far too easy; she was not a challenge any more. Roseanna was always far too ready to raise her skirts, far too ready to share her charms.

He allowed his kisses to trail up her arm to her lips, and she answered by leaning into him so closely that his own body began to harden with interest. He trailed kisses across her jaw and down her neck to the glorious swell of her breasts. Her nipples were hard nuts of desire peaking above her bodice, longing for the lips of the man in whose arms she reclined, and he did not hold back.

It was pleasing to take the roseate peaks into his mouth, to titillate and torment, to suck and bite until she groaned, almost fainting away with elation. A hand snuck into her gown and dragged one full breast into his palm. She loved a little rough with the smooth; she might well act the lady in public, but in the confines of her bed Roseanna was a whore.

'Oh, Gideon,' she cried giddily. 'Take me to bed. I have missed you so much.'

'And I, sweeting,' he said, tweaking her other breast a little too hard, 'have missed you. And I have certainly missed these,' he said thickly, nipping them one at a time with his teeth till she had cause to cry out in pain.

She drew him into the house and up to her boudoir, where she ordered fruit and wine to be served immediately. She began to undress, leaving each garment where it lay on the floor, stepping out of each piece of cloth delicately, like a ballet dancer during a performance. Each movement, each gesture aimed to titillate, to please.

The serving maid brought the wine and fruit, her eyes lowered respectfully. She was well aware of her mistress's voracious appetite for sex, and knew that if she should raise her gaze any higher the Lady Roebuck would use the whip she kept in her bureau, having no mercy until her chemise had been beaten from her body.

Even so, she had seen enough this day to be able to report back to the other servants of the goings on in the lady's boudoir with the handsome Captain Tempest.

Roseanna took an orange from the bowl on her nightstand. It had been peeled ready and she set her white teeth into the juicy flesh, allowing it to dribble down her chin and breasts. She ate it greedily, caring nothing for manners as the juice spurted hither and thither, giving her lover a secret smile as he undressed.

Gideon had to admit that although he was jaded with this particular lady, her body would always be of interest to him, as would the way she used it. She knew all the tricks and Gideon was more than happy to play her little games.

When he had disposed of all his clothes her eyes shone as they glided over the long legs, narrow hips and broad shoulders of the seafaring captain. She took another bite of the succulent flesh, and as the juice ran from her breasts down over her belly, she offered it to her lover.

Gideon took a segment from between her teeth, biting to capture both her lower lip and the fruit in one. And though she let out a cry and shuddered at the spot of blood that issued from her mouth, and at the discomfort as the acidic fruit smote the wound, so too did she sigh when he kissed away the pain. And when he continued on down her ample curves, lapping at the juice with his tongue, she sounded almost like a cat purring.

But Gideon was not about to give her an easy time; that was not what she wanted. She wanted to be loved and adored but she also yearned for pain, for a long time ago Roseanna's body learned that pleasure and pain were different sides of the same coin.

78

The captain, well tutored in the art of pleasing a woman of her persuasion, nipped her stomach with his teeth, smiling slyly when she shivered at each little bite. And when he had finished licking the juices from her flesh he licked the spillage that had leaked down into the black curls at the junction of her thighs.

Roseanna sighed and opened her legs welcomingly as Gideon's fingers reached lower for the lips of her inner labia. They hung like ripe plums between the black hairs that framed them; he had never seen such large nether lips on any woman before. It was as though they were there to let her lovers know of her sensual nature.

He dug his teeth into one, taking it into his mouth and sucking at the same time. Liquid seeped from her vulva and Gideon slid a finger inside this verdant core, then two. He fucked her with his fingers, gliding in and out of her, pausing occasionally to nip her labia with teeth that sent her into tremors of delight. Then he decided to crown it all by nibbling her nubbin, the stiff protrusion of her womanhood that begged more than anything for his attention. He nibbled and sucked and bit and tormented until her shrill cries echoed through the elegant house, and when she shuddered into climax, so he led his stiff member to the weeping core of her and ploughed inside roughly, until she was wont to another bout of loud noise that told the servants that she was well serviced that day.

Afterwards they lie abed, with Roseanna beaming her satisfaction. ''Tis wonderful when you take me at the second of climax,' she purred. 'It thrills me like nothing else.'

'But I thought your favourite pastime was being fucked up the arse, Lady Roebuck,' he said lightly.

'Oh, that too. And this.' She pulled his fingers to her nether curls and he gave a sly grin; the lady wanted them tugging. To keep her sweet he stretched each curl and pulled hard, but each time he strayed away from the area she dragged his hand back. For this was another personal favourite of hers, and if he did it long enough it would lead her to another climax.

But this time Gideon was not quite so malleable. 'You never did say…' he murmured quizzically.

'What is it, Gideon?' she said, impatiently pushing his hands back to her nether curls.

'What happened to Mistress Brown when she left here…?'

She turned her head on the pillow, quite disinterested in his turn of conversation. 'She went in my coach, of course.'

Gideon give a mighty tug of the black curls, and at the same time he pinched her labia between finger and thumb, keeping up the pressure until she screamed and shuddered mightily and her second come of the day brought a smile to her lips.

'Of course,' he said, acting almost as disinterested as the lady herself, 'but where to? You see, the family are worried. Her father has passed away and they need to get in touch with her.'

'Alas,' she said on a sigh, 'I do not know of the wench's whereabouts. I know only that she was talking of seeing a lover.'

'I will make enquiries of your coachman.'

'It will do you little good,' she said quickly. 'I had to get rid of him. He was beginning to be far too familiar. I have been obliged to take on another who will know nothing of what happened that evening. Gideon, my love, can we not talk of pleasanter topics? You make me jealous speaking about other women… even one as common as Leah Brown.'

Gideon knew by her tone that she was lying. It didn't bother him, he would talk to her servants and they would tell him anything for the toss of a coin.

As usual Roseanna soon fell asleep and began snoring, no doubt dreaming of the handsome captain making love to her again.

Gideon dressed swiftly and looked out Cedric, the coachman, who in spite of Roseanna's lies had been in her service for many years. She had obviously thought he would take her word, but he knew better.

Cedric had great respect for the captain and could not get enough stories of his travels and adventuring. Although he had a yearning for being a sea rover, his stomach had always been too weak for a sailor and so he had to content himself with tales.

He shook his head when Gideon asked him about Leah. 'I didn't take her, sir.'

Gideon produced some coins and Cedric's eyes lit up. 'I am very worried about the lady and will pay well to find her.'

Cedric looked around the stables nervously, but apart from the restless snorting of the horses there was no one about. 'I had heard that she went by river,' he said quietly. 'Heard tell she was taken to the home of her lover, Percy Darlington, who resides at Dunstan Hall.'

He was about to tell the tall captain where Dunstan Hall was when Gideon forestalled him. 'I have passed there many a time. But are you sure of this?'

Cedric nodded his clear eyes, as honest as it was possible to be. 'Aye, captain sir. The gardener took the young lady and says as how he was paid well. Trouble is any coin he gets hold of gets pissed away in the gutter so he couldn't keep his mouth shut.'

Gideon thanked him, and with rounded shoulders went straight to the *Three Eels* tavern, where he was soon joined by Dr Fitzherbert, who wondered why his good friend was drinking himself into insensibility. It was a rare occurrence for the captain, who was usually a moderate man in all things. But he was bent on forgetting a certain golden-haired wench who had wormed her way under his skin.

'Women are the devil's spawn, Fitz,' he muttered, leaning on the bar, quite oblivious to the admiring stares of the barmaid for his handsome physique in his wine-coloured doublet and hose. Even then, in his hours of repose, his basket-hilted sword was at his side, hanging staunchly on his baldric, which was secured over one shoulder. 'Lead you

81

on with their soft words and pretty ways and then crack! Before you know where you are they've changed their minds, leaving you gasping and gaping like a damnable fool.'

Fitz patiently questioned his good friend, and slowly the story poured out. 'It's a rum business, Gideon,' he agreed. His heart had been broken too, and he sympathised with his friend.

'They enjoy seeing you drooling, Fitz,' Gideon said miserably. 'The prettiest are the worst. They smile and fine words tumble off their tongues, but all the while they are planning to break your heart. But I won't make the same mistake again, oh no,' he was heard to mumble as Fitz and the coachman hauled the hefty captain to a waiting carriage.

Gideon awoke with a headache and a tongue as thick as mud, but the inevitable had to be faced – Leah Brown was not the young woman she appeared to be. He was tired of the opposite sex and intent on ending his relationship with Lady Roseanna Roebuck, for she was another who was only happy when she had a dozen suitors. Up to then her indiscretions had not bothered him. It had been convenient to have a warm bed to lie in and welcoming, perfumed arms in which to reside when he returned from his trips at sea. But he was disenchanted with her lies.

Upon arrival at her residence he was shown into the sitting room, where Roseanna was resting. 'Gideon, what a pleasant surprise,' she said happily, immediately tugging down the bodice of her gown so her charms should be on better display, recalling his skilful lovemaking of the previous day. In all of London, and that included the court of King Charles, there was not a better lover.

Gideon's eyes wandered restlessly over her fine gown, barely noticing the curves beneath. 'It's about our relationship, Roseanna. I think it's run its course, don't you?'

Roseanna grasped the folds of her blue gown, tearing her darker petticoats in her anger. 'How could you? After… after…' Her shoulders shook but Gideon was not rising to the bait. He turned and Roseanna, realising her ploy was not working, spat vitriol at him. 'Why? Have you been playing the ministering angel again? The handsome hero who saves wenches from all manner of dangers before spiriting them into his bed, just as you did with that whore Leah Brown.'

'Watch your tongue, Roseanna,' he warned, his voice deceptively quiet.

'You couldn't wait for my husband to be cold in his grave before you bedded me!' she wailed.

Gideon's face was a cold mask. 'You tried to seduce me and half of London when your husband was still alive,' he spat. 'I just wish that when he passed away I'd had the sense to keep resisting you.'

Lord Cob had been a friend, and he would have none of Roseanna when the poor man was alive. After his death, his widow played her cards well by leaning on Gideon's broad shoulders and asking his advice in all she did. As he was meant to, he finally took pity on her and she managed to wheedle him into her bed.

'You are quite unable to resist anything in a skirt,' she spat back.

'Just as you couldn't resist sleeping with Lord Stanhope the night you told me you were comforting a sick relative.' His grin was sardonic. 'But of course his coffers are full and one must prepare for old age, for you aren't getting any younger, are you Roseanna?'

Roseanna was incandescent with rage as she waved her fan in his face. 'How dare you? The gossips have provided you with the correct information, captain. That is my business. But pray tell, how can you point the finger at me when you brought that little whore to my house?'

'I advise you to speak with respect when you mention Mistress Brown.'

She fanned her flushed cheeks. 'Mistress Brown, indeed!

Why, if I hadn't had her sent to Sir Barnaby's you would be lying abed with her now, wouldn't you?'

He viewed her levelly. Sometimes gossip was spoiled when it had been told many times. 'Sent? So the lady did not go of her own volition?'

Roseanna realised her mistake too late. 'What… what else was I to do when you were obviously bewitched by the besom?'

'Instead of laying the blame at someone else's door, Roseanna, had it not occurred to you that I may have merely grown tired of you?'

Roseanna lifted her hand to slap him, but he restrained her, holding her wrist firmly in a grip of steel.

'You are a bastard, Gideon Tempest!' she spat virulently.

'And you, Roseanna, are no lady,' he replied coldly, and perceiving that the fight had temporarily gone out of her, he released her, then as she rubbed her sore wrist he left her and strode down to the river.

So Roseanna had the lovely Leah Brown whisked from under his nose. No wonder he had gone on a fool's errand when she sent him to the docks.

Roseanna followed furiously, snapping her fan against her palm. 'You will be sorry for making a fool of me!'

Gideon stiffened before swinging round to face her, his eyes bright with rage. 'Hold your tongue!' He felt like striking this woman grown ugly in her jealousy, but instead he turned on his heel, his expression grimmer than ever. 'I will leave now to try to undo the mischief you started. I'll send someone for my things. Be sure to have them ready.'

She watched him go in disbelief. He did not fall to his knees and beg for forgiveness as she had expected, as she was used to with her other paramours. She slashed at the pots of geraniums that decorated the garden, overturning one in her rage, before storming back into the house muttering outraged oaths. Captain Tempest would be sorry he had crossed her! No man living had ever ended a relationship with her, she had them march to her tune, and she would have it no other way!

She ran up the stairs and into her bedchamber, where she flung open her jewellery casket. Seizing a ruby pendant she held it up to the sun, where it glowed like dripping blood. A laugh sprang from her throat like an explosion, filling the empty room and then dying down as swiftly as it began. Roseanna stared into the heart of the jewel, her eyes glazed with revenge.

Leah squinted up at the bright candles that lit her bedchamber. To her surprise and delight Percy had not come to her the previous night, and that morning she'd been fetched from the cellar and taken back to the room she had first occupied at Dunstan House. A bath was prepared for her and Daisy was busy lathering her back. ''Tis a crying shame you were unable to escape last evening,' she consoled.

'At least I was left alone,' she replied with a sigh. 'I was afraid Percy might come looking for me.'

Daisy smiled. 'When I knew you'd been found I put a little sleeping draught Lady Darlington often uses in his wine.'

Leah took the soap from Daisy and lathered her legs. 'You are a good friend.'

Daisy grimaced. 'But not good enough, mistress. You see, 'tis Sir Barnaby's birthday and there's going to be a party.' She paused and surveyed Leah sorrowfully. 'These affairs can be pretty wild and I fear for your safety.'

Leah swirled the perfumed water around her; how good it was to feel clean again. She knew that most people bathed little and that some were even sewn into their clothes for the winter. It was also the fashion to carry a pomander to hide the bad odours of one's person; but Dr Brown had been of the belief that a dirty body was not conducive to good health and brought Leah up accordingly.

She finished her toilette and stood up so Daisy could dry and powder her. 'I am in the hands of wicked people, Daisy.

But God is good. Someone will come to my rescue, I know it.' She didn't mention that she hoped she knew who that person would be. Captain Gideon Tempest had lit a bright light deep inside her and she knew it would never be extinguished, no matter what was done to her.

Daisy pampered her skin with a soft towel. 'I'll be running around all day. The mistress has already had me treat her warts with slaked lime and lye. And later she will 'ave me ply 'er with even more cosmetics than usual. Mark my word she will look like a court jester by this evening.'

Leah giggled. 'You mean she can look worse? I didn't think it possible.' The two girls laughed heartily thinking of the unappealing looks of Lady Darlington.

'I would have said Sir Barnaby was handsome in his day,' Leah mused as Daisy helped her into a gown that Phyllida had long grown out of. 'Whatever did he see in his wife?'

Daisy lowered her voice. 'Her family had money, but the baronet is a one for the gaming tables and the ladies. Or at least he was before he got so mad.'

Leah felt much better when Daisy left, and she began to look for a means of escape, but the door was well locked and the room was far too high up to venture out of the window.

When it was dark and the candles were lit Thomas came for her. Leah hoped there might be some sign of the submissive from the previous evening, but to her disappointment Thomas was every bit as aggressive as ever. She was taken to the main hall and made to wait outside, wondering why several servants came to slyly peak through the double doors that sectioned that room from the rest of the house.

Noting her curiosity Thomas beckoned her forward. 'Want to see the rich at play, do yer?' He opened the door a crack for her to peer through. 'Feast your eyes, girlie. Feast them good.'

Leah blinked at the sight of the assembled company. The Darlington's had invited many guests who were noisily dining from a table that groaned with food, and she surmised that they would be paying for this party for a long time to come.

Most of the guests' attention was given to some sort of entertainment put on for them, but for the moment Leah was more concerned by the fact that some of the ladies were sitting on gentlemen's laps in a sorry state of dishabille. In fact a few seemed to have lost the top of their gowns completely and were revealing rosy-tipped bosoms. Many of the gentlemen were playing idly with the pink-tipped globes and Leah's mouth gaped.

But when a rousing cheer from the guests seemed to be directed at the entertainment, she turned to look. She hadn't known what to expect but it certainly wasn't what she found. Two servants were holding up what looked like a piece of bed linen, which was lit from the back by an assortment of lanterns and candles. A naked lady danced exotically behind this screen and her shadow was thrown into stark relief on the linen. Her dainty breasts bobbed as she moved sinuously through her routine, and her perfect figure was breathtaking. There were catcalls and bawdy sayings, but the young woman seemed completely oblivious to the coarseness around her.

Her display was awe-inspiring and Leah watched in fascination as she was joined by another female, and then another. As the three nymphs whirled elegantly and performed an exotic ballet, so the guests egged them on with the vilest language.

'Show us your tits,' said one gentleman garbed in brown velvet.

'Let's see your arse,' said another, his cravat askew, his long curled periwig hanging off the back of his head. His legs rose in the air as he tipped his chair in excitement, and the great loops of ribbon that decorated the outer sides of his gathered breeches caught in the false hair of his companion and she screamed as it was torn from her head.

But no one took notice, for they were all either far too

inebriated or too caught up in the performance of the naked dancers to care. And in the midst of all this sat Lady Darlington and her husband, Sir Barnaby, who was clapping his hands with glee and shouting as loudly as the rest. Percy, on the other hand, was far too busy with his hands between the thighs of a beautiful brunette to take much notice of the entertainment.

Thomas nudged Leah away from the scene of debauchery and gave her a triumphant smile. 'I bet you ain't seen nothing like that before.'

'N-no,' Leah stammered. She could hardly believe her eyes. She had known the place was evil, but she had seen things take place in this house she'd never dreamt of. 'Why am I here, Thomas?' she asked, her hands trembling fearfully.

'Who knows?' He shrugged. 'I was told to bring yer, the rest is up to them,' he declared, nodding towards the doors that led to the drunken baying crowd.

Just then the double doors opened and the dancers appeared, their heavenly bodies wrapped in blankets. 'What a bleedin' mob,' cursed one.

'That dark one put his hands on me fanny,' said another.

'Aye, and that old fool had his cock hanging out of his breeches,' muttered the last in disgust. 'I'll be glad to be out of this mad'ouse.'

The others agreed just as she spied the white-faced Leah. 'Yer not going in there, are yer?'

Leah nodded. 'It seems so.'

The young woman shook her head sorrowfully. 'Then watch yer cherry or they'll pop it as soon as look at yer.'

Leah had heard the expression from Rose, unfortunately understood its meaning, and her pale features went even whiter. 'I don't dance, so I'm not sure why I am here,' she replied weakly.

'I don't think its yer dancing yer need bother about,' one tossed over her shoulder as she scurried away after her sisters.

88

'I can't go in there,' Leah pleaded, deeply afeared by the dancers' warnings, but as she spoke a head appeared through the double doors and announced to Thomas that they were ready.

He covertly slid a mask that sported eagle feathers over her face, propelling her forward through the doors, and she was suddenly deafened by the din that met her. The screen, she was glad to see, had been taken down and she shrank back against the wood of the doors, trying without success to open them so she could escape from that hotbed of lust. But she was drawn deeper into the room to be exhibited to all and sundry, and a smiling Lady Darlington twirled her around.

'There you are,' she said slyly. 'How well my old plum gown suits your complexion. 'Tis a shame the petticoats will be up over your arse before you can look down that saintly nose of yours.'

Leah's breath came in short sharp bursts. 'W-what do you mean?'

But the over-painted lady was far too concerned with trying to stay on her feet to take any notice of the terrified girl. 'Here she is,' she said carefully, lest she slur her words, 'the star of the evening. And do you not think she has a fine figure?'

'Superb,' shouted a gentleman, his enormous stomach barely contained in his breeches. 'Strip the wench; let us see that she's as perfect as you say!'

Leah almost swooned at the fellow's audacity. Lady Darlington smiled affectionately, holding her firmly at her side. 'Come, Sir Robert, have patience, you know the game.'

Leah's ears pricked up at this; so she was to be part of some game, was she? She hoped it would be over quickly, for she did not like the look of the Darlingtons' friends.

Phyllida's words had been met with shouts of disapproval and she quickly changed her mind. 'I suppose it will not hurt to give you a sample of what to expect,' and to Leah's horror the woman dragged her bodice down, quite easily

89

owing to its ill fit, exposing her breasts to the drunken gathering. Then her next unexpected move was to lift Leah's petticoats so that her legs and blonde mound were on show to a very happy audience.

A handsome cavalier prodded her and Leah shied away. 'Unhand me, you wretch!'

The man laughed his admiration. 'So the wench has spirit, eh? I will offer for her.' He took off his plumed hat and luxuriant chestnut hair tumbled down around his shoulders, and Leah realised that the handsome cavalier was not a man, but a beautiful woman in disguise. The woman wrote on some parchment, tossed it inside the hat and handed it around.

While there was much muttering and writing on parchment Lady Darlington remarked to Leah, 'Lady Marchmont flies both ways and is much taken with you. You will be lucky if she wins you.'

'What do you mean?' Leah asked anxiously. 'How can she win me? I am not a fish to be won at the fair.' But the lady's next words sent chills down her spine.

'No, but these dear people are bidding to see who will pay the highest to own you for a night.'

'Own me for a night?' she gasped in confusion.

'For goodness sake buck up, Mistress Brown, you are beginning to sound like an echo.'

When the hat was full of pledges Phyllida greedily went through each one to find the highest bidder, and finally flashed a smile at the assembled company, who held its collective breath. 'Lady Marchmont,' she said, returning the hat to its rightful owner. 'I vow that you have bought yourself a fine filly for the night.'

The chestnut-haired enchantress tossed the heavily plumed hat into the air and her shoulders were patted from all sides. Leah watched the scene in silence, her head whirling to make sense of what she had just witnessed.

Lady Darlington viewed Lady Marchmont equably. 'Before you bear your prize off, my lady, you must give the rest of us some fun. The rules have not changed since the last time.'

She beckoned someone forward and Thomas, who had been standing to one side of the hall, sidled up to Leah and upending her, tossed her over a chair, dragging her skirts up over her blushing bottom. She was far too startled and her mouth was much too dry to enable her to speak, but she watched in amazement as the lovely lady who had purchased her took a sturdy whip from Phyllida and began to swish it for effect. It snapped loudly through the air, and Leah let out a cry of horror.

Chapter Six

Leah trembled, her pretty cheeks quivering with fear, for she knew what to expect. This aristocratic gathering was waiting for her naked rump to be beaten by the beautiful woman who had latterly been in disguise. From the corner of her eye she was able to see the appalling way they behaved; the dandies molesting their partners in all their intimate places, and the ladies not batting so much as an eyelash in return. They disgusted her!

But Leah was to be even more horrified when the lady in question handed the whip over to Percy, who had deserted his partner in order to do the honours. As Leah wished she could run and hide he spat on the handle of the whip and then inserted it into her vagina, twisting and turning the object patiently as Leah cried and begged him to stop. But ignoring her he went about his mission diligently, until it fitted snug inside her.

''Twill make things easier for my passage later,' he explained smugly, and the crowd clapped and cheered raucously, throwing hats and feminine underwear into the air in excitement.

'Make her scream,' shouted a man and a woman who had

stopped masturbating each other in order to watch the entertainment.

'Stick it right up her, and then whip her arse with my cane,' yelled another, waving his walking cane in the air.

Leah held back her tears; let them stare, let them leer; she would take no notice, for in spite of their breeding they were acting no better than the bawds in the alleyways. But she gave a startled cry when Percy began to use the handle as a cock, thrusting the object in and out of her vagina as fast as he could.

The hall erupted into even louder cheers and she shut her eyes against the pain and the mob that were baying for more. When she opened them it was to see Percy's expression in a silver tray that stood on a side table in front of them. His eyes were wild, his cheeks reddened with excitement, his penis almost bursting the seams of his breeches.

She knew he would not stop, no matter how she pleaded with him, so she braced herself against the discomfort of the handle as it rode back and forth inside her, against the appalling humiliation he was inflicting upon her. But then a strange bloom of desire surged through her lower belly, spread through her loins and, as she relaxed and her natural juices covered the whip handle, so it became a fount of pleasure. She rode with it, pushing down on the implement so she could gain more purchase, more delight from its thrusting head. She slid her fingers into her wet vulva and began to stroke the little nubbin that was begging for attention, throbbing with so much need she cared little who saw; she was on a mission to satisfy the urges Percy had inspired in her.

The sight of the lovely young woman enjoying Percy's attentions in such a sensual manner soon became far too much for some. Dishes were pushed aside on tables, ladies were lifted onto the surface from which they had supped and their legs pushed apart as lusty gentlemen rutted like animals, driving their cocks into the core of feminine bodies. Some were not satisfied with this and urged their companions to open their sweet mouths for their pleasure. Soon they were all having sex, and to Leah's surprise, readily changing partners afterwards.

She came with a loud groan and Percy, seeing that he was missing out, found a nubile young earl whose buttocks were bobbing in the air. He creamed his bottom hole with butter from a handy dish, freed his penis and thrust it up the earl's arse. The earl, who was riding a rather striking duchess, rolled his eyes in delight.

Leah cast her eyes around for the lady who had outbid every other person in the room for her favours, and found her sucking a portly gentleman whose balls slapped urgently against her chin on each thrust of his penis. Even Thomas was on his back while one very lovely lady of the aristocracy rode him wildly, shouting, 'Tallyho!' whenever she became overly excited.

Leah knew it was the very opportunity she'd been awaiting, and made for the door eager to make her escape. She would away while the lady and gentlemen guests of the Darlingtons satisfied their lascivious appetites.

But it was not to be, for she immediately found herself ensnared by the chestnut-haired enchantress, who had satisfied the portly gentleman and was now claiming her prize.

Tears of frustration made Leah's eyes bright, anger made her voice shrill. 'Let me be,' she pleaded, her emerald eyes never more beautiful. 'I have been held prisoner in this house and crave my freedom.'

Lady Olivia ran her fingers through Leah's golden hair longingly. 'I cannot. You are mine for a night and as such my needs will take precedence.'

She opened the door and snapped her fingers at the tired footman, who immediately gave orders for her carriage to be brought round. Leah's borrowed gown and her chemise were pulled off over her head, and a leather shirt without arms was pulled on in their place. It reached down to her hips and was laced up at the back so that she was unable to move her upper limbs, and she was mortified with embarrassment. Her mask had been dislodged during the change of clothes and Olivia replaced it carefully, licking her lips provocatively.

She allowed her hazel gaze to travel over Leah's figure in the tight, armless garment, and she smiled enigmatically at the sight of the leather smoothed tight over her heaving breasts. They rested there a while before travelling downward, to where the tight garment finished on the hips, leaving her pouting cunny with its pretty golden curls of nether hair naked to her perusal.

Her eyes sparkled with lust, and Leah, completely unable to move her arms, bit her lip in embarrassment. When the lady had finished her appraisal she snapped her fingers, and Leah was taken roughly between two servants and led out to the waiting carriage. She felt the night air on her thighs, on the naked flesh of her cunny and, as strange as it sounded, felt her cunny blushing.

Flaming torches outlined the handsome vehicle, the coat of arms gleaming like jewels on the door, highlighting her dilemma for all the servants outside to see. The men had the same reactions as the Lady Olivia, their eyes glinting in the light from the torches, their mouths slack with lust.

Leah was pushed inside and her bottom slyly patted by the footman who manhandled her onto one of the seats. The lady with the chestnut curls followed, and settled down on the red velvet upholstery opposite. Leah felt the coach tilt and looked up to see a leering Thomas climb up beside the driver. So she was not to be left, as she had expected, in the sole charge of this lady. The Darlingtons were making sure she had no avenue of escape. Her freedom had been snatched from her and it wouldn't easily be given back.

The Lady Olivia did not speak or even glance at her during the journey, and they travelled a goodly distance before the coach changed direction and the fine horses pulled it up a handsome drive, lined with elm trees and lit by flaming torches set in fancy sconces in the ground. They stopped at a palatial mansion, and after the sweet-smelling Olivia decamped from the coach, Leah was hauled out and taken inside.

She was left momentarily in a huge hallway, lit by a chandelier wherein at least a hundred candles burned, and she looked around in admiration. This house was beautiful indeed, everything screamed elegance and money.

She wasn't kept waiting for long, and when two servants guided her up the stairway she was taken into a lovely chamber where the hangings were in deep plum and leaf green, the tester bed a soft haven of plum satin quilts and pillows. It was a place in which dreams were woven, but she bit her lip in vexation; what treatment was she to expect in this household?

She wasn't left to wonder for long, for the lovely Olivia appeared from an adjoining chamber, her night-rail, all lace and froth, sweeping out behind her. She inspected Leah carefully, her eyes taking in her bright curls, her body in the leather jacket without arms, and her shapely legs. As before her eyes targeted the blonde triangle at the juncture of her thighs, and she knew her cunny lips would be visible for the lady's pleasure.

Leah blushed deeply at the close inspection and dropped her eyes demurely, lest the lady find her whip and have her beaten. She had never felt more vulnerable than she did standing there in nothing but the restraining leather top and mask, her sex open to anything.

It was still very warm and she longed to remove her arms from the leather to alleviate the heat, for it was extremely sticky in the costume and terribly uncomfortable. She tried giving the lady imploring looks, but all she met was a stare of desire and triumph.

'M-mistress,' she stammered, 'would you kindly have me released from this garment? I am overcome with the heat.'

Olivia laughed softly. 'I cannot allow that, Leah. You see, you must learn obedience. It is important that you know you're my slave, and as such a willing vassal to anything I might order you to endure. Besides, I can't have you escaping and missing what I have planned for later.'

Leah licked her dry lips. 'What would that be?' she asked uneasily.

Olivia sighed. 'Oh Leah, what a naughty girl you are, licking your lips like that. How do you expect me to concentrate?'

Leah swallowed and arched her neck to ease the aching that had overtaken her, no doubt from the tension fear had inflicted on her. 'I… I don't understand.'

Olivia came closer, and Leah could feel her sweet breath on her face. 'Don't you want to know what happens to naughty girls who pout sexily and flick pink tongues at me?'

Completely fazed by the turn of events Leah took a deep breath, and her breasts, so obvious in the tight leather, rose and fell enticingly. Olivia was captivatingly perfumed, her night-rail completely diaphanous in the soft glow of the candles, showing off her divine curves. It reminded Leah of the graceful ballet at Dalton House, silhouetted on the sheet in front of the debased friends of the Darlingtons.

She did her best to ignore the sensual expression on Olivia's face, or her own mounting excitement, and she was powerless to move as the woman delicately moulded her leather-covered breasts with her elegant fingers. There seemed to be mirrors everywhere in the satin-hung bedchamber, and Leah was appalled to find that her reflection, and Lady Olivia's, was staring back at her from many angles of the room.

Olivia, noting her dismay, gave a tinkling laugh. 'Does it not fascinate you to be portrayed so?'

Leah fumbled for words. 'I… I find it nerve-racking and quite inappropriate.'

'Oh, my dear, what a sheltered life you have led!'

Leah inhaled swiftly when the slender fingers increased the pressure on her breasts through the confining leather. 'Un… until recently,' she ventured to whisper. After all, amongst other atrocities had she not been abducted, abused, exposed to the indignities of being put up for sale and having her bottom shown to all and sundry while Percy Darlington abused it with a whip handle? She recalled her own reactions to the dire act and blushed to the roots of her hair. Her own body was traitorous; how did she know what else it would desire?

'Do you not think it exciting to watch yourself being touched so?' Olivia went on artfully.

Leah watched the mirror image of the gorgeous creature in the diaphanous night-rail as she moulded her breasts, caressing the nipples as only another woman would know how. 'Yes...' she admitted, feeling far too aroused for comfort.

Olivia ran her fingers down over the firm stomach covered by the sensual leather. 'Good, then you have learned well.' Those fingers massaged her pubic mound, and Leah thought she would faint at the urges that spread through her like needles darting through tapestry. They lingered in the blonde curls, and Leah couldn't help but try to tilt herself a little so that the lady would touch her nubbin, for it pulsed with need.

Leah nervously flicked her tongue over her lips, and Olivia caught the soft flesh with pearly teeth before stabbing her own tongue at Leah's, who closed her eyes as the fingers kneaded her breasts, as the velvet tongue fenced with her own, eliciting such strong feelings she thought to collapse in a heap at this lovely being's feet.

Their hot breath mingled, and when the lady slid one questing finger into Leah's wet furrow the girl's legs almost gave way and she sobbed a small cry of delight.

'Do you like that?' Olivia purred.

Leah could not deny it. 'Oh yes,' she said, trembling slightly.

'Then perhaps I should use two fingers to plug your cunny. What do you think?'

Leah trembled even more. 'Oh yes, yes please.'

Olivia gave another tinkling laugh and fed a second finger

inside her. 'And perhaps I could frig your nubbin with my thumb. Does that appeal to you, Leah Brown?'

The woman's soft lips moved to Leah's throat and a jolt of pure delight shot down her spine. 'It does,' she agreed hoarsely, pushing herself down on those questing fingers, sighing and gasping when the lady began to gently rub the small nub where so many nerve endings pulsed for release.

'Look, Leah,' Olivia murmured breathily. 'Look in the mirrors. Does it not look disgustingly rude as I play with your nubbin and fuck you with my fingers? Do you not wish I could always love you?'

Leah was completely carried away, hypnotised by the sensual lady doing such wonderful things to her body. 'Oh I do, I do,' she agreed instantly, allowing her eyes to feast on the reflected sight that should have been taboo.

Thoughts of the debased William Penrose crept unbidden into her mind and she momentarily stilled. Olivia felt the slight change in her and began working even harder on her clit, and Leah watched in the mirrors, hardly recognising the girl who stood so lewdly in front of the gentlewoman, her expression glazed, her body responding so luridly to the titillating fingers.

Leah convulsed in Olivia's arms, her climax flowing over her like warm honey. She was so weak that she didn't demur when Olivia guided her to the bed, and rang for some wine and small beer to refresh them both. And even though the servant gazed longingly at her shapely legs and the fair bush and pearly lips that ran with love dew, Leah cared not for she was still wrapped in a sensual haze. Her lashes began to flutter and close and she lay down on the soft eiderdown, wriggling awkwardly in the restraining leather garment, trying to find some comfort.

'Come, Leah,' snapped Olivia. 'I have you for the night. You are not allowed to sleep.'

Leah looked at her wearily, but Olivia took her by the shoulder and shoved her up from the bed. 'I have something to show you, and I want you completely cognizant when I do.'

Leah obediently followed her into an adjoining chamber, every bit as magnificent. It was decorated in dark blue with rare paintings on the walls, and from behind the confines of the bed hangings appeared a large figure that viewed her with interest.

'She's quite lovely, Olivia,' he declared, hovering over Leah threateningly. She was able to see him more clearly now. He was tall and obese, his belly hanging over his breeches. He had probably been handsome at one time; until his greed put paid to his figure, but now his chins wobbled and one of his fat hands reached out to caress her golden hair.

Olivia smiled. 'I knew you would approve, sweetheart. Did you like what you saw through your peephole?'

He roughly tugged at Leah's mask, pulling it from her face. 'Oh yes,' he drawled, his chins wobbling all the more as he spoke. 'She has the most divine cunny, and her arse is to die for. And her face isn't to be sniffed at, either.'

Leah was watching him in confusion. What had Olivia said? Had he really watched them through a peephole? Her face reddened and he sniggered.

'My wife and I have a little pact. She gets hot for other women and I let her enjoy them as long as I can watch.' He pointed to a small hole in the panelling that led from his chamber through to Olivia's. 'I thought you looked very well together. Night and day, light and dark, a bewitching mix. Now, sweet victim, lie yourself on my bed while I get ready to have you.'

Leah backed away from him, shaking her head in disbelief. She would not allow this fat pig near her! She turned and tried to run, but Olivia dug her long fingers into her shoulders, and then grabbing the laces that tied the leather jerkin together, dragged her backwards to her husband.

'Ungrateful bitch,' she cursed. 'I paid well for you. Now do your duty and open your legs for my Drake.'

Leah trembled as the fat man lunged at her, and catching her by the neck of her jerkin threw her onto the bed. 'I did not ask to be bought like an animal at auction, and I do not wish to have sex with your husband,' Leah protested valiantly when she got her breath back.

But Olivia merely slapped her cruelly across the cheek. 'If you wish to stay in one piece you will do as you are told.'

The chestnut-haired lady no longer looked attractive with her face contorted with anger. Leah glanced fearfully from the wife to the husband, and cried out when he pulled a wicked knife from his breeches and loomed over her. Leah shrank down into the mattress, silently praying to be spared, but with a flourish of one flabby arm he slit the leather jerkin from top to bottom, leaving her completely naked and open to his perusal, his mouth cruel and his dark eyes glinting with relish to see her so terrified, tears stinging her eyes as the blood began to rush painfully back through her arms.

From his breeches Drake lovingly hauled his manhood, and she let out another frightened scream, for she had never seen anything so huge. 'No, please,' she begged. 'I am a virgin.'

He leered at his wife. 'You have done well this night, Olivia. I have not had a virgin for a long while.'

'Let me break her in for you,' Olivia offered eagerly, routing around in a drawer and retrieving a wooden penis-shaped tool.

'Don't be greedy. You've had your turn.' He studied Leah's curves with slack lips, his podgy hand reaching out to touch her perspiring breasts. 'It's been as hot as Hades these last weeks. Having a virgin will make up in some part for my misery.'

His fingers pinched her soft flesh and she bit back a strangled sob. 'This one's perfect,' he murmured with delight. 'Firm tits and a lovely yellow bush. And she shakes and shudders like a junket. You can have the emeralds you so lusted after, my dear.'

100

Olivia pressed her hands together and did a little dance, her luscious breasts bouncing beneath her diaphanous night-rail, the shadow of her dark sex a scintillating triangle beneath the gauzy material. 'Thank you, Drake. They will go well with my new gown.'

Leah was stunned; the woman was thinking of naught but frivolous items when she was about to be ill-used by her insufferable husband! But little did she realise that her fear put a sparkle in her eyes, added roses to her cheeks, made her even more attractive to the man whose penis she was sure would tear her in two.

Desperately she cast around for a weapon, and seeing the candle on the night table, made a grab for it. But despite his considerable mass, Drake was faster and caught her grasping arms in an iron grip.

'Fetch me some rope,' he commanded. 'The she-wolf has fangs!'

With a sly smirk on her lips Olivia left the room, and returned with a coil of rope, which she wrapped around Leah's limbs, tying her securely to the bedposts. 'That's better,' she sneered. 'Now you remind me of a butterfly mounted in a glass case.'

Drake chuckled rudely and mauled Leah's breasts, kneading them like pieces of dough meant for the oven. 'Aye, but the only mounting to be done around here will be done by me!'

Leah cringed at his crude joke, clenching her fists as his clammy hands wandered over her body, marking the pale flesh cruelly. His fist snuck between her legs to be met by arid flesh. He slapped her face and she turned it into the pillow, where her tears fell like rain.

'So you can turn it on for another woman but not for me, eh? Well, I'll soon fix that.'

To her distress he pushed one bloated finger inside her, impatiently following it with another. Leah winced at the pain inside her, and then shed more tears as her rogue body answered his prodding and her dew coated his fingers.

'That's more like it.'

Before she had time to catch her breath his huge cock was pushing at her vagina... and then actually sinking inside her! The chamber echoed with her screams as her insides were stretched to ridiculous proportions to accommodate him. Then once fully embedded in her virgin flesh he grunted his smug satisfaction like a huge, sweating pig, and began his obscene dance of possession.

Leah screamed at every lunge of his huge tool as it made a fiery path inside her, wanting to gag against the disgusting body that had taken her for its own. His belly slapped and squelched against her, and she could just see Olivia watching with delight. Then when she was beginning to think the pain would never end the most extraordinary thing happened; her wayward flesh began to accept and even enjoy the demands made of it, and she was sick to the stomach to think that these appalling people had won.

'Oh Leah, what a dirty bitch you are,' Olivia said slyly, seeing the change that had come over her. 'You have excited me and now I need you to make me come.'

The woman pressed her hot lips to Leah's, who tried to squirm her face away, but Olivia held it fast between her hands. She was persistent with the passionate kisses, but Leah was disgusted by her and held fast to her principles. Then she lifted her night-rail, giving Leah free view of her dewy sex, and she closed her eyes against the petal-like display. She would not be swayed this time. What Olivia wanted was wrong.

But Olivia was even more determined, daintily arching herself she lowered her cunny onto her face, and Leah breathed in the honeyed tang, tasted the salty dew that coated her rosy sex.

'Please me and who knows, I might well forget that you are naught but a prisoner. Why, I may even forget to take you back from whence I found you.'

Leah knew she had no choice but to please this spoilt lady, whose every whim was catered for, so with a heavy sigh she poked her tongue inside the slippery funnel.

Olivia giggled triumphantly. 'That's right, slave, fuck me with your tongue. Do it well. Please me as I pleased you.'

Leah did her bidding, pleasuring the lady while her husband rutted on top of her, struggling loudly to reach his crisis. When Olivia moved a little so that her nubbin was more accessible, Leah sucked and tongued the small root until the woman began to moan with delight, and soon her love dew ran freely, culminating in a hearty scream as she reached her climax.

Drake, however, was still driving sturdily into her, and as Olivia rolled away Leah concentrated on that huge tool as it plunged in and out of her, longing to be free of the man who slobbered and slapped his fat belly against her. She tried to ignore the warm buttery feeling in her stomach, the quickening in her sex, but it was so difficult.

The sweating bulk on top of her shuddered and gave a bestial bellow as he came, and Leah breathed a hearty sigh as he too rolled off her. She wiped at her tears, her vulva sore from his unwanted attentions, her virgin blood staining the bedcover.

Olivia appeared through her glistening tears, and Leah was amazed to see that she had changed into a riding habit and was donning a plumed hat, just like the one she had passed around at Dunstan House. She inspected the bed and gave a satisfied nod.

'You have been obedient and satisfied our needs. Now come, the night is still young. I intend enjoying the game a little longer.' A young maid carrying a china bowl of water entered at the snap of Olivia's fingers, and giving Leah a furtive look of pity, placed the bowl on the nightstand beside the bed and began loosening the rope restraints. 'The maid will bathe you and help you into a costume for your next role. Play well and I may keep my promise and turn a blind eye when it's time to return you to the dull Darlingtons.'

'But what of Thomas?' Leah asked wearily.

Olivia hooted. 'Thomas is snoring in the kitchen, no doubt

dreaming of your sweet little arse.'

Leah's relief was overwhelming; she would do *anything* they asked in order to win her freedom. So rubbing her sore limbs she allowed the maid to wash her with the warm water from the bowl, then dress her, and as she did it occurred to her that the apparel was strange, but she was far too excited by Olivia's statement to care. It was only when she gazed into the cheval mirror that she realised how bizarre it really was. Her breasts were completely naked, pouting prettily above her narrow waist, around which was a thin band of red fur that also ran between her legs. Attached to the back band of fur was a tail. Her footwear was of thin leather and claw-like in appearance, upon her head was a mask with ears and a snout, and she realised that she was supposed to resemble a fox! She turned wide, alarmed eyes on Olivia. 'W-what abomination is this?'

Olivia smirked slyly. 'All will be revealed soon, my dear. Do not fret.'

Leah watched as Drake joined them, also dressed in riding apparel 'Ah, very nice,' he drooled throatily. 'My little red fox is all ready for the hunt.'

A cold hand of fear clutched at Leah's throat. 'You... you are going to *hunt* me?'

Olivia smoothed on leather gloves. 'Of course,' she confirmed breezily. 'It is the next phase. While we have been delightfully indulging in your charms the servants have been well occupied. Look to the window and you will see how well they have lit the woods, so we may find our little fox more easily.'

Her face pale with fear, Leah went to the blue-draped window to see that the woods had been illuminated with torches. There was nowhere for her to hide! 'And what will happen when you find me?' she asked shakily, not really wanting to know.

'That depends on your captor.' Olivia gave a small toss of her head. 'I omitted to say that we have invited some neighbours to join us in this night's activities.' She gave an imperious wave of her hand and a liveried servant entered the chamber. Taking Leah by the arm he forced her to walk with him down the elegant stairway and out into the starry night. Olivia's and Drake's friends were gathered in the courtyard, while servants hovered around serving hot rum.

Horses snorted and steam from their bodies rose in the humid night, to meet the smoke from the torches that lit the courtyard. When Leah was hauled out before them there was a burst of applause and cultured voices raised in their approval.

The odour of animals, smoke and humans was overwhelming, it found its way down her throat and she almost vomited. But there was something else in that night air, something menacing. It was prevalent in the sly glances that raked her body, in the dissolute faces that towered over her as they sat high in their saddles, weighing up the girl who to them was worth less than their lowliest servant.

A thin man with a squint and a stooped back leaned over from the great height of his stallion and fingered her face, allowing his hand to drop lower to her quivering breasts. He pinched the nipples cruelly. 'She's a fine wench. You have outdone yourself, Marchmont.' He spun her round and eyed her bottom. 'Fine flanks, too. We'll have good sport this night.'

'Take your vile hands off me.' Leah smote him with her eyes, and as the horse danced backwards she cowered away from the large animal that didn't look any less evil than its master.

Raucous laughter met her brave words, and a haughty woman in a russet riding habit viewed her more closely. 'She has spirit; it will make the hunt more interesting.'

A man said something to one of the servants in green livery, who grabbed Leah by an arm and dragged her through the crowd, parading her charms for everyone to see more clearly. Leah tried to pull free, but the tall servant slapped her hard across her face, almost rendering her senseless. She tottered on unsteady legs, her head whirling.

The incident increased the excitement of the crowd and incited even more comments.

One man grabbed her nearest breast, slobbering like a pig. 'I'd like nothing more than to master this one. I'd soon break her spirit.'

'That pleasurable task will be mine,' said a man with a dark, full-bottomed wig that was beginning to part company with his head, giving everyone a glimpse of the shiny pate beneath. 'For I'm sure I shall keep my record,' he bragged. 'I bagged three last month, and this little fox will be my fourth.' He slid his riding crop between her legs, prodding cruelly. 'A fine specimen indeed.'

'Your luck's run out,' a portly cleric boasted, slapping her bottom hard with his riding crop. 'The prize is mine.' For all the might of his cloth the cleric was obviously as perverse as the rest, and his jowls wobbled with excitement.

But none of them frightened Leah as much as the dark rider with the hooded eyes who stayed a little apart from the rest of the group on his black stallion. His stare branded her with the look of possession, and Leah's blood ran cold.

One of the servants saw her tremble and felt pity. 'You'll do well to fear that one,' she whispered a warning, and Leah thought that even she seemed uncomfortable. 'He's the Duke of Cullingham, a man you never want to cross. He 'as strange powers over people, and I've heard tell it's unwise to look into 'is eyes, for he can steal your very soul with one mean glance. Seems 'e be a fierce one with the whip and cane. I've never heard of anyone escaping 'im. 'Tis said he chains them up in 'is dungeons.'

Chapter Seven

Jane was busy marketing, the old adage that life must go on swirling ineffectually round in her brain. Her eyes were still red from the tears she shed and the lack of sleep. Each time

106

she thought slumber would take her into its restful arms, so she thought of her lovely Leah out there somewhere in terrible danger. Everyone she loved seemed to have been taken away from her. But she trusted the captain, he'd given his word and somehow she had the feeling that he would soon find her mistress.

It seemed that Smithfield was busier than usual, everyone jostling for room. Jane sighed, and hearing her name being called urgently turned to see Violet, Lady Roseanna Roebuck's maid, beckoning to her.

'Oh, Jane,' her voice was strained, her manner apprehensive, 'I bin hoping to see yer.'

She dabbed at her eyes and Jane took her arm and escorted her to a quieter spot. She had met Violet when she took a fresh gown to Lady Roebuck's for Leah to change in to, and they often met at the market. 'What is it?' she asked, alarmed by her demeanour.

''Tis Captain Tempest,' Violet gasped through trembling lips.

'Captain Tempest? What's wrong with him?'

Violet shook her head despairingly; the handsome sea captain had made a favourable impression upon her and the news she'd received was upsetting. 'Oh, the poor man,' she wailed to Jane's impatient ears.

'For pity sake, tell me!' Jane shrieked, now cold with fear.

'Seems the captain's in Newgate,' she sobbed.

'Newgate?' Jane's legs almost gave way and she leaned on a stall of vegetables. She tried to speak but words would not come. She swallowed and tried again. 'But why? What's he done?'

'Lady Roebuck told the law he pinched a valuable ruby pendant.'

'I don't believe it; he would not do such a thing!' Jane was shocked to the core.

'That's the rub,' Violet said miserably. 'He didn't steal nothin'. I hears 'em arguing, see. The lady were peeved 'cos he likes your mistress, she calls her a...' Violet clicked her

107

tongue in disgust. 'Never mind, but it weren't nice. The captain tells her to mind her tongue; says Mistress Brown could teach her some stuff about morals.'

'And then?'

'She calls him a bad name, and he tells her she ain't a lady. He says someone'll get his things and goes.' Violet tittered. 'She was in a right mean mood by then, knocking flower pots over and cursing like a fishwife. After that she goes to her bedchamber she does, and being curious, I follows.' She lowered her voice a little and Jane had to crane her neck to hear.

'She goes to her jewellery casket and takes out a ruby pendant, holding it up with a strange look on her face. Then she gives a queer cackle. I was afraid for her sanity. Then just as I decides to slip away she packs the captain's things with her own hands, and what do you think?' Without awaiting a reply she continued, her eyes bright with the telling. 'She slips the pendant into the middle of his belongings. Then she calls for his things to be put ready for collection.'

'She set a trap for him?' Jane was appalled.

Violet nodded sadly. 'The captain's man picked his effects up later that day and not long after the captain was arrested.'

Jane shoulders stooped miserably and her red-rimmed eyes filled with tears. 'Oh Violet, he was my last hope. What will happen to my lady now?'

If Jane knew how Leah had passed her day she would have been heartbroken. But come the night and she was to be treated even worse. The lords and ladies tossed hot rum down their throats and watched eagerly as Leah, garbed as a little fox, ran into the woods, lit by the flaming torches that were placed at intervals, the acrid fumes of the smoke stealing down her chest making her cough.

The hounds were brought and the armless jerkin she'd been made to wear earlier thrown to the pack in order for them to obtain her scent. They obediently sniffed it, their

108

tails curled high over their backs, their teeth snarling in anticipation.

Leah ran until she thought her heart would burst, the thought of being caught terrifying her. She had been allowed a small start and she intended to use it to her best advantage; surely there would be somewhere on this huge estate where she could hide away until they tired of searching for her. But when she reached the woods her breathing became laboured and she realised that her earlier assumptions had been correct; they were far too well lit for that. Even so, she had put a goodly space between her and her pursuers, thanks to her fear and the fact that she was free of constricting petticoats.

She had almost flown over the lawns but she found the woods harder going, for her feet were only shod in thin material and sharp twigs and stones dug into them. Tree roots and ivy tripped her, but she picked herself up and ran on, praying for a hiding place. After a few minutes she heard the sound of horns and of dogs barking and thought she would faint. But she girded herself with resolve and ran on.

A stream divided the woods and she waded through it, panting heavily, glad of the cool water as it splashed up her legs, reviving her flagging spirits. The stony bed dug into her feet, but she would not be swayed from her path; thought of the devils behind her pushed her onwards.

With her feet cut and bleeding, her legs cramping and her breathing ragged she was eventually persuaded to stop for a short while. She dived into a bed of parched ferns, gasping for air, freeing herself from the awful mask that only added to her discomfort.

And it was there he caught up with her, the devil on the black stallion! Lord Cullingham's black eyes crawled over her as before, promising evil.

Leah saw the man and fear slid down her spine, squeezed her lungs. She pointedly avoided his eyes, though whatever power he had seemed to be working already. As she viewed his fingers grasping the horse's reins so her breath wheezed through her parched lips; it was as though those brutal fingers held her windpipe. Never in her life had she been in contact with so much malevolence, it was there in his satanic features, in the menacing way he held his head. She cast around her but there was nowhere to hide, nowhere left to run. He circled her, his mouth set in a cruel slash, his lips curling into a sneer over his teeth.

Thanks to the servant's warning she still avoided that dark gaze, the foul stare that would steal her very soul. She had no doubt that he was Satan's spawn and she crossed herself and said a quick prayer for safe delivery. She was more afraid of him than the dogs that snarled and bayed at her heels.

With a commanding flick of his whip and a stern command the dogs drew back and he smirked. 'I have you, little fox. You are mine now and soon your tail will run with blood, for I am your master now and always. You will adorn my bed and feel the taste of my lash. And I shall train you to obey my commands, to appreciate and even welcome the sting of leather on your flesh.'

She heard his taunts and, in her mind's eye, could see the picture of herself hanging from mighty chains in a dank dungeon, grateful for the lashes he applied to her body, grateful for sight of another human being – no longer a young woman, but a cowering slave.

It was this vision that moved her to action. There was a flaming torch behind her. The second she took to measure its distance and the possibility of the horseman guessing her plan and reaching it before her seemed like an eternity. But she depended on his vanity, for while he was busy boasting about mastering her he was not paying attention to detail. Stealing her chance she snatched the torch from its sconce and threw it into the wilted fern. It was like a tinderbox and the space between them instantly became a wall of flames. She heard him scream, saw the horse rise up on its hind legs, heard the pack barking frantically and the flames obscured her vision.

She ran from that hateful place as fast as she could. The fire was spreading like quicksilver; it had already spread to the trees. It crackled and spat, belching foul-smelling black smoke that invaded her throat, making her cough, stinging her eyes so that they watered. She knew her pursuers would be turned back by the force and heat of the flames, which were making fast work of destroying the woods, but she still wanted to put a goodly distance between them.

When it seemed as though she'd been running for hours she dropped down in some long grass, and exhausted, fell instantly asleep.

Dawn was spreading sheets of gold and pink across the sky when she awoke, shivering with the chill of the early morning dew, realising immediately that although she had escaped Olivia's dreadful plans for her, she would have to get rid of the fox costume. It wasn't the kind of thing ordinary people wore and would attract nothing but horror and disgust. And it seemed luck was with her now, for she spotted a scarecrow in the very pasture in which she'd been sleeping.

Admittedly it wasn't the best dressed scarecrow, but she had no thought for fashion at that moment. She quickly stripped it of its hat, coat and breeches and changed into the tattered clothes behind a stout oak, gladly casting the bizarre costume aside. She hurriedly bunched up her hair and stuffed it into the hat, feeling relief wash over her. From a distance she would appear to be a country boy. It would arouse far less curiosity.

Although she had managed to acquire a little sleep she was feeling weary again, but she knew she had to go on. Somehow she had to find a way back to the city and home. She walked a little way before spotting a farmer taking his goods to market, and the kindly soul gladly gave her a lift, despite her scruffy appearance, and as the large wheels rumbled along the uneven rode she quickly fell asleep in the back of the cart, snuggled up to the sacks of vegetables.

Leah was received with glad hearts and much love back in the house in the city; even Rose sobbed into her apron to see the mistress safe. While she tried to explain some of what had happened to her, leaving out the most perverse parts lest Jane have apoplexy, so the woman fed her and helped her bathe. And although the house felt empty without the presence of her dear papa, she was glad to be back.

There was so much to be done even though she had sadly missed papa's funeral. One of her first tasks was to receive her father's solicitor, Jonas Clements, and his words only led to the confirmation of her suspicions after overhearing the conversation between Percy and his mother.

'I am to inherit some money?'

'Indeed, mistress.' He adjusted his shirt cuffs. 'Your maternal grandfather, Lord Harold Sherwood, was a very wealthy man, and although he lost some of his estates to Cromwell he retained one in Essex, which you are to inherit, along with the majority of his fortune.'

'Why was I not told?' she asked dazedly.

'Your grandfather left explicit instructions that the monies and estate be held in trust for you, and that you were not to learn of your inheritance until your marriage, unless your father's demise preceded that event. Also you will not receive anything until you marry the man of your father's choosing. That is why you are to marry one William Joshua Penrose by proxy. As you are aware, your father arranged all the details before his death. I am merely awaiting the papers signed by your betrothed allowing me to choose a man as his proxy.'

Leah's head was spinning, everything was moving far too quickly.

Jonas Clements was uncomfortable at the young lady's obvious distress, and cleared his throat loudly. 'As soon as I receive the papers I need I will be able to tell you the date of your wedding. I can understand your shock at these disclosures but I must follow your father's instructions, as I am sure you can appreciate.'

Leah sat stiffly, hands tightly folded in her lap as the man's voice droned on. Everything else went over her head; the only thing that registered was that her father was determined even in death to see her married to William Penrose.

When Jonas Clements was finished Leah mumbled something fitting and Jane saw him out.

Would you like some hot chocolate, my dear?' she asked on her return, distressed by the girl's darkly ringed eyes, her expression of defeat.

'No, Jane, thank you. I need to think.'

Jane gave a distracted shake and made for the door, closing it quietly behind her. Leah's head slumped back onto a cushion; she had the beginnings of a headache. Before her was a glass-fronted cabinet that held the fine china Jane had said was her mother's pride and joy. Thaddeus had kept it thus from the moment of Elizabeth's death. She bit her lip as tears came to her eyes.

Her thoughts were a maelstrom of emotions, and glancing at her father's muddled bureau she decided to put it in order. There was nothing like idle hands for accelerating worries. She sat on the finely turned stool and began her task, feeling closer to her dear papa than she had in weeks.

She dextrously tidied and sorted, thinking how strange it was that her grandfather had relented and left her all his money when he had never even seen her. She thought about the estate in Essex where her mother had been brought up, which was apparently being looked after by an estate manager. But even so her spirits stayed the same. Money never brought anyone happiness, though she supposed it meant they would not starve.

Her thoughts went back to the day her papa expressed his wish that she marry William. It had upset her and she argued with him. Papa had looked tired and ill, perhaps too ill to continue the discussion, for shortly after he died. If only she had realised, but he never mentioned it, never complained.

Her busy fingers were fast making order from chaos,

when she happened upon a letter in her father's handwriting addressed to her. With shaking fingers Leah opened the missive and read her papa's last words to her.

My Beloved Daughter,

There are things I have been meaning to say to you, but somehow I never found the opportunity. As you know your mama and I married without her father's permission, they being of the aristocracy and I being naught but a poor physician,

Your grandfather completely disinherited your mama, but over the years he must have had second thoughts because he made you his heiress. And although he had little faith in me as a son-in-law, he obviously trusted me to do right by my daughter; because you see, my dear, you can only inherit upon marrying the man of my choice. I have pondered long on this matter and settled on William Penrose. As he no longer resides on these shores I overcame the legal difficulties by having papers drawn up which William will sign, enabling you to be married by proxy, allowing you to claim what is rightly yours.

Richard Aitkin, who manages the estate, is a good man. You can put your faith in him and trust him to do what is best.

I hope to be there to wish you every happiness in your future, but if that proves to be impossible I will be there in spirit, my dear. If, as I suspect, I do not have long upon this earth, I forbid you to wear mourning for me. I have always loathed dark, depressing colours.

Finally, thank you for leading me from the brink of despair when your mama was taken from me. You were only a babe but you gave me as much happiness then as you have every day since.

I am sure that with William you will find the joy and love I shared with Elizabeth. God bless and keep you, my dear child.

Your devoted Papa.

Leah blinked away her tears – papa had loved her! He had merely been making provisions for her. She folded the letter and placed the parchment back in the bureau, feeling sad. After all her father's plans and contemplation on the matter she still wished she did not have to marry a comparative stranger, leave her home.

Jane brought her some hot chocolate despite her earlier refusal, her eyes resting softly on her charge. She was sure she wasn't telling the whole truth about the affair with Lady Roebuck and the Darlingtons. She was probably too ashamed to tell all. Jane had been asking around and told by a few folk that the goings on at Dunstan House was even worse than the antics at court.

She wondered how she had coped. She caressed the blonde hair lovingly, hoping the girl would be all right. She had cause to worry, for Leah's mother had been an extremely sensual person, and she should know as her own mother had waited on her. She herself was naught but a child, but had lost count of the times the mistress got herself in scrapes with the opposite sex. 'A handful' was what her father called her, and he didn't know the half of it!

One morning her mother had found her climbing up the apple tree outside the house in order to gain access to her bedchamber through the window, her hair a mess and straw hanging all over her. But she had no shame, did Mistress Elizabeth at that young age.

'So what?' she'd asked brazenly when the housekeeper had words with her, being afraid to call on her father. 'There's no harm in having some fun. The blacksmith's son is very handsome and his dick's mighty fine.'

Mrs Grant had blushed to the roots of her hair and fainted clean away. But the little minx was incorrigible! When Jane had been off on some errand for her mother she saw Mistress Elizabeth in the orchard; her thighs open wide while some village lad rode her hard, the sweat pouring off his back as he laboured over her. And as if that wasn't

115

enough, there were three others waiting in line as she cried out her excitement at the joys of her sexual liaisons.

Although Lord Sherwood had to be told something of his wayward daughter's antics, he was never told the full story, or she was sure he would have had her locked in the cellar and thrown away the key.

She reckoned the worst trick she ever pulled was when she went after the young pastor of the parish. The poor man was newly ordained and very shy when Mistress Elizabeth first spotted him. That first sight of the handsome, god-fearing gentleman made such an impression on her she declared then and there that she would have him.

He had been unsure of the pretty girl's attitude towards him. When she threw flirty glances his way he gave her texts to read from the bible and spoke long sermons about the wages of sin. When she visited his home with naught on but a cloak, flinging it back to expose her naked body, he tried to restrain his natural urges, but Mistress Elizabeth's sensuality won hands down.

They met most evenings after that until caught fucking in the churchyard. The pastor was sent away in shame, his career in ruins, and Lord Sherwood had strict words with his daughter. It was shortly after that she met Thaddeus Brown and fell head over heels in love with the young doctor. The upshot was that she ran away with him, taking Jane, and his father washed his hands of her. However, when Mistress Elizabeth found love it was the making of her, and she never looked at another man after marrying Thaddeus. Jane sighed, theirs was such a romantic union, 'twas a pity it was so short lived owing to the death of the mistress.

Jane was torn from her reverie when Leah announced that she was to order a carriage so they could take the air in safety. As it clattered over the cobbles Leah sat back looking aimlessly out of the windows at the town. She needed to clear the cobwebs from her mind. She had so much to do, so many arrangements to make, but her heart was not in any of it. Her father had been dead for weeks and she was no nearer reconciling herself to her marriage. Of course she had expected her father to arrange a match for her one day, but not so soon and certainly not to a man so far away.

She must write to William telling him of her bereavement. It would be difficult putting her feelings into words, but she had to try. He must be prepared for her to settle into her new life, her marriage slowly. She was trying to change her opinion of him; after all, he had kept his word to her father despite believing she was naught but a poor physician's daughter, so he must have some love in his heart for her.

Leah ordered the coachman to take them to St James's park so they could observe the scenery. The horses shook their fine heads and broke into a trot, their hooves striking the cobbles loudly. On the ride through the park she recalled Lady Roebuck's words when she was pretending to be a fine dinner companion, and how she had extolled the king's tennis playing. She moved in a different world. She had the ear of the king himself. No one would believe Leah if she accused her of having her kidnapped, even if she swore on a thousand bibles.

Forcing herself from her introspection, she noticed that Jane appeared jittery. 'What is it?' she asked worriedly.

Jane wrung her hands. 'I've been wondering how to tell you, not wanting to add to your grief.'

Leah looked at her speculatively. 'You are upsetting me more by keeping whatever it is to yourself.'

Without further ado Jane told her what had happened to her saviour and the man of her dreams, Captain Tempest. Leah shook her head in shock. 'Lady Roebuck did this?' Jane nodded. 'The woman has no shame! She bundles me off to rogues and accuses a good man of a crime he did not commit.' Leah was determined to do something, but what? Kindly eyes that crinkled just like her father's came to mind. 'If only I knew how to contact Doctor Fitzherbert. I'm sure he would know what to do.'

Jane smiled brightly and flourished a piece of parchment

in her face. ''Tis the doctor's address. Violet gave it to me; he and Captain Swan are supposed to be great friends.'

Acquainting the coachman of their new destination, Leah sighed worriedly. 'I hope the good doctor is available.'

Leah rapped on the door a second time, but the doctor was not at home. There was no one to help them in their troubles.

But just then a carriage rumbled up beside theirs and the doctor stepped down, followed by a servant. 'To what do I owe this honour?' he asked.

'Doctor Fitzherbert,' Leah gasped in relief.

'Ye gods, the last time a lady was so glad to see me I was but four and twenty,' he said with a laugh. Leah smiled weakly, and doffing his plumed hat he opened the door and stepping aside directed Leah and Jane ahead of him.

'I've been visiting some friends,' he said when they were comfortably seated in his sitting room. 'I can see this is more than just a social call, so if you will wait while I order some refreshments I'll be all ears.'

'Don't trouble on our behalf, please,' Leah replied earnestly, eager to get the news of Gideon's incarceration off her chest.

The doctor poured himself some whiskey from a sparkling decanter. 'Then please, dear lady, tell me what I may do for you.'

'So you don't know about Captain Tempest?' she returned anxiously.

'I have not seen him for, let me see…' he twirled his whiskers, 'oh, must be a sennight. If I remember rightly he was on his way to visit Lady Roebuck.' Seeing the strained faces in front of him he frowned. 'What is it?'

Leah quickly explained everything Jane had learned from the maid Violet, and the doctor sat in stunned silence for a few moments.

'In Newgate, you say? Hm, always knew that woman wasn't to be trusted. Too flighty for my liking, aristocracy or no.'

'Can you do something to help him, Doctor Fitzherbert?' she asked desperately.

'Call me Fitz, my dear,' he said kindly. 'And if I may I shall call you Leah. If we are going to put our heads together on this we shall need to relax and forget about formalities.'

'Then you think there is some way of helping him?'

Fitz smoothed his beard, deep in thought. 'I will need to confer with a body or two before I can give you a satisfactory answer. So, if you will forgive me, ladies, I must beg your indulgence for perhaps an hour or so while I make some enquiries. My man will provide you with some refreshments while I am gone.' He bowed politely and made his exit.

A tall, thin man in green livery served them hot chocolate and sweetmeats, but neither had much of an appetite. Leah could not rest and incessantly paced the room. She had heard dark tales about Newgate, and visions of Captain Tempest lying in a dirty dark cell tormented her.

Just over an hour elapsed before the doctor returned with an encouraging smile on his face. 'The person I have been to see seems quite confident that, God willing, we will soon bring about Gideon's release,' he said brightly.

'His release?' Leah cried jubilantly. 'But how?'

'All will be revealed on the morrow. But now I must hasten to the prison.'

Swiftly making her mind up she got to her feet. 'I'm coming with you.'

Fitz glanced at her doubtfully. 'I really don't think that would be a good idea.'

'I insist,' Leah replied firmly.

Seeing her determination, Fitz nodded reluctantly. 'Very well, but it will not be a pleasant experience,' he warned soberly.

Chapter Eight

Leah was to remember those words later when they dropped Jane off and went on to Newgate. Its forbidding appearance unnerved her, and trembling slightly she followed Fitz through the gate, gazing wide-eyed at the figures of Justice, Mercy and Truth standing in niches above the entrance.

Inside the prison a turnkey led them into the Keeper's House, beneath which was the condemned hold that was also used as a holding cell. It was entered by a hatch, about twenty feel in length and fifteen in breadth, which the turnkey opened so they could look for Gideon. It was heaving with bodies and they were quite unable to see him. The stench was unbelievable and men screamed out to be saved and some flung vile oaths, causing Fitz to pull Leah away. He led her outside while the turnkey spat at the ground impatiently.

'Wait outside in the carriage, Leah,' he said. 'You can see this is not the place for you.'

'Please, Fitz, I must see him. I will not rest until I do.' Jane had told her he'd promised to find her, and as a result gone to Lady Roebuck's in order to prise information from the woman. Therefore Leah felt partly to blame for his incarceration.

The lovely green eyes pleaded silently up into his, and Fitz sighed and gave way. 'Let me see what I can do to gain better quarters for Gideon. '

While Fitz spoke in low tones to the turnkey, Leah slipped back to that portal of damnation and glanced inside. It was dimly lit, but she was able to see the steps that led down to the dungeon, and her heart full of seeing Gideon, she slowly descended. Her eyes strained in the bad light, but it was impossible to recognise anyone among the tangle of bodies.

Feeling her stomach lurch against the stench in that pit, she held a handkerchief to her nose. She was quite unable to see much in the dark confines and was beginning to regret her impulsive action when something grabbed her ankle, holding it fast while a hand crawled up the inside of her leg. A scream froze in her throat, for terror had rendered her speechless. She tried to move, but the man at her feet held her cruelly with steel fingers while he climbed to the junction of her thighs. She was rooted to the spot, the hairs on her neck standing on end fearfully. She could hear his laboured breathing and she cast her eyes downward to see a filthy rogue leering up at her.

Fitz was in heated argument with the turnkey and had not noticed that she was missing. Leah glanced up at the hatchway longingly; what had she done? With her ankle clamped tightly in the grip of the fiend on the floor, and Fitz so far away, she was completely at his mercy. There was a spectre of terror encompassing her and she tried to calm herself. As her mind cast around for ways to rid herself of the beast, so he reached that which he sought and triumphantly inserted his fingers in the soft petals of her sex.

By now several more men realised what was going on and began hissing nastily, their excitement and unexpected shock at having such a jewel in their midst registering in their filthy oaths and licentious muttering.

'Let me give 'er a length.'

'Let me 'ave a piece of that arse.'

'Grab 'er and we'll soon teach 'er what a real man wants.'

'Give me a suck of them titties.'

Soon many hands were mauling her, bearing her down into a corner. Darkly shadowed forms, no doubt men long starved of the touch of a feminine body, strained to have a piece of the golden girl who had somehow been magicked into their hellish existence.

Leah almost fainted at the appalling stink of their collective bodies and a scream almost escaped from her mouth, only to be cut off by a piece of filthy cloth that was stuffed between her lips. Her body was an offering they had not expected, and with hoarse breaths and vile whispers of what they were about to do to her they converged like an

121

army of ants.

Her arms were pinned down and she felt her feet being sucked, the skin between her toes licked eagerly and with great precision. Hands fought to feel the silk of her legs, the curve of her knee, others nudged impatiently to gain more access. The soft tresses of her hair were torn out of its ribbons and its perfume inhaled. Her throat was arched backwards and mouths pounced on the sweet flesh, rubbery lips ground into her fragrant skin and Leah's breasts were grabbed and pinched roughly. Her shoulders were caressed, her arms prodded and her gown was soon torn from her body in lustful anticipation of what lay beneath.

And though she struggled it was all in vain, as a weight like iron pinned her to the filthy, straw-strewn floor. Fingers once more invaded the tender petalled flesh, the treasure chest of her femininity, and though she tried to kick out that was impossible too. Her limbs ached as she strained for freedom, and her skin ran with sweat and spittle from the intrusive mouths and panting bodies that consumed her.

Fingers impaled her, one, two, and three at a time. A tongue rimmed her anus and snuck inside. A huge penis infiltrated her private tunnel, ploughing into her with a great hunger. She was turned and another tumescent cock nudged at her vaginal opening, filling it with surging flesh that had no pity. Her breasts were pressed into a channel and used in the same manner. One after another they came, while Fitz's voice rose higher and she lay there, an unwilling victim of their lust.

But soon her cringing being seemed to ring with new life as her sensual side emerged, and the men who had once tortured now bore her to a new plain, a place of pleasure. Her pain deviated into a burning desire for satisfaction and she feverishly welcomed the hands that pulled at her greedily, ignited with lust as several cocks strove to fill her at once. Men long dreaming of a moment like this whispered into her ear.

'Suck my meat, sweeting.'

122

'Open yer legs wider so I might fill yer crack.'

'Ye gods, the slut's loving it!'

And Leah embraced it all; she was drowning in male attention, her skin soaked in spunk. Every part of her body was used lustfully, even her sweet-scented armpits, and every delicate membrane inside her pulsed and burned as though seared by fire.

'Leah. Leah, where are you?'

She heard Fitz call her name, his voice rising with alarm when he could not see her. The mass of men magically faded away and she was left to wonder how to face the good doctor in her state of dishabille. She got hurriedly to her feet, gathering her gown around her, glad of the poor light that hid her from questing eyes.

She hurried up the steps and through the hatch, and finding a cloak hanging on a nail in the Keeper's House, draped it over herself, pulling the hood up to hide her features. 'Here I am, Fitz,' she said breathily. 'I had thought to find Captain Swan, but 'tis impossible in this light.' As he moved closer she put her head down and a hand to her face so he was unable to see the state of her. 'But now I am overcome with the stench of this awful place and must find some air.'

Fitz was all concern. 'I knew it was a mistake to bring you here. Are you all right? I will come with you and set you in the carriage. Home is the best place for you, my dear.'

She nodded. 'I think you're right. But please stay or I shall fret. Do what you can for Gideon, and please call on me.'

Fitz was uncertain as to his next course of action. But knowing that Leah had but a little way to go to the waiting carriage, and that Gideon needed him much more at this moment, he acquiesced to her pleading tone. 'Very well, but be sure to rest when you arrive home.'

Leah fled from the prison, glad Fitz had not noticed that she'd entered in a gown and departed in a cloak. The coachman thought nothing of it when she approached him all cloaked up, for it was an unhealthy and upsetting place for any gentile female to visit; no doubt she was hiding her red-rimmed lids from prying eyes.

Safely in the confines of the vehicle, Leah rested her aching form against the heaving velvet seat, her head hanging in shame. What had she done? What was she thinking of entering such a place alone? And even worse, how was it possible for her to even contemplate enjoying such a dire attack? What was it about her that made her so diverse? She'd been brought up strictly, though she had received plenty of love. And up until lately her life had not been anything other than dull. She had always been gentile and respectable; what was happening to her? Was her nature so different from others, or did other women lust after such deviations of the flesh, too?

She could do nothing but ponder and pray that Jane would not see her on her return. As luck would have it she heard her arguing with Rose in the kitchen and quickly ran up the stairs, divesting herself of the spoilt gown. She would have the cloak returned to the prison later, but for now it was imperative that no one should find out what had happened to her at Newgate. Her main regret was that she had not had the chance to see Gideon, and her heart went out to him. That stinking hole was not for men of the captain's calibre! And neither was the gallows. The thought shook her rigid. She prayed the person Fitz had spoken to earlier that day knew what he was about, for she could not bear it if Gideon were to be taken to Tyburn to be hanged by the neck until he died.

Fitz had made a deal with the turnkey, though the man was a greedy beggar, no doubt thinking he could wring even more coin from him than he did, owing to the good cut of his cloth. He stood at the hatch, watching as Gideon was brought up, his limp more pronounced than ever, the light of the lantern exposing bruises on his face, his hair matted with blood.

'Darn! His wound's troubling him again,' Fitz murmured

under his breath.

'Fitz, what are you doing here? This is no place for you.' Gideon's voice smote him like a dart, not the violence of his tone but the shame behind his words. It was not right that this proud man, who was so decent and good, be made to feel so demeaned.

'Nor you,' he averred briskly. 'We know that you are innocent. Mistress Leah Brown came with me, but was overcome by the stench of the place.'

Gideon's head shot up. 'Mistress Brown? How is she? What happened to her when she left Roebuck's?'

Fitz held up a hand, not completely sure what his friend was talking about. 'All in good time. Now then, do not fret, we'll have you out of here in the twinkling of an eye,' he said with false camaraderie. 'Can't you get rid of those things?' he asked the turnkey, nodding at the manacles. 'And surely there's somewhere else he can stay beside this filthy hovel.'

The guard nodded. 'I'll show yer to the master's side to wait for his lordship here while 'e be having his irons struck off. Got to leave one set on though, 'tis the law.'

Another gaoler was summoned and Gideon was led away. Fitz was taken to a spacious hall he was told was called the Gigger. Here he was also charged an entry fee of 1s 6d. The cellar man who had borne him down brought him a quart of beer, and one for Gideon. He sat at a table and awaited his friend, quaffing the beer that had never tasted so good after the trials of the day. He realised that Gideon could have looked worse, but he had a strong constitution, better than most, which had served him well in the darker times.

When the door was flung open the turnkey reappeared, with Gideon now in lighter shackles. He sank onto the bench opposite Fitz, his face white with pain.

'Let me take a look at you,' Fitz ordered, anxiously examining him. 'Where on earth did you get all these bruises and abrasions from, man? Someone must have clubbed you hard. Good thing your skull's so thick!'

Gideon grunted as Fitz felt his scalp. 'I didn't take kindly to being arrested for something I didn't do,' he replied, with a touch of his old humour.

While Fitz dressed the old wound in his leg Gideon sipped his ale and the men conversed in low tones, bringing each other up to date with their news.

Gideon's eyes softened when he heard about Leah's dealings in the situation. 'God bless Mistress Brown. But they won't take Violet's word against Roseanna's, you know. You're just wasting your time on me, old friend.'

'Don't you believe it,' Fitz replied with a sly wink. 'I have friends in high places.'

Gideon blinked his thanks, knowing he must obtain his release somehow. He owed Fitz and he was aching to see the lovely Leah again.

The door opened, admitting the turnkey. 'He will take you to your new cell, where you'll be given food. Eat well and rest that leg.'

Gideon gave him a roguish grin. 'There's not much else to do here but rest.'

Fitz gave him an encouraging smile. '*Bon appetit*, my friend.'

When he was once more incarcerated, Gideon found himself in a room which contained a flock bed, a table and a bench. There was a kind of stew laid out for him on the table and some more ale. He limped towards it and swilled some ale down his parched throat. She was a fascinating creature, this doctor's daughter with the face and body of a goddess and the courage of a man. He would never have believed such a gentle-bred creature would dare enter the dark confines of this hellhole without swooning.

He attacked the stew on the trencher, he had not eaten properly in a sennight, stale bread and water was for dogs! His thoughts strayed back to the day he'd been taken. He left Roseanna and went to an inn for a strong draught of ale to rid the taste of her bile from his mouth. From there he'd

126

gone to the docks to view the work on his ship, which wasn't progressing as well as he'd hoped.

He sent a man to pick up his effects from Roseanna's and went back to Fitz's, using the key he kept for when his ship was in port and Fitz was not at home. When the man returned with his belongings three burly lawmen had descended upon him and demanded to search his things. They found the ruby pendant in amongst his clothes, not yet unpacked, and accused him of thievery.

His eyes glinted. He should have known Roseanna would not rest until she revenged him.

Leah Brown, on the other hand, believed his innocence without question. From the first moment he set eyes on her he knew she was different. There was something deep in those emerald eyes that had taken his heart and made it leap in his breast. He was a man of the world and well used to women. He had indeed lost count of the wenches he'd bedded over the years. They swarmed around him in every port in which he laid anchor. Yes, he had them all from tavern maids to duchesses, but Leah Brown was the jewel in the crown.

How he longed to be able to take her in his arms and make her his own, stamp his own brand of loving on her. He had no doubt she was a virgin and imagined what the first time with her would be like. Would she cry out when he pierced her maidenhead, sigh when he sheathed himself deep within her core? The more he thought about it the more excited he became – indeed, it made him consider taking her to wife.

The more he thought about it the more the idea appealed to him. She had no one to care for her except the maid Jane, and she needed a man to protect her against life's hardships. She was all he could think of now and he prayed he could be freed soon so he could pay courtship to her.

He was a man who made his mind up quickly. There was no sense in shilly-shallying; it served no purpose in the end. He had always known what he wanted and he wanted Leah Brown, in his heart and in his bed.

Leah sat stiffly on the edge of her seat in Fitz's drawing room, like a coiled spring waiting for this personage Fitz still had not put a name to. She had tossed and turned all night worrying about Gideon and what would become of him if he wasn't released, and when she eventually fell into slumber it was to dream of him at Tyburn. The crowds were cheering, eager for blood, the smell of unwashed bodies assaulting her senses. Gideon stood tall and proud, his face set in a cynical smile.

They placed a noose around his neck and in her dream she tried to close her eyes to shut it all out, but she couldn't. The crowds screamed excitedly, shouting oaths and obscenities. Many had brought food with them; it was a day out, something to be savoured, enjoyed. Hawkers moved among the crowd selling meat pies, chestnuts, pastries and gin. Whores sold their wares and gentry rubbed shoulders with common folk as all strained to see the prisoner.

Gideon blew her a kiss, and in that second he was turned off and left dangling in mid-air. The noise from the crowd came in a mighty whoosh that deafened her. This time she did look away, for she dare not cast her eyes on the body of the man she loved as it swung from the gallows like a limp doll.

A noise in the hall attracted her attention, and Fitz entered the room followed by two ladies, one of whom was extremely beautiful.

'Leah, allow me to introduce Barbara,' Fitz said, 'Lady Castlemaine.'

Leah fell into a deep curtsy. Never in her wildest imagination had she expected to see the king's mistress walk through the door.

Barbara Castlemaine gave her a broad smile. 'I hear you have a grave problem, Mistress Brown, but I think I can help.' She studied the wan face before her. 'I know what it's like to love, my dear. It can take you to the heights of heaven and the next moment plunge you to the greatest depths. And Captain Tempest is a very handsome man, is he not?'

Leah blushed. 'Yes, ma'am.'

'Roebuck never deserved him. But I don't think he ever cared greatly for her.' Her liquid eyes sparkled with mirth. 'Men need their diversions, Mistress Brown.'

Leah nodded, trying to hide the high colour in her cheeks. The lady laughed. 'You have a lot to learn, and if my plan works you will gain much in the good captain's tender arms. Now if you will kindly show us where we can set to work, Fitz, we will get started.'

When they were settled in a pleasant green and cream bedchamber Lady Castlemaine waved Fitz away, and he bowed and left good-naturedly.

The manservant brought them some hot chocolate, and as they sipped the king's mistress sat on the tester bed, quite at home in her surroundings.

'You may be wondering why I am willing to help you. Well, it's not entirely unselfish. Roebuck tried to usurp my place in the king's affections.' She sniffed indignantly. 'As you will have perceived she has a certain attraction, but luckily his majesty did not succumb.'

Noting Lady Castlemaine's fine figure and lovely complexion Leah could understand why she was the king's favourite. 'Lady Roebuck could not hold a candle to you, ma'am,' she said shyly.

She smiled her thanks and motioned to her maid, who went to the door and clapped her hands. Immediately two servants appeared, one carrying a beautiful gown of white silk, the other a wig box and cosmetics. Barbara Castlemaine commanded Leah to stand before her, and she did self-consciously as the lady studied her face and figure closely.

The woman giggled girlishly. 'I think we can pull it off. You are blonde where Roebuck is dark, but with the help of the wig and cosmetics cleverly applied by Cathy here, no one will know the difference. You have a well rounded bosom, but are far more slender than Roebuck. A little padding will take care of that. As for the difference in eye colour, it is a small detail and not to be fussed over.'

Leah listened to Lady Castlemaine's remarks in alarm. 'I am to pass for Lady Roebuck?'

Barbara Castlemaine put a hand to her bosom. 'Forgive me, Leah, I am so excited I forgot to mention it. There is a masked ball tonight at the Banqueting House. We will carry out our plan there. It is all the more exciting, for the king has banned ordinary dominoes in favour of elaborate disguises.' She smiled coyly and dropped her voice to almost a whisper. 'I have decided to go for an unsophisticated costume that will make me appear far more striking in its simplicity, than all the other bejewelled and over made-up ladies whose attire will be as elaborate as their purses will allow.'

Leah smiled; the good lady was indeed clever! It was no wonder King Charles found her the most fascinating lady of all. But her insides roiled at the thought of attending a masked ball with all the titled ladies and gentlemen of the court. In fact she was near to hysterics. Little Leah Brown at a masked ball thrown by the King of England! It was ridiculous!

Lady Castlemaine giggled at her expression, obviously cognisant with her thoughts. 'Come now, Mistress Brown, do not be overwhelmed. I was brought up with the concept that you are as good as you believe yourself to be. And If you were able to see some of those so-called ladies and gentleman of the court, at times you would be quite shocked, I can tell you.' She glanced wickedly at Cathy. 'I have no doubt my maid will give you plenty of information on the conduct of the court whilst preparing you for your roll-playing. And if that does not work use an old trick I have used for an age – imagine the haughty darlings in their underwear. Some of those portly dowagers and their husbands must look quite ridiculous thus garbed.'

Leah giggled conspiratorially. Barbara Castlemaine was

full of fun and good commonsense and she echoed her own father's opinions on some of the upstanding noblemen and women of the country. 'I shall strive to remember your words,' she promised.

'To all intent and purpose you will be Roseanna Roebuck, but in your heart of hearts you must remember that you are still Leah Brown, daughter of Thaddeus, whose good deeds are well known, even by the king himself.'

Leah gasped. 'I had no idea.'

Barbara Castlemaine nodded sagely. 'Oh yes, His Majesty never forgets a kind deed. And Thaddeus Brown will always be remembered as a fine, upstanding man.'

Tears of pride filled Leah's eyes. 'You don't know how much that means to me, ma'am.'

Barbara Castlemaine gave her one of her beautiful smiles. 'Now, enough talk, for I am afraid I will forget what is to be done. And as you can imagine, I have a great deal to accomplish this day. I shall leave you in the capable hands of the good Cathy here and see you later, my dear.' With that she swept out, leaving the fragrance of roses in her wake.

Leah tried to still her hands from shaking, but the more she thought of the task ahead the more nervous she became. While Cathy fussed with cosmetics she took some deep breaths. 'I am not sure I'm up to this,' she said shakily. 'When Lady Castlemaine was here she seemed to give me some of her courage. I am afraid it has fled.'

'Fie, mistress,' Cathy said reprovingly. 'You mustn't be negative! If my lady did not think yer capable she wouldn't've let me stay and carry on with the charade.'

'I suppose you're right,' Leah said doubtfully, willing herself calm.

Cathy did not allow Leah to dwell on her fate, for as her fingers skilfully applied colour to Leah's skin, like an artist to her canvas, so she chattered about the goings on at the palace.

'You'd never believe what went on there,' she said with a

giggle, her pretty face dimpling with mirth. 'I be going on an errand for my good lady one day when I decided to take a nice walk among the roses, the weather being so fine. And what do yer think I saw on the way?'

Leah shrugged her shoulders. 'I cannot imagine.'

'Well,' she said in a hushed voice. 'Lord Ogmore was playing Pell Mell, so he was. At first I took little notice, and then I spied as how he was naked from the waist down and it caused me to halt and duck down behind a bush. So shocked was I my 'eart was palpitating like yer wouldn't believe.'

Leah's eyes widened in surprise. 'What happened then?'

'What indeed!' said the maid in a voice laced with disgust. 'Lines up his shot with great aplomb when I hears a lady giggle. "Hurry up, Harry", says she, "for my bottom's fair stuck to this grass and my cunny's freezing".'

Leah gasped. 'What did you do?'

Cathy lightly dusted her face with ceruse. 'Well I peeks out from behind the bush to see a lady perched upon the lawn, her white legs open for all the world to see what lays between them.' She peered cautiously at the door. 'It was her cunny Lord Ogmore was aiming for.'

'No!'

'True as I stands here. Cross my heart and hope to die.'

'And, um,' Leah paused, quite unsure as how to phrase her next sentence, 'did the wood reach its target?'

Cathy nodded gleefully. 'Oh yes. Rolls right between the lady's thighs and right up to her cunny, it does.'

Leah's mouth gaped open. 'And then?'

'Lord Ogmore shouts his delight and runs up to his lady, rolls the wood away and takes out his cock.' Cathy looked guiltily at the door once more, and finding they were still alone, gave a relieved sigh. 'Then he plunges it between her legs like a donkey on heat.' She giggled. 'Least ways, he were as big as a donkey.'

'Were they not afraid of being seen?'

'I don't think they was worried. There she was a-screaming and calling out his name and he a-panting and

132

calling out hers when the king himself strolled by.'

'No!'

Cathy nodded fervently, helping Leah on with the white gown. 'Walks straight by 'em does he, saying, "It's a nice day for it, Ogmore, Lady Danbey".'

'How embarrassing!'

'I don't think they even noticed. They jus' goes on fucking without losing a beat, her with her legs wrapped round his waist and he a-panting as loud as ever. There weren't an ounce of shame between them!'

Leah wiggled on her seat as Cathy lifted the wig from its box, her secret place becoming moist from the maid's reflections.

'But that ain't nothing compared to the day I took a wrong turn in the palace and walked in on Sir Henry Fielding and one of the maids.' She pursed her lips in disapproval. 'There they was, her on his lap kissing and canoodling and he sliding his fingers up her skirts. ''E's a big boy is Sir Henry, and Jessie was impressed with his tool, I can tell yer. I shouldn't have been surprised to see her all over him; I always said she was no better than she should be, always hanging around the stable boys. I warrant her hair is often so full of straw it's a wonder they don't charge her for it.'

Cathy settled the wig on Leah's head and began combing it, her expression sober. 'Anyhow, Jessie moves over to one knee so she could curl her hand round his cock and he pulls down her top and begins sucking and squeezing her titties.'

'Didn't they notice you?'

'Not they, for they was far too busy with their own business.' Cathy brushed her hair off her face as she concentrated on styling Leah's wig. '"I have a treat for yer, my lovely" says he, assisting her from his lap. "I have travelled well and during these travels met many interesting people. One gentleman was much interested in fucking and told me how to enjoy the art by being more adventurous".'

Cathy's eyes grew wider with the telling. 'Then blow me if he don't sit on the floor with his feet crossed and his tool sticking up. Then he tells Jessie to sit on 'is cock and put her feet round his back.' The girl hooted her disgust. 'Well she don't need telling twice. Sits on that old cock she does and dances up and down on it with her bum going hell for leather.'

"Slow down, sweeting", says he. "Gently now or my crisis will come too soon". So he suggests she rocks back and forth on his cock instead. Jessie obeys his lordship, giggling with delight, and declares it a fine way to fuck. I left them to it and went back to me duties, but I certainly learned something different that day.'

Leah viewed the maid keenly; she wasn't as shocked as she pretended to be. Leah decided that the minx enjoyed rooting out the little amours at the palace. No doubt both Cathy and her tales were well received below stairs.

Cathy added a mask to her costume. 'There, all done,' she supplied triumphantly, taking a step back to examine her handiwork. 'And if I may say so, mistress, yer quite a picture.'

The girl held up a cheval mirror and Leah viewed her reflection with mixed feelings, for staring back at her was the beautiful Lady Roseanna Roebuck. 'I am at a loss for words.'

Cathy tittered. 'Yer will pass for Roebuck easily.'

The door knocked and Leah bade them enter. Dr Fitzherbert smiled broadly. 'You look a treat, though I much prefer you as yourself.' Seeing the questions in her eyes he patted her kindly on the back. 'All will be revealed at the palace. Now hurry, your coach is waiting.'

Leah stared about in awe; the Strand was busy as coaches full of titled ladies and gentlemen rumbled towards Whitehall. When she arrived to the glow of bright torches she was awestruck, everything was even more beautiful than she could have ever imagined. Everywhere she looked shouted elegance and wealth.

When she reached the Banqueting House she was shown

into an anteroom with ivory and red drapes. She looked about nervously, almost waiting to be pounced on by some oversexed lord or other after Cathy's stories.

She waited there for some minutes before becoming impatient and opening the door a crack and peering through... all was quiet in the long gallery, and she assumed that everyone had been announced and introduced to the king. She hoped they had not forgotten about her, but then muffled footsteps alerted her to a coming presence and she nervously straightened her shoulders and took a step forward.

As soon as he came into view she recognised him immediately, despite his turban and flowing multi-coloured robes. She would know that mincing walk anywhere and she wished she could sink into the carpet.

Percy Darlington smiled wolfishly. 'Ah, Lady Roebuck,' he said brightly, making a leg to her. 'I had hoped to see you. You are a bright butterfly in a colony of moths.'

Leah took a deep breath. He really thought she was Roseanna Roebuck! 'I am sure the other ladies would be much put out by that declaration,' she scolded, in the breathy voice of Roebuck, surprised at how easily the inanities rolled off her tongue.

Percy took her about her waist, making Leah think he and Roebuck were much closer than she had known. 'You know how you set me on fire,' he drawled, pushing her inelegantly against a pillar and lifting her skirts.'

'Pray desist,' she begged, trying to ward him off.

'How cold you are, my lady,' he said in great surprise. 'But then you haven't felt my cock in a long while. Mayhap you have forgotten how much you enjoy it burrowing into your sweet cunny. Let me remind you.'

To Leah's horror he found the delicate folds of her sex and inserted a finger in her funnel, then two. With great determination he finger-fucked her, and feeling her love juices escaping made a sound of encouragement. 'There, you have not forgotten how I pleasure you.'

135

Leah mumbled something, her body reacting shamefully to his overtures. When she was panting with need, her clitoris so engorged she almost snuck a finger into her own wetness and began rubbing it, he smirked and sensing her need did it for her.

His finger frigged her hard and, her knees sagging, she soon reached her crisis, shame colouring her cheeks. She hated Percy Darlington, what was wrong with her? But before she was able to answer her own question he was in her and they were like two animals rutting in a field. This occurred to her and turned her on all the more. It was dirty and dangerous to be thus employed, here in the corridors of King Charles's Banqueting House, but she loved every minute of it. She loved Percy's cock as it ploughed in and out of her, as attuned to her rhythm as a violinist to his instrument. She loved the way his hands pulled down her bodice and he took her nipples into his mouth, adding to her pleasure. And finally she loved the way they both came together, his last thrusts causing her to squeal her satisfaction and almost faint with the trauma of her second crisis. After all, it wasn't often one was pleasured in such regal surroundings.

She lent against the pillar, gasping for air, and he grabbed her bottom and pulled her close. 'Ah, Roseanna,' he said hoarsely, 'would that we had the time, I would beat your arse until you cried for mercy.'

She blinked in surprise. 'You would beat me after what we just did?'

'Don't act so coy. You know how much you love having your arse smacked and then filled with fine meat.'

She blushed, and was saved from his attentions by the sound of an approaching conversation. He quickly and deftly tidied his clothes and Leah hurried back into the room from whence she had come, wondering yet again what possessed her to enjoy such intimacies.

Chapter Nine

Leah was to wait no longer for her secret assignation, for the door opened and a beautiful shepherdess walked in. Leah recognised her straightaway despite her mask. Barbara Castlemaine smiled broadly.

'You look wonderful,' the woman said. 'Now then, in a little while I will call the king out on some pretence or other, and Roebuck will be summoned by a servant. She will follow with a smirk on her face, thinking that his majesty wishes to see her alone. However, she will find not the king awaiting her, but a lackey who will serve her a drink. Roebuck is fond of her wine and will sink it quickly, anxiously awaiting her monarch. She will be asleep in seconds, for the wine will be laced with a harmless sleeping potion.' Leah gasped. 'And then, Mistress Brown, you will come out of hiding and assume her identity.'

'To what purpose?' she asked anxiously.

'To persuade a very important judge of Captain Swan's innocence.' Lady Castlemaine smiled. 'Let me explain. Sir Jonathon Wilde is extremely fond of the ladies, but even more so of the coin.'

'You mean he is corrupt?' Leah asked in disgust.

'Quite so. But even corrupt people must be handled with subtlety. That is where you come in. You will flirt, flatter and generally give Sir Jonathan an unforgettable evening. And then you will confide your little secret to him.'

'My little secret?' Leah asked blankly.

'I will go into the details later.'

'But what if I cannot do it?' Leah was suddenly very afraid. 'The part calls for an actress of exceptional talent.'

'When you are in love you find reserves of talent and strength you never knew about. Believe me, Mistress Brown,' she said in a gentler tone.

Leah nodded; if it meant saving Gideon she would give a performance worthy of Moll Davies.

'Good. Now just a few little modifications as Cathy has done wonderfully well. She commenced to dust her face with a little more ceruse, adding more rouge to her cheeks. Then she fussed over the wig until she declared Leah to be perfect. 'Venus the goddess of love, Roebuck's choice of costume, according to her maid.' Barbara Castlemaine's lip curled into a sneer. 'The lady compliments herself too well. A wailing banshee from hell would far better suit her image.'

Leah was once more given the chance to view her image in a cheval mirror, and had to admit that Lady Castlemaine had indeed made the transformation even better. She looked slightly older, plumper; her face had a haughty expression thanks to the clever cosmetics. The white gown fell in soft folds from one shoulder, held in place by a large sapphire-studded brooch, leaving one creamy shoulder wholly exposed, and barely covering one luscious breast.

'Now let me hear you speak. You must use the breathy tones of Roebuck in order to fool everyone.'

Leah was confident about this, having already fooled Percy, but she thought better about relaying the earlier incident to the lady. Taking a deep breath she did her best Roebuck voice, and was met with peels of excited laughter and hearty applause.

'Very good. Now I think we must add this.' A patch over her breast was her last embellishment. 'Roebuck never goes anywhere without her patches, she believes they add to her allure!' Barbara Castlemaine laughed derisively.

Leah stared uncertainly at the stranger in the mirror, and her fellow conspirator patted her gently on the arm. 'Imagine you have been attending balls at the Palace for years. It will help.' She smiled her gratitude, and Lady Castlemaine gave her a few more instructions. Then Leah was ready for the biggest charade in her entire life!

Lady Roseanna Roebuck sipped her wine, idly perusing the other guests; how they preened and pranced, thinking

138

themselves unrecognisable behind their guises and masks. Fools, she thought sardonically, noting the fat paunch that obviously belonged to the Earl of Doncaster, and an over embellished bosom that denoted his lady wife. She sought better pickings. Where was the Lord Stanhope, the absurdly rich nobleman who seemed to find her irresistible?

A touch on her elbow brought an impatient frown to her brow, then seeing one of the king's liveried servants at her side, she smiled.

'Would you care to follow me, my lady?' he said with a stiff bow.

Roseanna nodded, wielding her fan, suddenly warm with anticipation. She hurried after the man and was shown into an antechamber, richly decorated in blue and gold. This could mean only one thing; the king was wearying of his other paramours; he had finally noticed her. How she longed to see Castlemaine's face when she learned of their passionate liaison, for she would take it upon herself to see that she did.

She removed her mask and a servant brought some wine, which she downed swiftly before spreading her curves seductively over a brocade sofa. She dragged her bodice even lower so that one ripe nipple showed to advantage above the white folds. Her fingers clawed the upholstery in anticipation. Castlemaine had boasted of the king's endowments; was he better in that area than Gideon? For a moment she felt a twinge of loss. Gideon Tempest – what a man!

She patted her elegant coiffure, banishing him from her mind. The bastard was getting everything he deserved for daring to trifle with her affections. Without doubt he would soon hang from the Tyburn tree, and a good riddance too!

She glanced expectantly at the door, a tingle of excitement encompassing her. Oh, how she had longed for this day; power and beauty melding together in hungry lust. After making love to her Charles would want no other. She would take him to the heights of passion and mayhap the good king

139

would show her who was master and put her over his knee. She trembled at the vision of the King of England pulling up her skirts and slapping her cheeks.

How exciting it would be, and how she would enjoy being mastered by him. She would whimper and cry, plead for mercy, secretly loving the feel of the hand on her flesh. Then he would kiss her nether lips, his handsome moustache tickling in all her sensitive places. He would exclaim loudly over the beauty of her cunny until she begged him to rub her nubbin.

Oh yes, soon Charles would be dancing to her tune instead of Castlemaine's. She glanced expectantly at the door, a tingle of excitement knifing through her loins. She yawned. God's teeth, she must not feel sleepy now! She must be at her most radiant in order to dazzle the king with her talents in the boudoir. But her eyes closed and her head dropped onto a blue cushion... and she slept.

A few moments later Barbara Castlemaine entered the room, giggling delightedly to see her hopeful rival sprawled inelegantly on the sofa, her open mouth emitting small snores. Unpinning the emerald brooch from the woman's shoulder she returned to Leah, who was waiting outside. 'Let me exchange that paste jewellery for the real thing. Everyone knows of Roebuck's famous emerald. Now you must follow the lackey into the ballroom. He will point the judge out to you, and you must bewitch him into rapture before captivating him with coin.'

Leah hesitated. 'But what if he doesn't find me attractive?'

Barbara Castlemaine smiled. 'There is little fear of that. And any woman worth her salt can bewitch a man if she is beautiful enough; it is a primary part of our characters. And should you waver in your task just think of your handsome captain.'

Leah glanced through the open door at the woman on the sofa, her bosom so wantonly exposed, and her ire rose. She would undo all that harlot's mischief if it proved to be the last thing she ever did!

The chamber was glittering with chandeliers and riches, sweet music drifted around her. Leah held her breath lest anyone see her mouth agape in awe. Not in her wildest dreams would she have imagined herself in this wonderful place, built by the great architect Inigo Jones for King James I. The magnificent ceiling had been painted by Rubens, and though Leah was completely dazzled she knew she had to contain herself.

She glanced at the large man, pointed out to her by the lackey, and sauntered over to him. A servant offered her wine from a silver tray. She took a glass and continued her journey. Close to he was far larger than she realised, and she almost lost her nerve. But she only had to think of Gideon to strengthen her resolve, so with a distressed cry she tipped her wine onto the highwayman's arm.

'God's teeth!' he thundered, wheeling around.

'Oh, forgive me my clumsiness,' Leah returned in the voice she'd been taught by the king's mistress.

The highwayman's eyes lit on her with great interest. 'No, indeed my lady, forgive my churlishness.' He brushed at the wine with a kerchief. ''Tis nothing that will not soon dry.' His pale gaze wandered lustfully over her costume. 'Venus the goddess of love. How apt a choice for one so lovely.'

And you, sir, a highwayman; more than apt, she thought wryly, the irony of the situation not escaping her. But she said, 'Why, thank you, sir,' in honeyed tones, fluttering her eyelashes furiously.

'Would you think it even more churlish were I to make a guess as to your identity?' he asked silkily, touching her cheek. 'I believe that beneath this mask lies the lovely face of the Lady Roebuck.'

Leah cringed at his touch but managed a sensual pout. 'Ah, my lord, you have found me out.'

'Don't be too disheartened,' he returned softly. 'For how could a red-blooded male not recognise the most perfect

141

bosom in all England?'

Sickened to the stomach by his lecherous grin Leah hid her feelings behind her fan. 'As any appreciative female would instantly recognise those manly shoulders, Sir Jonathan.'

His flush of pleasure eased some of her fears, it was easier than she had thought possible, what vain creatures some men were!

'Do you approve my attire, Lady Roebuck?'

'Indeed I do. The rakish air with which you wear it makes me think you would be devilishly good on the road. I daresay many a lass would lose their hearts to such a handsome rogue.'

She could not believe that such inanities rolled so easily off her tongue, any more than she could believe herself in this great Banqueting House surrounded by such wealth and beauty. They talked some more of the gay costumes around them, each minute Sir Jonathan's stare becoming a little bolder, Leah encouraging him with coy glances.

A lilting melody was struck, and Leah found herself watching the King of England take the Duchess of York on to the floor and dance a single coranto. They were then joined by other lords and ladies, and Leah had to fan herself hard lest her emotions overtake her. That was followed by country dancing, and she was quite breathless at the sight. Here she was, little Leah Brown, in the company of royalty; watching the king dance with the cream of society.

'Would you care to join in?' Sir Jonathan asked politely. She shook her head and the judge's fingers tightened possessively on her arm, his breath hot on her neck. 'Ah, madam, you plague me with your beauty. I have never seen you look so lovely... peaches and cream!' he exclaimed, drooling lasciviously over her bosom. 'Allow me to show you my apartments, for they are newly done and I would appreciate your feminine view.'

His eyes lit on her so hungrily she knew it was time to begin her spiel, glad that Roseanna's reputation was so well known. 'Ah, but I cannot give my thoughts over to such matters, for I have much on my mind.'

The judge's brow elevated. 'May I enquire as to what troubles you?'

She sighed. 'It is a very delicate matter, my lord, and one I am wary of discussing.' She allowed her fingers to wander to the front of his coat in a gesture of intimacy. He quivered and lent even closer.

'Then I insist that you accompany me somewhere quieter,' he announced importantly, 'for I am used to dealing with the most intimate situations…'

The carriage ride was short, and when the coachman pulled up outside a house every bit as splendid as that of Lady Roebuck's, she tried to appear quite unperturbed by her glamorous surroundings.

He showed her into the elegant drawing room, where valuable paintings decorated the walls, and made her comfortable with wine and sweetmeats before asking about her problem.

Leah gave him the full power of her tearful gaze. 'I was enamoured of a certain gentleman,' she began sadly, 'a sea captain. We had a falling out and, thinking that he had been unfaithful to me, I did one of the vilest things possible.' She clung to him, her eyelashes fluttering with dewy tears, her bosom heaving.

'I do not believe you capable of such an act.' He sat close, his fingers wandering to her waist, his thumb caressing the underside of her breast.

She wanted to gag, but dare not. She moved away from his grasp, her eyes flirtatious, her lips moist and inviting. 'Ah, my lord, how I wish I were free from this worry.'

'Jonathon, call me Jonathan,' he said eagerly. 'Unburden yourself, Roseanna, and I shall do all I can to help.'

Her hands fluttered to her throat. 'Very well, but remember that I am in your hands… Jonathan.' He nodded fervently and she continued, feigning reluctance. 'I am

143

ashamed to admit it, but I put a ruby pendant into his things unbeknown to him.' She looked up, her eyes swimming with regret. 'Then I had him arrested for stealing. Almost as soon as it happened I knew it was wrong, and… and I no longer feel anything for the wretch except pity. But I have little idea how to undo the terrible transgression I have committed.'

'Are you sure you feel only pity?' he asked urgently.

She gazed ardently into his eyes. 'Oh, Jonathan, how can you ask such a thing?' Her fingers caressed his wrist and she heard his swift intake of breath.

'Well of course it was a foolish action, but if you are repentant…'

'Oh, truly, and I would be more than willing to pay well the man who would relieve me of this cloud on my conscience.' She removed the perfumed kerchief that had been hidden between her breasts, and displayed some of the coin within. His greedy face lit up, so she tightened the screws a little more. 'Besides, I am unable to take another, um, friend, with Gideon Tempest on my conscience.'

He moulded the sweet curve of her breasts boldly, and though she wanted to slap him for laying hands on her she desisted. His fingers found her nipples and circled them deftly, and Leah was surprised at the sensual yearnings that invaded her.

He puffed out his chest. 'I could easily have the captain freed, had I the monies to oil the wheels, so to speak. I assume he resides in Newgate.'

'Yes,' she said, slipping the coin into his hand. 'I will arrange for a man to meet you at the gate at midnight. When Captain Tempest is free the man will give you the rest of the money.'

He appeared to consider her offer, sliding the money into a nearby drawer. 'I shall agree to help you,' he said, with what she thought was a sly smile, 'but I cannot allow your crime to go unpunished. So you must agree to me disciplining you first.'

Leah's heart pounded in her breast. What was she to do? If she refused he might well deny his help and Gideon would be left to languish in his filthy cell, or even be sent to hang, so she had no choice but to agree. 'Very well,' she said bravely. 'I daresay I deserve it.'

'Then I shall summon Jarvis.' Without another word he rang for his servant, speaking to the man in low tones while Leah sat nervously awaiting her fate.

The servant, a tall fellow in grey livery, beckoned her to follow him up the wide stairs into what she assumed to be a bedchamber, though the man didn't stop there but led her into what she assumed to be a dressing room. She looked about with sinking spirits, noting the small bed against one wall, the clothes-press and the cheval mirror, the table that contained a hairbrush and several phials which she assumed held perfumes.

While Leah was thus engaged she felt her hands being taken and forced behind her back, and before she could do anything at this intrusion she heard the clanking of metal. Her heart sank with dread upon sight of the manacles in the hands of the judge's manservant, but he had no qualms as he snapped them onto her wrists, and she wondered how often he had done the judge's dirty work, he seemed so adept at his job.

'I see Jarvis is readying you for your discipline.'

Leah turned as the judge entered the antechamber, her lips ready to plead with him, to beg him to spare her, her limbs trembling with fear. But she took a deep breath and resolved to carry her task through to the end, or Gideon would be undone. So with her head held high she faced him. 'So it seems.'

He had changed out of his costume and now wore just a robe. 'My, but you are a wonderful woman,' he averred in admiration. 'A weaker female would be fainting with fear.'

Leah chose not to answer him, she dare not in case her voice betrayed her terror. With purposeful strides he went to the clothes-press and took out some strange looking

145

garments. Jarvis, she noticed, was beginning to look quite excited and it accelerated her fears.

'I have decided to allow you the full benefit of the tools at my command.' Judge Wilde held up what seemed to be a leather mask, but there were no eyeholes, just a strange looking mouthpiece. Then he showed her a sort of leather suit; the jerkin and breeches sewn together to form but one garment.

'I must ask you to disrobe, my dear.'

Leah's insides recoiled. 'I cannot.'

The judge smiled. 'Of course your hands will be released while you carry out this task.'

Leah shook her head vehemently. 'I will not do it.'

The smile left his face, which darkened as he reached out and ripped away the delicate materials of her gown and chemise, the lovely emerald dropping to the floor with the material.

The air was suddenly chill on her naked body and her nipples swelled to welcome its attentions. The two men regarded her with great interest, each savouring the delicious curves and valleys and the pretty blonde triangle that pointed the way to her sex. Leah was shocked as the embers of sensuality now fanned into blazing flames inside her belly. Where each pair of eyes landed so her skin heated, almost as though she was being touched by invisible fingers.

'Even more beautiful than I expected,' he breathed. 'Though I wonder that one so fair always hides behind a dark wig at all times.'

If he was to find her out now was the time, she thought with dread. Surely her fair nether hair was a giveaway and he would notice that her shape was far slimmer without clothes. But there wasn't a glimmer of doubt on his face, either about his actions, or hers.

'It seems almost a shame to cover such a stunning body,' he drooled, caressing her breasts, inserting a finger in her sex.

Leah breathed in quickly as he stroked her nubbin, her

146

legs opening of their own volition to welcome him inside. She knew it was wrong but she was doing it for Gideon, so what was the harm if she should happen to enjoy it a little?

The judge nodded his satisfaction. 'Feel how wet she is, Jarvis,' he urged. 'How ready she is for fucking.'

Jarvis eagerly pressed his hand against her sex, stroking her while he had the chance to do so. The judge turned stern eyes on him and he removed his hand and licked her juices from his fingers. Leah was almost fainting with need, but she silently castigated her wayward flesh.

The two men converged on her and she was relieved of the restraints, then they began wrestling her into the strange leather garment. It took a while to encapsulate her, and when they did they pulled the straps at the back of the garment that were designed to tighten around her. Her arms were strapped to her sides and she remonstrated with them.

'This wasn't what I had in mind when I agreed to being disciplined,' she said as firmly as her trepidation would allow, 'so please get me out of this monstrosity.'

But her words were ignored, and when they finished buckling the straps she felt extremely uncomfortable and the breeches cut into her sex and bottom painfully. She continued to complain, but neither one took notice; indeed the judge was busy admiring himself in the cheval mirror. When Jarvis removed her mask and replaced it with a leather one that he strapped around her head, she was glad the judge had been occupied elsewhere, for it would have been heartrending to be recognised at this late stage.

When he finished fastening the mask she was left in a world of darkness. She felt extreme panic and claustrophobia cloaked in the all-encompassing leather, and found that she was unable to breathe. She started to cough and worried that she would suffocate.

The judge touched her arm. 'Breathe through the mouthpiece, Roseanna,' he instructed, and she found the small protuberance and inhaled deeply, relieved to find she was able to breathe adequately through the strange tube that formed the mouthpiece of this ghastly costume, but she still felt panicked.

'There you are, my dear,' he said gleefully. 'Now on the bed with you.'

She was lifted and pressed onto the bed face down. She struggled once more to breathe, turning her head until she was able to find the mouthpiece that had slipped from her. She felt them fiddle with the straps and then air on her bottom, and realised there must be a flap in the back of the costume, and she wondered at it. But she was not to wonder for long, for a hard object nudged at her sex and she knew her love juices were flowing. Almost as soon as the dildo was dipped in them, so it was removed and forced against her anus, gently at first, then pushed until her sphincter accepted it.

As tears ran down her face so another hard object was dipped in her furrow, and he lost no time in filling her vagina with the wooden phallus so that both her private holes were plugged.

She wanted to cry out, to rail at them for their dastardly treatment, but she was unable to speak and the sounds she did make were completely distorted. Once more she found herself gasping for air. Her bottom hole was plugged so tight she fought tears of pain. Held open as it was she feared she would disgrace herself, and her stomach churned. She prayed she would not shed the contents of her bowels; it was far too mortifying to contemplate.

The discomfort of the dildo continued to plague her and she struggled for air through her tube, fighting back anger. All was silent now, but she could hear him breathing, knew he was watching her, awaiting some reaction. After a while the tightness of the leather coat against her nipples made them hard, and as the breeches rubbed against her crotch so her nubbin began to throb. Her muscles flexed against the dildo in her vagina and she gasped loudly through the tube in her mouth. How strange it was to be gratified by a wooden cock. The plug in her bottom hole was beginning to give her pleasure too, and she marvelled at it. Here she was, bound in an ungodly costume and filled in both her delicate passages, and despite her shame and indignity she still felt extremely sexy!

'Are you enjoying that, Roseanna?' he asked, his voice honeyed. 'Is the mask taking away all thought of everything but the power in your body to feel sensations? Is the leather arousing you? Is the dildo in your arse leading you to ecstasy? Do you see that in spite of your predicament I have given you power? You are helpless in one way, but in another you are quite capable of giving yourself pleasure by flexing your muscles against the dildos and pressing your flesh against the leather. Is it not a sweet punishment?'

Leah was appalled at the way she was reacting to the confining costume, at the way her body surged and tingled, at the way her muscles clenched at the foreign objects buried in her most intimate places. What was she? Was her sensuality so great it blinded her to everything but pleasure? She didn't know, but she did know she was fast beginning to learn the secret of punishment and pain.

Chapter Ten

Leah lost track of the time she lay in the blackness of the stifling mask, in the strange leather costume. She had surges of anger at the depths to which the judge had brought her down, and minutes of gratification as her body took delight in the sensuality of her position.

There was nothing to distract her from the fact that all her pleasure zones were being stimulated by the snug garment, and the dildos that tormented her intimate areas. She moaned as her nubbin was frigged by the seam of the fabric as she strained against it. She was in heaven – she was in hell!

She inhaled, and tears meandered inside her mask at the

149

inadequacy of the ventilation tube. Each breath was laboured, her chest feeling heavy, leaving her weak from the effort. She had not heard the sound of a human voice for hours, and she was beginning to feel more suffocated and claustrophobic than before.

'Do you find your situation appealing, Roseanna?'

Leah jumped at the unexpected sound of Judge Wilde's voice, and instantly regretted the movement as her breath rasped through the breathing tube, sounding desperate even to her own ears.

'But then you are quite unable to answer me, aren't you?' He chuckled. 'But that is not my worry, for naughty girls must be punished, and I must admit that I find the sight of your good self encased in animal skin quite captivating.'

As he spoke he fingered her cunny and back passage through the leather, grinding the seams hard into her tender flesh, pushing the dildos even deeper. She inhaled loudly and heard him laugh at her exertion as air rasped through the tube. His fingers found their way inside the leather through the flap that dissected the legs of the garment. They slid down to her nubbin and rubbed until the already swollen nodule swelled even more and pulsed until she thought she would die with pleasure.

He did not cease from his task, and as she was so wonderfully stimulated by the wooden phalluses her crisis came with an explosiveness that left her whole body quivering and her juices coating his hand.

Before her spasms subsided he relieved her of the dildo in her back passage. But he replaced it with his cock, and she felt the difference immediately as the warm flesh sank into her, throbbing and vibrating with life.

She snorted loudly through the mask as her muscles clenched around his warmth, thrilling to him in the aftermath of her crisis. Her body seeped from the satisfaction of her orgasm and the stimulation of the man as his cock ploughed into her rectum, adding more pressure to the dildo in her vagina, allowing her to experience more pleasure.

Leah was besieged with such wonderful sensations she lost sense of everything apart from the force of her own gratification. She came again long before he rolled off her, and was beginning to think she could take no more excitement when she was released from the restricting leather garment.

As before she worried that the judge would recognise her as a fraud when her mask was lifted, but when freed she looked into the entranced gaze of Jarvis, the manservant.

He left the dildo until last, and Leah watched his face as his eager fingers trailed into her wetness, played there for a few moments before divesting her of the last wooden phallus.

Her channel flooded at the attention and her nubbin swelled with desire. Jarvis smirked. 'You've a rare appetite, me lady. Mayhap Jarvis can be of some more service to yer.'

Leah looked up at him helplessly, her body betraying her once more. It was no good denying what he saw with his own eyes. 'I think we have done,' she said without much conviction.

Jarvis grinned and smoothed his finger over the pulsing nut. 'No me lady. My master trusts me to do I all can for his guests. It would not be fair to leave you out of the equation, now would it?'

'I think you'd better tend to your other duties,' she said waspishly. 'Now unhand me; your master would not approve of you taking liberties.'

She moved away from him, attempting to rise from the bed, but with swift movements the man had her spread-eagled once more across the counterpane. He was wiry and though she fought hard he was far stronger than she. Their tussle ended in his snapping manacles onto her wrists and ankles, which he then secured to the bed by means of metal clamps she had not seen before. She wondered grimly how many more victims had struggled here only to be overcome by the brute strength of the men of the house.

'You will find little pleasure in taking a woman who does not want you,' she snapped.

Jarvis grinned and rubbed his hands together gleefully. 'There ain't no fear of that, me lady.' Without further ado he dropped his codpiece and hauled out his rampant manhood. 'I've a good length here. 'Twould be a shame to waste it.'

Leah struggled against her restraints. 'If you touch me I'll inform your master and see that you are punished.'

'I am entitled to master's leftovers, 'tis the perk of a good servant.'

Leah did have the satisfaction to see that, despite his arrogance, he stole a nervous glance towards the door, though his hesitation was quickly thrown off as he ran his fingers possessively between her legs. His lips rose momentarily as if a happy thought had occurred to him. 'Stay right where you are,' he said derisively, feeding his cock back into his breeches. 'I won't be long.'

She strained and fought against the cruel metal that dug into her ankles and wrists, but it was to no avail and her heart sank when Jarvis returned bearing a dish.

'Your little pussy suffered so much heat in that leather I thought it a good idea to fetch some ice to cool you down.'

With a leer he laid the dish aside, and Leah saw that he was left with a goodly sized piece of ice in his hand. She shrank back into the bed, but when he applied the ice to her clitoris she gasped. The frozen water was a shock to her system, and as Jarvis slid it against her sex lips, running it over her clit, she shed tears of anger, tensing as the chill bit into her delicate flesh and her sex contracted painfully.

She silently castigated herself; this was what he wanted, her tears and her anger. It showed him the control he had over her. She then vowed to remain passive, no matter what else he did. It would give him little pleasure to dominate a female who refused to react to his atrocities.

'There, is that better?'

'You are nothing more than a... a...' she began, quite unable to finish her sentence as the ice made her labia sting with an intense vitality. Jarvis grinned knowingly and Leah knew he had done this before.

'Is that nice? I haven't met a lady yet who didn't enjoy ice applied to her pussy. The more high-flung they are the more they enjoy their sessions on the bondage bed.'

Leah viewed the tent in his breeches doubtfully; the erection he had earlier seemed to have lengthened even more, and Jarvis noticed her nervous glance with some amusement.

'Look well, me lady, for I've a right boner all ready for yer when I've cooled your purse.' As he spoke he inserted the ice into her vagina and this time, in spite of her earlier intentions, she let out a weary sob. The ice was excruciating, a pain darted through her centre and she shuddered against it. He began to fuck her with it, and to her disbelief she found the stark cold a delightful contrast to the heat of the leather costume they'd forced her to wear earlier. She found it hard to describe the excitement she was caught up in; the overpowering irritation, the divinely exasperating numbness turning to a vibrant heat as the ice danced along the sensitive nerve endings inside her core.

Triumphant at her reactions, Jarvis tossed what was left of the ice aside and undid the flap of his codpiece, releasing the beast that struggled within his breeches. The friction of his hot cock in her vagina, after the cold of the ice, was a distinct turn on, and though she tried to remain lifeless beneath him she found it impossible.

His victorious grunts shamed and repulsed her, but Jarvis rode on, sucking her nipples, clawing at them in his desire to reach the pinnacle of his desires, and when he did he gave a louder grunt and collapsed on top of her.

After a few moments' rest he folded himself back into his breeches and became the obedient manservant again. Releasing her from her restraints he wiped away all signs of his seed with a damp cloth, drying her almost tenderly, and then he helped her into what was left of the clothes, muttering about his master's regret at the spoilt chemise and gown.

'My lord sends his apologies,' he reported, his eyes straining for any glimpse of flesh beneath the enveloping garment of her cloak, 'but says you will understand his absence as he hurries to do your bidding.'

Leah nodded. 'Of course.'

Her heart fluttered in her breast with hope; was he really about to obtain Gideon's release? With the thought of seeing Gideon Tempest again high on the agenda she entered the coach that had been sent for her and settled into its confines, prepared to forget everything that had happened to her at the hands of Judge Wilde. All that mattered was that he kept his promise.

Gideon was awakened, his irons cast off, and then he was led through dark passageways in silence. 'What's happening?' he demanded.

'Yer been set free,' the turnkey muttered, ill-tempered at having been woken from his peaceful sleep. 'Consider yerself lucky to have such influential friends.'

Soon Gideon was outside the gate of the prison, still bemused at the swiftness of his release.

'Gideon, is that you?'

He saw the flicker of a torch and the outline of his good friend walking towards him. 'Fitz, what's going on?'

Fitz caught him by the arm and led him swiftly to a waiting carriage. 'Come, 'tis best we leave this place, for it leaves a nasty taste in my mouth.'

Stepping into the comfort of the carriage Gideon looked to Fitz for an explanation. 'How did you manage it?' he asked in amazement. 'I owe you my apologies for doubting you, and my deepest thanks.'

'Not I, captain,' Fitz corrected. 'You owe this lady your thanks, for she was the one who brought about your release with her great courage.'

Gideon, in his haste to thank Fitz, had not noticed the other person in the dark depths of the carriage, and when he

154

did he studied the woman with narrowed eyes.

'Thanks!' he thundered. 'By all the saints I have this bitch to thank for having me locked up!'

'Don't you know me, captain?' Leah asked softly, removing her dark wig and shaking out her golden hair.

'Mistress Brown,' he said in disbelief. 'Is that really you?'

She laughed lightly. 'Aye, captain, 'tis I.'

'Will someone please tell me what's going on?' he asked, more bewildered than ever, and before Leah's home was reached the tale of her masquerade was told, and Gideon viewed her with undisguised amazement. 'You endangered yourself posing as Roseanna in order to free me?'

'It was not so dangerous,' she said modestly as the carriage came to a halt outside her door.

He climbed out before she did and, swinging her into his arms, pressed a kiss of thanks on her mouth. The door was opened and Jane appeared. 'Look after her,' the captain averred firmly, 'for she is a rare jewel.'

'Aye, she is that,' Jane agreed proudly, allowing Leah entry.

As the coach rolled away Leah was left with the pressure of those grateful lips on hers, and her dreams that night had never been sweeter.

Leah was so tired out after her adventure she did not awake until midday, and when she did it was to see Jane's smiling face.

'Get dressed quickly, the captain's here with two horses,' Jane said excitedly. 'He's taking you for a picnic. I... er... I don't feel well today so you'll have to go without a chaperone, I'm afraid.'

Leah was both amazed and delighted at Jane's words. It was not done to venture out with a gentleman without a chaperone, but something in Jane's face stopped her asking questions and she hugged her gratefully.

She was soon ready and presented a charming picture in the pearl-grey riding habit and military style coat that showed off her figure to perfection. Her wide-brimmed hat, fashionably decorated with ostrich feathers, shaded her face, and lent an air of mystery to her features.

Gideon's gaze lingered admiringly. 'You look wonderful,' he said, with a dazzling smile that made her stomach curl in pleasure. Leah blushed and thanked him. 'Shall we make a start? Now I have my freedom I intend to make the most of it,' he averred with a grin.

Leah's mount was a gentle grey and she patted her velvet nose in delight.

'She's called Duchess,' he said, 'and I've been assured she has the nicest temperament imaginable.'

'I'm sure we'll get on famously,' she said a little shyly, as Gideon helped her into the saddle. She took the reins and urged the animal into a trot as Gideon mounted a large bay.

Before very long they had left the confines of the city and were out in the glorious countryside. Though they conversed little Gideon's eyes spoke volumes. The sun seemed to reflect their pleasure, casting its warming rays to lighten her curls.

They alighted in a pretty meadow, and as Gideon lifted her down from her mount Leah trembled at his touch. 'I thought this a satisfactory spot for a picnic,' he said, hitching the horses to a bush.

Leah sighed. 'Yes, it's perfect.'

Their eyes met, the tension of the ride sparking a fire between them. He bent his head and kissed her, and everything else was forgotten as they swayed hungrily together, unaware of the lush grass that carpeted their feet, of the huge oaks and elms that swayed gently in the breeze, their leaves whispering secretly.

Their garments were swiftly torn asunder as the flames of passion that had been kindled from the first day of their meeting became an inferno. Gideon reverently anointed her body with soft kisses, holding himself back, not wanting to hurt her. But her nipples surged into his mouth willingly, and her sex lips, hot and pink with desire, opened like a flower to a bee. She was soft and slippery with need and he stroked her labia, gently caressing the nub of her clitoris as it begged attention.

Leah shuddered with delight and kissed the hard, furred wall of his chest, before taking his straining shaft into her hand, marvelling at the size of him. She slid her fingers up and down his silkiness but it was not enough, she needed to taste him, to slide her tongue down the length of him. The nest of black hair that surrounded his sex smelled sweet and clean, and when she took him into her mouth he made a sound deep in his throat that signalled his elation.

Soon they were head to tail, both wanting to taste the texture and sweetness of the other's sex. Leah thrilled to his firm tongue as it licked her cleft, slurping her juices, sliding into her warmth and fucking her like a cock. She fingered his balls, began kissing them, loving the contrast between their softness and the steel of his shaft. For a fraction of a second she wondered how he would feel when he realised she was not a virgin, but she was soon too overcome with passion to even think straight.

To her surprise he stopped her, bringing her lips to his own, whispering sweet words of love before opening her thighs once more and licking her pulsing nubbin, swirling clever fingers over her nipples. The more he licked the wetter she became and soon the familiar tension began in her loins, building to a crescendo of sensation that completely overwhelmed her. When he heard her sigh of delight he entered her in one clean thrust and she screamed, not in pain but in total elation as the steel of his cock sheathed itself inside her slippery vagina.

It was as though they were made for each other as he moved inside her, gently at first, then building, thrusting deeper and deeper until she thought she would die, leading her to a paradise she had never known before. Luck was with her that day, for when they were done there was a red sticky residue between her legs, and she realised it was the beginning of her flux.

Gideon, taking it for the sign of her virginity, held her close and they lay together, marvelling in the passion of first love. Leah was loath to disabuse him; the truth would only set him to worrying and no good would come of his anger.

She refreshed herself in the brook, tearing her shift to form a protective barrier so that her gown would not be stained.

They both dressed, she behind a bush as shyness overcame her. Then Gideon reached in his saddlebags for the food they'd brought.

They dined on pigeon pie, fresh bread and cheese, all washed down with a bottle of wine from fluted glasses. They ate like lords, their avid glances telling of their devotion. When they were replete he asked about her disappearance to Dunstan House.

Knowing the truth would only bring more trouble, she smiled. 'Percy thought it a romantic gesture, having me taken from Lady Roebuck's, and asked me for my hand. I could not accept his proposal. A short time later I took a fever, and was obliged to foist myself on their hospitality for a little while.'

He studied her closely and she gave him another reassuring smile, hating herself for having to lie to him, knowing it was for the best. 'He was foolish, I know. But a stricken heart causes people to do foolish things. He apologised profusely and the matter is at an end.'

He seemed unconvinced for a moment, but her humour seemed to convince him. Then pouring some more wine he made a toast that warmed her heart. 'To Leah, a beautiful sorceress who saved my life, the lady who has gained my deepest admiration and devotion.' She blushed and his avid gaze swept over her. 'I will never forget what you did,' he said gratefully, placing his glass aside.

'I would not hesitate to do the same again,' she replied quietly. 'I could not bear to see you hang from the Tyburn tree.'

'So you do care for me a little?'

'I thought I had proven my feelings for you,' she replied shyly, the buzz of insects and the sound of the brook tinkling over its stony bed the only sound to disturb them.

He kissed her, and she returned the kiss with the newly-awakened yearning of first love. 'You are a little witch,' he said with a chuckle. 'You've worked a spell on me and I am powerless to escape you.'

'And you, captain?' she teased. 'What are you?'

'I, sweet Leah?' He laughed softly. 'The son of a sea captain from whom I inherited my love of the ocean. My ship is my castle the ocean my domain.'

She caressed the deep cleft in his chin, and he captured her fingertips in a fleeting kiss. 'You are my lord,' she said softly. 'My lord of the sea.'

'Your lord?' he chuckled, but then his eyes became serious, held her in their thrall. 'Then grant me lifetime use of the title. Marry me, little witch, for you have burrowed so deep into my heart I swear I cannot live without you.'

The magic circle that had enclosed them all day shattered, and despite the warm sun she shivered. 'No, Gideon... I cannot,' she said quietly. 'Please don't ask it again. We must go,' she said insistently, her heart full of sorrow, knowing she could never be his.

When she returned home they clung together, her fingers on his lips as he tried to delve deeper into the puzzle. 'I can't see you again,' she whispered sadly, loath to spoil her wonderful day but knowing it had to be faced.

His face darkened. 'We have something special. Don't throw it away.'

'I am betrothed, Gideon. He was my father's choice and there is nothing I can do.'

He brushed away her tears, begging her to reconsider, but she was adamant so with love and anger vying for release he turned and left without another word.

Leah entered the house, her hair a riot of love-swept curls, her lips brushed red from passion, but her eyes held a haunted look that tore at Jane's heart.

Jane held the girl in her arms. 'I know what it's like to be in love,' she said softly. 'And like you I've known a man's passion.' She smiled at Leah's deep blush. 'Yes, I have a good idea what happened. When people are in love trying to stop their natural urges is like trying to stop the ebb and flow of the tide.' She looked soberly at Leah. 'Have you told him about William?'

Leah nodded, eyes swimming with misery, and Jane's held a faraway look. 'I lost my Robert, too. We planned to marry in the autumn. He knew I would not leave you and it was arranged that he would move in with us all. But it was not to be. When King Charles, at the head of the Scottish army, reached Worcester in the August, Robert rode out with a handful of friends to join him. He was a staunch royalist, you see.'

Her breath caught on a sob. 'But the Parliamentary armies, sweeping down from the north, had caught up with them and were laying in wait near the town. It was said they fought bravely, but they were defeated. My love was killed fighting for his monarch. Luckily the king managed to escape.'

Leah wiped her eyes. 'Oh Jane, I am so sorry.'

Leah went to her, and the two united by sadness clung together. Leah knew she would have to be brave too, for soon she had to go through the mockery of a marriage she did not want and then sail off to a strange land, to William Penrose, who would own her body and soul.

Chapter Eleven

Barbados

Wildwinds stood white and virginal against the blue, cloudless sky. The sugar plantation lay on the windward side of the island, where the trade winds arrived cool and fresh after crossing the Atlantic. A breeze whispered through the gaily-coloured vine that twined its sinewy tendrils through the trelliswork on the veranda of the plantation house. It stole through the open doors, fluttering the folds of the brocade drapes, disturbing the pages of a book lying discarded in its path on an inlaid table.

The place had been built for a beautiful bride, who with her grace and charm immediately became the heart of that great house. But she had been delicate and the burning heat of the tropical island soon took its toll, draining her strength, robbing the excitement from her laugh, the brightness from her eyes.

Within months she lay dead of a fever, leaving her husband to spend the rest of his life wallowing in grief. And although Silas Webster found some solace in a rum bottle and beneath the petticoats of the raddled trulls in the taverns, he tended the house well, for it was a shrine to the woman he worshipped.

But circumstances change and people move on, and the new owner, William Penrose, had no patience with human weakness. To him *Wildwinds* was more than a fairytale palace built by a besotted bridegroom, it was the realisation of a dream. Here he was master. Here his white indentured servants and his black slaves knew the sharp kiss of his whip. The younger more attractive ones, both male and female, were also privy to the enormous tool that was loath to stay in his breeches.

He had a personal preference for the blacks; they were more used to the tropical sun and laboured well in the heat of the day, and the gleaming, sinuous bodies of the women had a charm like no other.

Reclining in a leather chair a little to the right of the veranda doors, he unbuttoned the collar of his fine lawn shirt, welcoming the breeze from a palm frond wielded by a slave. He idly sipped a brandy, cursing as some of the amber liquid spilled onto his buff breeches, and swiped angrily at the stain with a lace-edged kerchief.

He clicked his fingers at the girl, who rushed forward to mop his breeches, her attentions causing his cock to stir within, so opening up his codpiece he forced her head into his lap. 'You have a good mouth,' he said as she guided her tongue over his glans. It was like being stroked with velvet and William clutched the wooden arms of his chair, more than ready to enjoy her ministrations. She took him into her mouth, then deep into her throat and he stretched his legs as she brought him to his crisis.

A servant announced a visitor and William's fair head tilted arrogantly to receive him, his fingers tossing aside the kerchief and beating an impatient tattoo on the highly polished wood of his oaken desk.

'Slade,' he acknowledged briefly as his henchman entered.

'There's trouble brewing,' the swarthy man replied without preamble, ignoring the girl who had fellated his master and was now licking him clean. 'Webster's crawled back out of his hole. He's saying you cheated him out of his plantation. No one's listening to his drunken bilge right now, but I reckon someone might get interested if he tells his story enough times.'

Crushing a sheaf of papers in his fist William pushed the girl away, and rearranging his clothes strode out to the veranda. He hadn't expected any trouble from that quarter. Webster had been taken in by one of his old bond servants who lived in a shack on the other side of the island. He had not seen or heard of either of them in months, and assumed they had whored and drank themselves to death by now, their bodies long eaten by sand crabs.

After a few moments' pacing he returned to his study. 'I think we'll deal with Webster after the ceremony tonight, Slade. It's a long time since we've sent someone to the twilight world. It will be good entertainment. What do you think?'

Slade nodded, his cavernous mouth revealing rotting teeth.

'Yes sir, a good idea.' He shivered, thinking of Webster's fate.

'The hungan will be pleased,' William smiled, referring to the black priest who attended all the dark ceremonies held on the plantation.

'I'll make sure the victim's here.' Slade grinned. It paid him well to be deferential to his master, for when he was in a good mood he allowed him the pick of the bondswomen. And there was one little blonde chit whose curvy backside was just crying out for the taste of his hand.

'Good. I would hate my new wife to hear any nefarious gossip, for God willing she will be arriving soon.'

He glanced down at the girl who still knelt at his feet. 'You can go. Send the new girl in.' William gave him a nod of dismissal and lit a cigar, his finely chiselled features set in a satisfied smile. He studied his slim fingers proudly. When he arrived in the Caribbean he had done some gambling, just enough to keep body and soul together, waiting for the main chance. His opportunity had arisen one fine evening in Bridgetown when the owner of *Wildwinds* strolled in to the tavern in which he had installed himself.

Silas Webster had been an easy target – his skills at the card table no match for William's. He cultivated him for a while, allowing him to win, then one evening when Webster was foxed he induced him to wager *Wildwinds*. The result was old news.

The new mulatto house-girl entered and William's gaze travelled greedily over her shapely curves. 'You are overly clothed,' he admonished, pointing to her tight bodice.

With a nervous smile the black-eyed wench slid out of her top and stepped towards his beckoning finger. Her breasts were pert and pretty. She walked tall and proud. Too proud! She would have to be taught a lesson. At the moment the heat was overwhelming. For now she could fan him with a palm frond while he watched her globes wiggle and jiggle like junket.

Smoke spiralled up from his fine Havana cigar, and as he

admired the girl's attributes the young woman of his dreams filled his mind. The lovely Leah Brown would soon arrive to share his life and everything would be just perfect. His eyes narrowed as he recalled his meeting with her father Thaddeus in the London alehouse, how easily he was hoodwinked into believing he'd been robbed. In reality he had invested his last coin in a good whore and was wondering where he would spend the night when the good doctor caught his eye, his successful spiel concluding in him being Thaddeus's guest for a sennight.

His daughter Leah had been a delightful surprise, but there was little opportunity to take advantage of the situation. His only pleasure was in following her shapely figure with his eyes, wondering idly if she lie abed exploring her sex with innocent fingers. He had imagined it often, and then imagined himself in that virgin bedchamber, ordering her to open her sleek white thighs for him so he could bury himself in the soft folds of her cunny. As it was he soon tired of fucking the cook, and after failing to bed Leah one drunken night, he decided to take his leave.

It was when he began to rifle the house, intent on stealing what he could before he left, that he stumbled on a very interesting document in the doctor's bureau; a document that told him Leah would indeed be a fine prize. It was then he became determined to win her. First he knew he would have to prove himself to Thaddeus by foul means or fair. But William had a golden tongue, and when he broached the subject the doctor was inevitably convinced.

All that was left was to find the monies for his voyage. That hadn't been a problem, for he had dallied with the landlady of the *White Swan*. She wasn't fair of face and it was easy to charm himself into her bed. He had not slept with such a large woman before and was amazed at what delights lay beneath her apron. Her breasts were like bolsters and he buried his head between the twin globes, squeezing them greedily with his fingers. She was a noisy lover, squealing and screeching as he pleasured her. William didn't mind – it let the world know how good he was.

He felt extremely randy that night, with thoughts of the lovely Leah Brown tormenting him, and the woman was more than willing to accommodate him. He fucked her between her huge breasts, making a tunnel for his shaft to slide through, and she loved every minute of it.

Then, after being refreshed by the good landlady's beer, he took his fill of the treasure between her thighs. Despite her size her inner sex lips were small and pretty, and her nectar was copious. When he had lapped her cunny well he ploughed his way inside her. To his surprise, though she wasn't in the first flush of youth, her purse was tight and it was his turn to shout out when he felt the tight muscles consuming him. He came quickly that time, like a young boy with his first love.

He was embarrassed by it, but she cradled him lovingly and he sucked the huge titties she offered, his hands wandering idly over the great expanse of her stomach. Lying close to her, suckling just like a babe, he called her mama. Then he laid his head on her, and with her enormous breasts and stomach almost enveloping him, he felt as though he was back in the womb and quickly fell asleep.

But he wasn't allowed to sleep for long, for the landlady was insatiable. She was all woman, a real handful for any man, and when she asked him to spank her on her enormous white bottom he did so with relish. She screeched with each slap and her thanks were profuse. He couldn't recall being so turned on by any woman, and gazing at the dimples in her podgy arse with great joy, realised her slimmer sisters were missing something. This fleshy woman looked really rude, turned him on more than anyone else ever had. She was a goddess of sensuality!

And so he'd been reluctant to part from her, and even more reluctant that he had to steal from her to survive. So he waited for her loud snoring to tell him she was asleep before taking her life's savings from the chest she kept in her bedchamber. Recalling how well he had serviced her went a little way to relieving his guilt.

He then set out on his adventure to the New World, certain that both Leah Brown and her fortune would one day be his. Although *Wildwinds* had once been a thriving sugar plantation he took to ignoring his factor's good advice, and his mismanagement was running it into the ground, so he needed Leah Brown's money more than ever in order to fund his expensive lifestyle.

He motioned to the slave girl to move closer, and while she wielded the huge fan he delighted in the smooth lines of her body. He reached out and jiggled one delightful breast, once more his cock stirring in his breeches. Opening his codpiece he pulled her to her knees and let her tend to him. It was merely a taste for what was to come that evening, so with a sly smirk he lay back and gave his attention over to the soft mouth and tongue that glided over his cock.

The drums pounded out their message, calling all the faithful to the ceremony. Their destination was a circle of palm trees deep in the middle of the plantation. Here, surrounding an altar that was lit on either side by flickering candles, the half naked followers of the dark religion gathered. As was usual at these times, a variety of different sized vessels were readied on the ground for whatever evil substance needed containing. The sacred altar held nothing but a wicked looking knife. Many sconces burned in the clearing, their fierce flames flickering like devils' tongues against the backdrop of the palms and the sugar cane in the distance.

Suddenly the insistent sound of the drums ceased and the gathering was silent, all eyes on the altar in their midst, their excitement almost palpable.

William watched from the shadows as the hungan appeared, draped in a white robe and a conical hat. The man began to chant, then taking up the knife, sounded as though he was calling up ancient spirits. The intensity of the situation made William's hands damp. It always affected him like this. Even though he didn't necessarily believe in

166

mumbo jumbo he knew it was wise to respect it.

He was eager to get started on what was, for him, the main event of the evening, but first of all the faithful had to have their fun. He allowed their nonsense only because it benefited him to do so. A goat was brought into the clearing – a sacrifice for the gods. Within seconds the hungan had cut his throat and, midst much chanting, his blood was drained into the waiting vessels.

A tall dark woman, her skin glistening with unguents, graceful movements reminiscent of a panther, moved towards the sacred shrine. She stood to one side, the ebony beauty of her flesh prevalent in the flickering candlelight. The woman's body was generously proportioned, her majestic posture regal. The only thing to relieve her nakedness, the sinuous body of a twenty foot python that wound itself almost lovingly around her curves, doing nothing to detract from her allure.

William watched Dominique with pleasure, his loins heating at the pure beauty of her. It was time for him to show himself. He walked into the clearing, an austere figure in a white hooded robe. With a motioning of his hand Slade came out of the trees, followed by two figures carrying a man who was bound by his feet and hands. The man was thrown to the ground at William's feet and the hungan stood aside.

William's lips curled over his teeth in a sneer as he glanced down at Silas Webster. 'You are to be allowed a special favour before you are sent to the twilight world, my friend. Give thanks for my generosity, which is far more than you deserve.'

There was an eerie quiet in the clearing, the call of birds, the scuffling of animals, all silent. William was always impressed by this; the old magic was a strong one, one to be respected. He called for the virgin he'd chosen to come forth, and she walked forward with grace, her dark skin gleaming in the wavering light, her naked body a target for eager eyes. She walked with what passed for confidence, though if you looked closely you were able to see a slight trembling in that shapely body.

When she reached him he held a cup to her lips and she drank deeply, some of the warm blood seeping from her mouth and down her chin. It dripped slowly onto her curvaceous breasts, which William licked, lapping at the blood with gusto. It seemed to revitalise him, to add weight to his resolve.

He motioned to Slade to untie the ex-owner of *Wildwinds*, and when his bindings were cast aside the man was hauled to his feet. Cushions were placed before the altar and the girl lay across them, her legs parted wide, showing the damp pink folds of her sex. Webster was stripped and pushed towards her, his drug-induced stare barely registering the naked girl.

William's henchman caught the back of his neck, pushed him down between the sweet thighs, insinuating his face against her sex. The heady scent of her seemed to reawaken something inside him, and he gave a throaty groan and lapped eagerly at the virgin vulva. His hands reached out for her flat belly, his fingers gliding over the glistening brown skin, the dimple in her naval. And as the drums pound out their rhythm his hands reached her breasts, trembling as they felt the feminine roundness.

The drugged man raised himself above the girl, and the drums stopped. His cock rampant, with one swift movement he plunged inside her. As she screamed and her virgin blood soiled the cushions so the drums began their insistent beat once more. Silas Webster rode her long and hard, ploughing into her depths as though he registered that it was the last time he would be able to love a woman.

Dominique held the snake over the couple and wove a spell that was more ancient than the land itself. Then loud voices joined in with the sound of the drums as the worshippers of Damballah-wedo, the serpent god, Oguferaille, the warrior-god, Shango, the storm-god, and dozens of other gods far too numerous to mention, threw themselves into a frantic dance, their multi-hued bandanas and loincloths melding into a kaleidoscope of colour that lit the clearing.

The energetic dancing ceased almost as abruptly as it had begun, leaving the participants panting and soaked with sweat. Then the faithful cast off the rest of their clothes and began pairing off, as there on the verdant floor of the plantation they thrust cocks into vaginas, into mouths and into arses. Men coupled with men and women with women, all driven on by the restless pounding beat.

William watched, his eyes glowing with lust as the faithful played out the ancient dance that was as old as time. When Webster rolled off the girl she rose gracefully and retired to the outskirts of the clearing. Webster was retied and bundled aside like a piece of rubbish.

William held his hand out to Dominique, and giving her snake into another's hands she came to him with a smile, regal in her bearing. She lay down in the virgin's blood intermingled with sweat and semen, and he flung aside his robe. He too was naked underneath, his cock a mighty staff that soon worked its way inside the vagina of the ebony-hued beauty.

She wrapped herself around him like a writhing serpent and he spent his desire in the feminine softness of her, tangling his hands in the raven-black hair, the twin moons of his white bottom bobbing, standing out in bold relief from the dark bodies around him.

When he was done he drank some of the magic draught that brought his shaft alive again, and throwing himself into the writhing sea of bodies found an empty arse that he used with gusto, caring not whether it belonged to a male or female.

When the orgy drew to its conclusion the hungan ordered the participants to be quiet, and began the ceremony to turn Silas Webster into one of the living dead. William was no longer interested in the proceedings. Leaving them to get on with their mumbo jumbo and strange magic, he gave

169

Webster a pitying glance before striding away from the clearing.

Leah and Jane were both eager to leave the *Christina*, it had been a wearisome voyage, in the small confines of the sailing ship. Even a welcome turn around the decks had not lifted their humour overmuch. They became tired of seeing nothing but the inevitable stretch of ocean everywhere they looked. And although the other travellers were pleasant enough, they soon tired of the same faces.

Leah suffered from seasickness and longed for the day she could once more feel firm land beneath her feet, instead of the constant sway of the ship. Unfortunately for them, they had been forced to weather a bad storm, when both ladies were convinced they would be nothing but fodder for the fish.

But when they anchored in the river, that was really an arm of the sea, they both sighed gratefully, eager to be near land once more.

Settled in the small rowing boat that was to take them to the shore at Bridgetown, Leah and Jane watched the lighters taking cargoes back and forth between the other ships and the shore. It was a fascinating sight of the world, and one they would have surely missed had they not boarded the *Christina* to take them to Barbados. The weeks preceding the trip Leah had often threatened Jane she would not go.

'Papa will not know,' she had wailed. 'What difference would it make now? Besides, I have no wish to marry William Penrose or anyone else of his ilk.'

Jane pleaded and persuaded, knowing in her heart of hearts that Leah meant none of it. It was just her way of readying herself for the task that lie ahead. When the proxy marriage was performed the young woman had gone through it dry-eyed, though her skin had taken on the cast of parchment. Jane worried she would pine away with love for Gideon Tempest. She wished Thaddeus had lived to see that young man, surely he would have seen the love they bore one another and been sympathetic. He had married for love and knew how it felt.

As it was Leah lost her appetite and consequently lost weight, and the sea voyage did not help. The constant upheaval of the ship had upset her and she could keep little down, and Jane was looking forward to settling on the plantation and feeding her up.

Safely on shore once more, Jane bowed down and kissed the earth at her feet. But Leah had eyes for nothing but William. She looked at him uncertainly as he strode towards her at the quayside and bent his head in order to kiss her fingers. 'Welcome, my dear wife,' he said. 'I have awaited this moment so very long.'

She blushed, during her six week voyage to the New World she had tried to acclimatise to the fact that she was a married woman, but somehow her brain could not come to terms with the fact. She knew that if the groom had been Gideon Tempest her heart would have soared with elation. But that would never happen now; she would never see him again. The only thing to be done was for her to throw herself into her new life with William with as much enthusiasm as she could manage.

She was amazed by his good manners and appearance. His wig was handsome, his skin had acquired a wonderful tan from the sun, and clear blue eyes observed her keenly. His face was wider than Gideon's, though his jaw line appeared far too feminine for a man. And though he was nowhere near as handsome as her love, it was a pleasing face and he had a nice smile. He was of average height and build, but he carried himself well and his innate magnetism made one immediately aware of him.

Had he been so attractive, so charming when he visited her home? Or had he merely gained these qualities with maturity? Then again, perhaps she had been at fault. Perhaps she had been too young to appreciate the man's attractions. As for the foray he made into her bedchamber, that must be put down to the drink and his strong male libido.

As he escorted Leah and Jane to the carriage that awaited them in the bustling Caribbean port, she realised he was much more fashionably dressed than she'd expected in this out of the way place. His neck cloth was a pleasing claret, his white shirt of the finest lawn. His knee length coat was slit at the back and of dove-grey like his breeches, which were gathered at the knee and decorated with beribboned garters. His hose was of the finest quality, his black, square-toed shoes decorated with shiny buckles, and he exuded confidence.

She felt far from confident in her own dress. Although she was in a pretty gown of peach that was held back by ribbons to expose pretty petticoats, she knew it did not fit as well as it should, owing to her seasickness, and she wondered if William was regretting sending for her.

All around them she could hear the speech of many nations as people went about their business, and the tall sailing ships anchored downriver were a romantic backdrop for the cosmopolitan scene. William's carriage was in the charge of a Negro and they were ushered into its confines, everything seeming strange and alien.

Leah began to feel a little better when they left the noise and bustle behind, and William pointed out some huge fig trees with gnarled trunks and a curtain of straggly roots, which resembled beards, which grew along the coast.

'Portuguese named the island after the fig trees. Los Barbudos, meaning "the bearded ones",' he explained. 'Which of course translates to Barbados.'

'How fascinating,' she replied a little breathlessly, smiling at Jane's obvious bemusement with the entire place.

They were soon travelling through acres of green cane fields. Before they reached the plantation house they skirted a village of small thatched-roofed huts that she learned belonged to the slaves. She knew her father hadn't agreed with the notion of buying and selling human beings, and meant to bring up the subject when she knew her husband a little better.

172

There were several buildings dotted around the plantation house, but Leah only had eyes for the house itself. Even in her wildest dreams she had not imagined so much beauty. On the voyage she had been told that the first settlers had been hard put to find any land free from trees. That and the flat sandy scrub had almost driven them to distraction, despite the glorious beaches that surrounded the island. It had worried her, and for a little while she was afraid William had been lying to her father and actually lived in nothing more than a shack.

But here was the proof staring her in the face, for the plantation house, made from imported stone, was a sight to behold. It seemed to be rooted in the earth along with the brilliant flowers of the bougainvillaea vine that wandered the trellis of the wide verandas. Huge shuttered windows, open in the heat of the day, would bring safety in storms, and she allowed a little smile to tilt her lips. 'It's quite wonderful,' she exclaimed excitedly.

William beamed widely. 'Even more so now it has a beautiful mistress to tend it.'

Leah was touched by his words, and when she and William sat on cane furniture on the veranda a little later, when she had changed out of her travel dirt, she found out just how charming he could be. The first thing he did was to remove his wig, declaring that it was far too hot to wear it overlong, which she found quite endearing. They shared a light repast, as he explained how the very first English planters had to clear the dense forests on the islands before planting any crops. Then he asked her about her voyage.

'It was something to be endured,' she replied with a laugh.

'You have lost weight,' he remarked.

'I was unfortunate in suffering seasickness,' she explained, and he clicked his tongue sympathetically.

'We shall have to see about putting the roses back in your cheeks and the flesh back on your bones. I hope you are able to sleep in this heat.'

She blushed. 'After being aboard the *Christina* I believe I could sleep almost anywhere that did not roll and tip like a cork on the ocean.'

His eyes scanned her avidly, and then he smiled. 'I don't believe you need worry about that. I think I can safely promise you that I will not tip or roll you out of my bed, Leah.'

She blushed deeply now, recalling his words, as she and Jane sat in her bedchamber some time later. He certainly seemed to have changed for the better. Jane helped her out of her gown and a servant brought water for washing. The man's skin was almost a grey colour, and he had a glassy stare that unnerved her. His movements were slow and lethargic, he reminded her of a sleepwalker as he set a jug of water near a basin that stood beneath a window. A woman followed him into the chamber, dismissing him with a wave of her hand.

'I am Dominique, the housekeeper.'

Where Jane and Leah had looked askance at the strange manner and appearance of the male servant, so they now looked at the woman in amazement, for she was quite beautiful. Almost as tall as a man, with generous curves, her skin was like black satin. Her hair was caught up in a bright bandana that accentuated her wonderful cheekbones.

'Water is scarce in these parts,' she said a little stiffly. 'We need to take care of every drop.'

Leah watched her turn down the bed and her fingers trembled. This was where she would share her body with the man she had married by proxy – the man she had hated when he stayed at her father's house. She wondered if he would take her forcefully, or be gentle with her. Would she care for her feminine needs, or would he merely fill her with his meat until he was satisfied and roll away from her?

Dominique finished her task and her dark eyes surveyed Leah insolently. She was appalled at the dislike in them. 'Thank you, Dominique,' she said softly, wanting to make friends with the lovely creature. 'You have a very pretty name.'

'My father was French,' the girl replied coldly. 'My mother was raped by him, but he wasn't all bad, he threw a few coins at her as she lay in the fields bleeding into the earth.' She was pleased with the shocked expressions she left behind as she tossed her head and walked from the chamber.

Far too tired to dwell on Dominique's attitude, Leah dismissed her and Jane helped her sponge her hot body down before she retired.

'How I would love to slap that young woman's face!' Jane hissed. 'She has the manners of an animal. I've never known anyone so rude.'

'We are strangers, Jane. Perhaps she will come round in time.'

Jane grunted and began to brush Leah's waist-length hair, which glistened in the candlelight. 'What is that strange sound? Though not unpleasant, 'tis strange when one is not used to it.'

Leah smiled. 'They are bush frogs. William said they strike up after dusk each day.'

Jane sighed with relief. 'Do you have everything you need?'

Leah looked around as though searching for escape. 'Oh, Jane, I am dreading this night. If only it was Gideon.'

Jane patted her tenderly and left her to her fate, for there was little else she could do.

Leah was trying to allay her nerves when her door was opened. She looked up expecting to see William, but Dominique appeared, closing the portal behind her.

Leah glanced at her expectantly, wondering if she wanted something, but the woman's expression told her more than words ever could, and she reeled back from the poison in her face, feeling quite weak with the impact.

Dominique, still beautiful in her anger, stood over her as she pressed herself into the mattress. 'Do not think the master belongs to you,' she spat. 'You are here to breed from, that is all.'

With a snarl of hatred she turned and left, leaving Leah reeling. What did she mean? Why was she so jealous of her? She didn't have to cast far for her answer; it was obvious that the woman had been sleeping with William. She wasn't sure how she felt about that, but she did know that she had unsettled the creature; Dominique was afraid she would usurp her position in William's affections and in his bed.

She decided to put the matter from her. William had been guilty of nothing more than loneliness, and in his wifeless state had bedded the nearest woman, his beautiful servant.

She was sitting up in bed, on top of the spread, when he came to her, her hair a tumbling cascade of gold. He sat beside her and kissed her gently. 'You are mine, Leah,' he breathed, and there was a pride in the way he said the words that touched her heart.

'Yes, William,' she whispered, deciding to try to forget Gideon and to give their marriage and William the chance they deserved.

He was dressed in an expensive blue robe which he shrugged off his shoulders to expose his naked form. He was a well made man, and though he did not have the same breadth of shoulder as Gideon, did not have as much sinew in his arms, she hoped she would learn to love him.

The bed gave as he joined her, pulling at a pretty curl, kissing her face, her neck, with soft kisses that eased her nerves a little. Outside the air was barely stirring and the sounds of the tropics reached her, as strange and alien to her as the man whose arms she was in.

When he brought her closer she lent to him without demur. She slid her fingers into the thick blonde thatch at the base of his neck and heard him give a groan low in his throat. His fingers combed through her hair as his lips shifted to her mouth and he plundered inside, barely giving her time to breathe.

'Fie, wife,' he exclaimed in remonstration, plucking

disgustedly at her night-rail. 'What is this? I am your husband now. You cannot threaten me with knives and throw candlesticks at my poor body any longer.' He referred to the time he had come to her bedchamber at her father's house. 'And I need to see what I have given my name to.'

Leah's breath caught in her throat, and he saw the change in her and laughed. 'Just a joke, sweating. Now, let us away with this gown so we may lay skin to skin like normal folk.'

The nightshift was drawn off her in seconds and William gasped when he was given full benefit of her satiny skin. 'An English rose,' he said as his hands caressed her shoulders. 'How long I have waited for you.' His hunger was that of a ravenous animal and he took her breasts, moulding them roughly to his hands, scratching with his nails and pulling the nipples so hard she bit down on her lip.

His mouth rasped over hers, any sign of the gentleman he had seemed to be earlier forgotten in his rush to have her. His fingers scratched down over her belly, kneaded the flat plain. 'You need to gain some flesh,' he said accusingly. 'I like a woman I can get hold of.' He began exploring her sex, prising and pulling, scratching her labia until she begged him to be gentler.

'Quiet!' he spat. 'A wife must be subservient to her husband at all times.'

'Please, William,' she began in earnest, for this was not the way to win her heart, 'you are hurting me.'

'Oh yes,' he said gruffly, 'and taking your virginity will hurt much more. But you must bear it.' With that he abruptly stabbed his cock into her and routed about before setting a comfortable rhythm for himself. His cock was large and Leah was not ready. He had not bothered to make her wet with desire and she screwed her eyes up with pain as he rode her hard. When he came he rolled off her and delved between her thighs.

'Where is the sign of your virginity?' he snapped without subtlety. 'I was led to believe I was wed to a gentile lady, not a whore!'

Leah paled and began to fashion the words of an excuse as he produced a leather belt from a drawer. With a sly smile he took both ends, and folding it over, snapped it together.

'You must admit that this is a fine bit of leather,' he averred, as the folded leather was snapped time and time again. I dare say you've never seen finer, have you, whore?'

Leah was determined to hide her fear from him. He was a bully, and bullies flourished on other people's terror.

'All fine airs and graces,' he snarled, 'but beneath it all you're no better than the trulls that frequent the taverns.' He laughed mirthlessly. 'How well you played the part of a tight-arsed bitch, how cleverly you pretended to be a lady when in reality you come to your wedding bed as soiled goods.' Slipping into his robe he strode to the door. 'I cannot bear the sight of you, but the fortune you bring will certainly make up for that.'

Leah's lips were tender from his ardour, but she licked them nervously. 'Fortune?'

William's face twisted into a nasty mask as he viewed her through narrowed eyes. 'You didn't think I wanted you and you alone, did you? You are a tasty morsel, it's true, but it was your inheritance I craved.' He sneered at the shock on her face. 'Your father was a do-gooder, a naïve fool who believed every lie I told him. But now you are my chattel all you own belongs to me.' He glanced out of the window. 'I have been well enough here, but 'twill be nice to visit the green meadows of England and to know that I can give my name to a part of that land.'

The sound of him besmirching her dear father's name stirred Leah into action, and leaping from the bed she slapped his face so hard his head snapped back.

Shocked by her retaliation he was momentarily stilled. But then the enormity of her digression hit home and his face twisted into rage. 'So, wife,' he snarled, 'you have more than asked for your punishment. I trust you will enjoy the kiss of leather on your arse.'

He rang for a servant and Leah covered her nakedness

with a sheet, wondering what he was about. She wasn't kept waiting long before the door knocked and Dominique entered the room.

William nodded towards the bed. 'You are just in time to watch my dear wife being punished. You see, Dominique, she did not come to me in a virgin state. The bitch is sullied.'

Dominique smirked. 'It does not surprise me. She looks the sort to open her legs readily.'

'How dare you?' Leah railed.

Dominique began to disrobe and Leah watched open-mouthed as the woman stripped down to her stays. 'Give me the belt, William,' she said softly. 'I would like to punish her for you.' She took the belt from him, a beautiful dominatrix who stood all of six feet tall in her bare feet. Her breasts were large and rounded, the nipples a dusky delight as they peeked above the top of her undergarment. Her hips flared generously from a narrow waist and her legs were perfect.

William was eyeing Dominique lustfully, and with a quick intake of breath he began to fondle her breasts. 'Now this is what I call a woman,' he drawled, his hands straying to the dark thighs, which he smoothed lovingly. 'Can you imagine how wonderful it is to climb these shapely stalks?' he goaded, with a tremor of excitement in his voice. 'To reach the treasure at her centre?'

He delved into the black nest at the junction of her thighs and Dominique wriggled against him. 'Oh love, that feels wonderful. But I need to teach your simpering wife a lesson first.'

Leah watched them speechlessly. The brazen hussy looked even more beautiful with a smile on her face. 'Touch me and I shall make you sorry,' she vowed.

With a sneer William pressed the bell once more and two Negroes appeared. He ordered them to take Leah outside.

Despite her struggles they rolled her in a sheet and transported her down the stairs and to the back of the house.

She was unable to see anything, muffled as she was in linen. But when they rolled her out on the rough ground in front of the barn she gasped at the hot air gratefully.

Flares lit a massive cartwheel that was secured to the outer wall of the barn. Leah was manhandled to this contraption and her wrists and ankles secured to the rungs. 'Let me down!' she hissed at Dominique, who had slipped a red robe loosely over her stays.

The dark woman laughed. 'It is time to brand you as a whore.'

As William stood beside her, a broad grin on his face, so Dominique raised the belt and snapped it across Leah's buttocks. 'That's for William!' she snarled. 'And that's for me!' she added, laying into her again.

Leah screamed as the leather bit into her bottom, once, twice, and then a third time. 'Stop,' she cried. 'Please stop!'

But Dominique was in her element, and William's gaze was straying from one to the other in swift succession – to Dominique, whose unbelted robe billowed out around her showing off the perfection beneath, and to Leah, whose creamy curves were turning scarlet thanks to the hands of his mistress. 'Beautiful,' he sighed. 'Light and dark, the sun and the moon.'

The Negroes watched without a flicker of expression on their faces, lest they face the same fate as Leah. But their dark eyes were alive with appreciation and from time to time they wiped sweat from their foreheads.

'Whoever stole your virginity needs to be punished also,' said Dominique. 'But as we only have you here, madam, you shall take the blows for him.'

She rained blow after blow on the girl tied to the wheel, until the perfect cream of her flesh, from her shoulders to her ankles, was crisscrossed with livid marks. But Dominique was good at her trade, and though the weals were painful she had not broken the skin.

Leah was almost unconscious from the cruel treatment, and when Dominique tossed the leather belt aside William

180

called out to the Negroes. 'Cut her down and do what you will with her.'

Leah was quite unaware of what was happening until she felt eager hands crawling over her body, and eager cocks, dripping with pre-come, ploughing into every hole of her person. She vented her anger into the earth, and swore that William and Dominique would pay well for this night's work.

Chapter Twelve

The *Black Spade* tavern in Bridgetown was occupied by a mixture of seafarers and the kind of women who knew it boded well to prowl such a place in order to sell their charms. Gideon Tempest lounged languorously in one corner, his pose deceptive. For anyone who knew him would tell of how deadly the captain could be when trouble came a-calling. Years of seafaring had honed him well, and since losing the merchant ship the *Pride* to a bloodthirsty Spaniard, who murdered his crew and blew his ship to bits, he had been even more daunting.

Gideon and his first mate, Muffy, would have gone the same way had they not been saved by Francis L'Olonnois, a privateer from Tortuga, and one of the Brethren of the Coast. Gideon joined forces with these men who pillaged the shipping of Spain, vowing to find the *Santa Maria* and the devil who destroyed his ship and slaughtered his crew.

A green-eyed blonde wench, who sat with a fair-haired girl a few tables away, constantly returned her gaze to the dark hairs curling riotously on his bronzed chest beneath his jerkin, to the handsome smile that flashed above the deeply cleft chin. The bright baldric that slashed across his chest held a sword that was never far from his side, two pistols were stuffed into a belt at his waist, and though she did not know it the highly polished boots that adorned his feet concealed a knife.

He was talking to a planter, and something the man said caused his smile to change to a scowl. A few men who were making their way in his direction steered away.

Lillian's green eyes flashed in amusement. She possessed far more courage in her little finger than any of those lacklustre pigs did in their whole bodies. And she certainly didn't feel threatened by the scowl on the handsome blade's face. On the contrary, he intrigued her.

Dragging down her bodice in order to display her charms to their best advantage, she sashayed up to him, her friend at her side. 'Do yer fancy buying a lady a drink?'

Gideon glanced at the pretty wench in red with interest, and his heart missed a beat. On first glance she could be mistaken for Leah, but with grim determination he cast those thoughts aside, for they could lead nowhere. By now Leah Brown would be married to another and he was left to deal with the knowledge in the best way he knew. So hiding his thoughts behind a smile he said, 'I don't see why not.' She was a beauty, and her friend wasn't to be sniffed at either.

He bought them both a drink before they retired to one of the rooms on an upper floor, where there was a comfortable bed just right for what they had in mind. Thinking of Leah had brought the ache back to his loins as it always did, but the young women would assuage his urges.

The girls were far from shy and immediately jumped on the bed, opening their legs invitingly. Lillian was impatient to get her hands on the stranger; he was the best looking man who'd been in the *Spade* in a long time. As for Daisy, she followed where her indomitable friend led.

'See, cap'n,' Lillian boasted, nodding to her nether region, 'we be clean an' free of pox, so you have nothing to fear.'

'I am glad to hear it.' He grinned at her honesty and stripped off his clothes before joining them on the bed, playing with the luscious flesh on display. Daisy's breasts were large with tiny pale nipples, fair flowers that tempted. Lillian bared breasts with deep-red aureoles, and Gideon

182

took it in turns to tongue and caress each one.

'Ah, but yer've a gentle mouth,' Lillian cooed, brushing her fingers over the furred chest, delighting in the corded strength beneath. 'I like that in a man. Many are too rough an' hurt us.' She was the product of a bondsman and his woman, and Daisy had been indentured to one of the plantations, but her time was up. They had decided to get together; it was safer that way and most men delighted in their diverse charms.

'Wastrels,' Gideon declared sympathetically, as she fingered the length of his manhood.

'Le's make sure we don't put this to waste,' she purred, holding the rampant cock lovingly.

As she stroked him Gideon played with Daisy's pussy. Lillian swept her hair out of the way and wrapped her lips around the straining shaft, sucking it lustily. Daisy kissed him, nibbling his lips with white teeth. Her breasts swayed above him, and Gideon sucked each one in turn, taken up with the fire Lillian was creating in his belly.

Lillian swapped her mouth for her cunny and rode him expertly, twisting her hips and grinding down on him till he gasped with pleasure. But before he reached his congress she left him, and Daisy slid down on the powerful shaft her friend had already made slippery. Then Lillian reared over him, her dark sex still slick from need, giving Gideon the chance to eat the tasty morsel. He sighed contentedly; with Daisy on his shaft and his tongue fucking Lillian his needs were well tended.

Lillian smiled. He was a rare find. She was tired of servicing the dregs of humanity that mainly landed up in the tavern, sick of pretending to enjoy the attentions of old men with gnarled fingers, or grouchy ones who had escaped nagging wives. Sometimes there were spotty youths fresh off a ship and eager to lose their virginity between her shapely thighs. She liked their innocent adoration, but Gideon pleasured her like no other, lapping her bud until she reached her climax, her love juices running freely over his

183

face. He licked the tangy secretions from her and she purred like a cat. Most men had no idea where her sensitive spot was, but the captain was an expert!

When Gideon shot his seed into Daisy she did him the service of licking him clean, before she smiled prettily and rolled away. He ordered more drinks, and as they lay sipping the beer he said, 'I have found there is no one like a tavern maid when a man needs information.'

The girls beamed and Lillian was the one to reply. 'We ain't brainy like, but we'll help if 'tis possible.'

'Do you know of a William Penrose? He has a plantation known as *Wildwinds*.'

The green eyes clouded. 'Aye, I knows him, he's a pig. He cheated a good man out of his plantation and the poor soul landed up living with his own bondservant.'

Daisy nodded her agreement and shrugged her shoulders sadly. 'We ain't seen nothing of him lately. He used to come in the *Spade* and we'd keep him company. Such a sad man.' She sighed. 'I 'spect as how he's drunk himself to death on cheap rum.'

Gideon listened sombrely. 'And Penrose?'

'Comes here when he's tired of fucking his slaves. But he ain't a nice man. Why d'yer wish to know about him?' she asked curiously.

Gideon took a deep draught of his ale before replying, a look of fury masking the handsome countenance. 'Just over a year ago I set off for Barbados with provisions to sell to the planters on the island. There is so much land taken up for sugar cane there is little spare to grow food, and I have always found my presence welcome. Unfortunately, on the way I was taken with a fever and forced to take to my cabin. My first mate, Muffy, took charge.

'Penrose was one of the planters to purchase some of the cargo, but when it came to payment he made a feeble excuse about being temporarily low on funds. He was told no money no cargo, so he reluctantly paid up.'

Lillian and Daisy listened intently. 'And then?' they asked

in unison.

He gave a sardonic laugh. 'Muffy celebrated the success of the venture in a tavern. When he came out a little worse for wear Penrose's henchman was waiting for him in the shadows. He clubbed him senseless and made off with the money. You see, what he didn't know was that Muffy glimpsed his face before he almost caved in his skull.'

'So yer've a debt to settle with the scum.'

'Aye. I later lost my ship and had other pressing business to attend to. But now I've made time to settle up with Mr William Penrose.'

Lillian grinned wickedly, feeling the steel that lay under the well-furred chest. 'If he's any sense he'll be pissing hisself.' She guided his hand between her thighs. 'How about seconds, cap'n?'

Chapter Thirteen

Leah reclined on the day-bed near the window. She lay awake listening to the song of the bush frogs, which were no bigger than a thumbnail and yet together they were quite an orchestra. As was usual she had tossed restlessly, wondering if William would come to her bed. Sometimes he did not disturb her for weeks, and then there would be a spate of cruel sex, where inevitably she would be left with bruises and bites all over her person. He often roped his mistress into punishing her for some imagined misdemeanour, and Dominique went round with a supercilious smile on her face, questioning her every month on whether she'd had her flux or not.

'You will give William many sons,' she taunted. 'But I have his love.'

Leah would ignore these jibes; she certainly didn't crave the love of William Penrose. There was only one love for her, and thanks to destiny he was now lost to her forever.

She wondered what her father would think if he knew the man he betrothed her to was fast eating his way through her fortune. He was a drinker, a gambler and a spendthrift. He had even sold the estate in Essex in order to fill his coffers. Apart from her life, she had nothing left for him to take.

She heard a footfall outside her door and her heart accelerated. She knew that sound; it was her husband. He would walk to the door and stand outside for a few seconds, knowing she was cringing in fear lest he entered.

But this time there was the sound of another joining him, and of whispering. Leah prayed they would pass by, but the handle turned, the door opened and William and Dominique were clearly illuminated in the flickering candlelight.

William smiled at her. 'Dominique has brought you some hot chocolate.' As the woman handed it to her he watched Leah closely as she sipped the sweet brew. 'It would seem our island agrees with you, wife. Your looks are bonnier than ever. But then our climate is most benevolent in comparison to a lot of the other islands. Even hurricane season occurred with little trouble, the worst of the weather passing us by to the north.'

'I find the island acceptable,' she said, her tone clipped with sarcasm. ''Tis the company I cannot agree with.'

William laughed her comment away. 'As you can see, Dominique has decided to give us the pleasure of her company this evening. I sometimes find you a little tepid for my taste and need something to liven things up.'

Leah ignored the barb, and trying to appear unconcerned drained the cup and laid it aside. 'I despise you and your mistress. Pray do me the honour of relieving me of your odious company.'

Dominique, in a robe of crimson that looked fine against her dark skin, was for once without her bandana. Her dark luxuriant hair curled in great profusion beyond her shoulders. Her lips were rouged and as she flicked her robe aside Leah was able to see that her dusky nipples had been given the same treatment, so they now pouted a pretty red.

The woman moved towards the day-bed and Leah shrank back into the cushions as she caressed the blonde tresses that lay against the headrest. 'You are indeed beautiful,' she soothed. 'I will take great pleasure in you this night.'

Leah shook her head in disbelief. 'No, don't touch me!'

Dominique laughed, and it was then Leah saw the knife she was holding. 'You protest too much. I know by the sensuality in your eyes when you look at me that you want me too.'

Leah flicked her hair back from her face. 'Don't be ridiculous! There is nothing in this house that I find in the least appealing.' The knife arced over her face and she bit her lip in terror. 'P-people know I'm here. There will be a hue and cry if you kill me.'

The woman's laugh was even more amused. 'You must not be afraid, Leah. That is not my intention.' With one smooth movement Dominique sliced through the bodice of her night-rail, ripping the rest of the material from her body. 'You see,' she said without a beat, casting her robe aside, lying down beside her, 'I merely wish to see all of you.'

William licked his lips, his cock standing to attention in his breeches, now that the two women in his life reclined on the bed as naked as the day they were born.

Leah's head began to swim and she rubbed her eyes. 'What's wrong with me? What have you done?'

'Do not worry,' Dominique soothed. 'I slipped a love potion into your drink. It will relax you; help you enjoy yourself even more.'

Leah tried to move away from the other female, but Dominique had perfumed her skin, and though Leah strained away from her she suddenly longed to caress the firm globes with the rouge tips that jutted against her own breasts, almost with a life of their own. 'You're both sick,' she snapped, angry at the feelings that rushed through her like molten fire.

'And you desire me,' Dominique said triumphantly, watching Leah's nipples swell. 'And I know that your cunny

187

is at this very moment running with dew at the thought of lying with me.'

As she spoke Dominique took Leah's fingers and forced her to fondle her breasts. They were warm and firm beneath her touch, and without even realising it she was soon caressing them freely, quite taken with the way the aureoles were darkly puckered, so different to her own.

A soft breeze wafted through the window, swept over Leah's creamy skin before feathering over Dominique's curves. The dark woman sighed with pleasure. 'Even the breeze is entering into our desires.'

Leah wanted to run to the door and flee from the depravity in the room, but as Dominique's hot flesh pressed close she had little choice but to listen to the other voice inside her, the voice that told her she wanted the woman, longed to touch and pleasure her, to do things with her that were forbidden.

Dominique smiled slyly. 'Touch me, Leah,' she urged. 'Feel how my heart beats with an urgent need to possess you.'

Leah's nervous hands touched the silky skin over her heart and felt the strong pulse that beat beneath. She was driven to stroke her divine breasts until the other woman gasped and began to fondle her too. Dominique reached for her chin, and lifting her face to her own, brought her mouth down in a lingering kiss that was as gentle as it was passionate.

Leah was drowning in desire, and when the kiss was over she took one rouge nipple between her lips and sucked, rolling the other nipple between finger and thumb, and Dominique's gasp of delight filled her with a feeling of such power she was almost delirious.

William undid his codpiece, and taking out his cock began to work it with fingers that shook with lust. 'That's it, girls,' he crowed. 'Suck and fuck yourselves silly and then I'll have you both.'

Leah was turned on all the more, seeing him masturbating as he watched them making love, and she groaned and

188

kissed her way to Dominique's naval. She rimmed it with her tongue before dipping inside, adoring the taste of the exotic unguents the girl had rubbed in her skin.

Dominique found the swollen nub that was straining out of its hood, begging for attention, and stroked it tenderly. Leah reciprocated and they lay back on the day-bed, mouths on nipples, fingers on clits, bringing each other female pleasure.

Dominique's channel was soon flooded with her juices and Leah smiled; it was a wonderful feeling to know just how much the other woman was enjoying her ministrations. But the smile soon left her face as a glorious fire seeped through her veins, flamed through her nerve ends, shook every last fibre of her being. She flung her head back and screamed as her climax ripped through her, leaving her sapped of strength and completely sated.

Dominique took her finger from Leah's nubbin and began to stroke herself, and with one hand squeezing her breast and the other frigging her clit she soon brought about her own crisis.

As Leah lay back on the bed, her skin feathered by the soft island breeze, so Dominique strapped a belt around her waist, watching as William tried to toss himself off. 'Don't overdo it, my love,' she purred. 'I want to feel you inside me soon.'

William insinuated a finger in her juices before sucking it with gusto. 'My sword still has plenty of play in it, never fear.'

Dominique smiled. She knew better than most that the steel of his cock usually outlasted every other man's, and she kissed the tip of it lovingly. She finished strapping herself into the sex toy, and with another surge of excitement saw how wide Leah's thighs were still spread, her nether lips rosy, seeping with her creamy juices.

'That is a sight no one could resist,' she whispered, as Leah's eyes blinked open and she viewed her with horror.

'What... what is that?' she demanded.

Dominique straddled her, a belt around her waist that held a huge phallus. The second phallus attached to the belt faced the other way, and was buried deep inside Dominique's vagina. Dominique smiled slyly and coated her fingers in Leah's juices, then smoothed them along the shaft of the phallus. 'I think that is self-evident,' she purred. 'As I promised, I'm going to fuck you until your little cunny is raw,' she boasted.

Leah shook her head, but her eyes were on the wicked object jutting from Dominique's belly, already slick with her juices. But then a stab of raw excitement filled her and she opened her thighs wider as Dominique bore down on her, plunging the false penis into her centre.

A howl of delight broke from Leah's throat as the dark girl rode her, giving them both pleasure as the twin phalluses did their work. William watched them with satisfaction, and then took some of Dominique's love dew from her gyrating cunny and rubbed some on his penis, and the rest inside her anus. Then with burgeoning desire he knelt behind the woman, and holding her still for a few moments, fed his meat slowly into her arse.

Soon they were fucking in unison, and if anyone heard the cries of lust and debauchery that issued from the windows of the plantation house that night, they only spoke about it in whispers, for to be caught talking about the goings on up at the house only brought twenty lashes of the whip.

It was a glorious balmy day, and Leah felt positive for the first time in a long while. William was every bit as cruel and demanding as ever, and though her body often bore the bruising from these liaisons, she had found a way to keep her mind completely separate from the wickedness that surrounded her. It was an art she learned in the Darlington's cellar; the art of self-preservation. Gideon Tempest was the one her brain sought at these times, and thoughts of the handsome sea captain kept her sane.

She and Jane spent much of their spare time exploring the

island. William did not object to them using the carriage, but the huge Negro who accompanied them was always vigilant. On the east coast waves roared and crashed over rocks, reminding Leah of how wild and dangerous it was living at *Wildwinds*. In contrast, the coast of the west and south of the island was calm and quite beautiful, as the ever changing sea seemed to throw up different shades as the day progressed. Barbados was not completely flat as she had expected, and she found that the view from the island's highest point, Mount Hillaby, was breathtaking.

It was on her return from such a sojourn that William cornered her and suggested she ride out with him. 'I have something to show you,' he said equably.

Jane, calmed by his unusually friendly tone, was quite happy to retreat to her quarters, and William sat in her place. As the carriage rolled through the cane fields, the harness jingling, the snorting of the horses filling her with a false calm, Leah recalled her conversation with William about the slaves.

'Can you not make them free?' she had asked innocently.

'And how shall I run the plantation without them?' he snapped snidely. 'The indentured servants are less than useless in the heat of the tropics. And if I freed the blacks they would not bother working so well. As it is the overseer has to watch them like a hawk and whip their lazy backsides when they don't do enough.'

He was determined not to listen to her pleadings, so she contented herself by trying to ease the life of the children and the pregnant and nursing mothers as best she could.

William was putting himself out to be pleasant to her on their ride, pointing out the tall green cane with pride. 'This is what our children would have inherited,' he intoned with narrowed eyes. 'This and the emerald fields of the English estate, before I was forced to sell it.'

She viewed him with distaste. 'Forced, William?'

He nodded. 'Had I been happy, had a wife who gave me children, I would not have resorted to gambling. As it is there has been no issue. You have proven to be barren and I shall have to make other arrangements.'

Leah was taken aback by his words. 'I don't understand, William. It has not been two years yet. These things take time.'

He gave instructions for the driver to slow to a halt at a corner of one of the cane fields. 'Time is precious,' he pointed out coldly, 'and I've given you the benefit of the doubt long enough. Elias Wilson has brought his very pretty sister over from England and I am quite taken with her. She has good childbearing hips and will make a pleasant wife.'

Leah looked from the towering green cane to William's stern face. 'But I am your wife,' she pointed out, as a small pain of fear niggled in her gut.

'Not for much longer, my dear.'

He stepped from the carriage and helped her down, her green eyes clouded with doubt. He paused beside what appeared to be a shallow grave, newly dug.

'Look well, Leah,' he said blithely. 'For this is your grave.'

She rounded on him with fearful eyes. 'What are you saying?'

''Tis not too hard to grasp, surely. You have disappointed me, and your constant carping has given me grief. You have often asked me about the drums you sometimes hear at night, and I'm now willing to reveal that they belong to an ancient religion the slaves brought with them. It has much magic that even I do not understand, but I do know that they have certain poisons that can render anyone chosen to become one of the living dead.'

Leah went cold despite the balmy weather. She glanced from the shallow grave to William's sombre countenance. 'You have decided this?' she said shakily. He nodded and the blood in her veins seemed to turn to ice. 'And how do you imagine you will hide the signs of my demise?' she returned as bravely as she was able. 'For as I have said before, our neighbours will soon wonder what has happened to me.'

William was quite unfazed. 'Ah, my dear Leah, that's no worry. You see, I shall make the excuse that you have fallen ill to a fever and died. A not unnatural occurrence in theses parts.' A feral smile passed over his mouth. 'In truth you will attend one of our ceremonies and the priest will put you into a zombie-like state. You will be buried, and after my wedding you will be dug up and brought into the house to serve my wife.'

Leah laughed nervously. 'You are talking foolishly. Such a thing is impossible. Anyway, I would be recognised.'

He looked at her gravely. 'I once thought as you do, but I soon learnt my mistake. Think of the man who serves in the house now, the man who goes around with grey skin and sunken, staring eyes.'

Leah swallowed. 'You are talking about Jacob, are you not?'

'You know him as such. But his real name is Silas Webster and he is the man I stole the plantation from. I had him turned into a zombie because it pleased me to do so. Now I can watch the wretch fumbling his way around my house and know that he can cause me no torment.' He paused and his eyes glinted evilly. 'As I shall soon be able to do with you.'

Leah fainted clean away, her body lying unconscious beside the piece of earth which, if William Penrose had his way, would soon be her grave.

The drums beat an insistent tattoo into the night, calling the faithful to meet in the sacred place that lay within the circle of the palm trees in the heart of the plantation. The clearing pulsed with life, each person very much aware that the air was redolent with promise.

On brightly coloured dishes on the altar gleamed the special mixtures of poisons and tinctures that would help the magic the hungan performed that night. A fire danced in the midst of the gathering, sparks flying away to appease the gods. This time roosters were sacrificed, their blood caught in the vessels laid around the altar.

The cultists spread the blood over their torsos, dancing wildly to the ever present beat of the drums, their semi-naked bodies glistening blackly against the flames of the fire and the torches that surrounded the clearing.

Dominique walked through this scene, her hair wrapped in a crimson bandana, her stance as regal as any royal, her black skin lustrous with unguents, the python coiled around her body as snugly as another woman would wear clothes. She was glowing with happiness; the young woman who had been a thorn in her side for almost two years now was to be banished from them forever. Even when she was roused from her deathly sleep she would be no threat, for no one would recognise the grey face and staring eyes as the vibrant, beautiful Leah who had been William's bride.

Ever since the girl set foot on the island Dominique feared William would fall in love with the green-eyed enchantress – thankfully that fear was gone.

The hungan chanted over the altar, stirring the poisons and incanting sacred words that would help them work. Dominique danced around him, the python curling threateningly in her arms, as though ready at any time to sink its fangs into the nearest flesh.

William watched from the outskirts of the clearing, his excitement almost palpable. Dominique was adorable and he could hardly bear the wait before their flesh met and they became one. But first he was to have the virgin. He had to admit it was the highlight of the ceremony, as he took what was due him by unburdening her of her virginity.

The girl was marched in, and he had to admit she was one of the most beautiful thus far. She appeared far less nervous than any of the others had, and William was looking forward to piercing her maidenhead, to hear her scream as he showed her who was master. He was the one who trembled with the drama of the moment, and he watched the frenzied bodies of the faithful as they threw themselves around, twisting and turning to the drumbeat that pierced the ears, sent fevers down the spine.

Suddenly the drums stopped and the black bodies ceased their movements, turning towards the altar. He pulled his white hood over his head and strode into the clearing where the girl stood before the alter awaiting him. Her mouth was open slightly, her eyes bright with promise. William offered her the chalice of warm blood and she drank deeply, barely spilling a drop.

His eyes took their fill of her. She was small-boned, almost boyish in the way she was formed. William didn't mind, he was partial to the odd change of sex occasionally, it never hurt to experiment. Besides, her small breasts were very pleasingly formed, the nipples large considering their size. The fuzz at the apex of her thighs was glistening with unguents, and William knew by experience that she would smell and taste of exotic spices.

His cock surged and he bore her with him to the ground, biting her lips so that she bled. He could taste the blood of cockerel and human and it set up a primal urge deep in his gut that made him lust for more blood. He clawed and bit her breasts, enjoying the way she cried out, loving the way he rid her of her arrogance. Soon she was gabbling hysterically, and knowing he definitely had the upper hand he entered her fiercely, without pity or care, and swiftly took her virginity. She was a good fuck despite her innocence and William decided she could adorn his bed at any time.

He sometimes wondered about these girls. Considering they were virgins some of them had a knowing look in the eyes that belied that sacred state. William often wondered if they spent time with young black bucks, their fists full of cock while the man diddled their nubbins. It would be a way to retain their purity while harmlessly receiving and giving pleasure.

With this one it was as though she had been ridden before, her every move geared to sensuality, and he supposed some were born with a secret knowledge. Whatever the reason he would definitely take her again. He smiled slyly. As master of the plantation it was his right to take any woman he chose. How his father would disapprove of his lifestyle. If the old man were here now he would force him to watch every debased act he had ever practiced before tying him to the wheel and laying the lash across his back.

The girl was rolling her eyes in delight at the master's staying power, murmuring something about his mighty weapon. Some of the slaves only spoke broken English; many spoke nothing but their own tongue. But William had managed to pick up enough to know what she was saying, and his ego expanded even further.

When he was spent he left her and watched as Slade brought Leah from out of the shadows. For a brief moment he felt sorry things had turned out so. She was a beautiful fiery wench, but she was completely untameable. It was her own fault; she had brought it all on herself.

Though her eyes were glassy from the drugs that had been administered, she still portrayed the spunk he had never been able to beat out of her and his heart hardened. Let her become one of the walking dead, let her suffer the woes he had suffered bringing her here, in trying and failing to break her spirit.

A huge Negro laid her on the ground before the altar, his cock enormous. Within seconds he had taken her and she flailed and squealed beneath him. Even in the throes of her soporific condition she felt his huge prick and railed against it. The Negro flipped her onto her front, and greasing her bottom well, drove into her anus, his teeth gleaming white in his handsome buck's face. Leah screamed as he stretched her, and William felt slightly jealous.

The man was named Saul; he would have him brought to his bed. It would be good to have his anus rimmed with that greedy tongue, to have him stretch him, drive him to delirium. Somehow it would feel right, almost holy after he had taken Leah.

When Saul was finally done with her she was laid aside,

196

to await the final rites of the ceremony.

As before, the serpent taken from her into other safe hands, Dominique took her place. She opened her thighs to William with a broad smile and he took her with expertise. He never had to wait long for his shaft to come alive again, and this time he was as fresh as ever. He had tasted blood, no less than he had before, but somehow this time he craved for much more.

Sensing a change in him Dominique's eyes opened wide, questioning. He felt his thirst for blood surge deep within his belly and he bit her throat, sucking until his thirst was partially quenched. Dominique scratched at his back, her long claws digging deep, a warning he ignored. He burrowed his cock deep inside her, clawing and biting her in turn.

She reciprocated, biting and clawing back, and soon they were rolling on the ground, each thrust of their hips accompanied by stabbing nails and sharp teeth. Their bodies bled into the earth, which stuck to them, making him almost as brown as the woman. But it was far too late for caution, they were both caught up in the frenzy of the moment and they tore at each other, their lust seemingly unquenchable. The drums resumed, beating in time with the lunging of the man into the woman's body, and the onlookers were silent as the fight for domination continued relentlessly.

When William was finally through he lay on the dry earth, sweat and blood-stained, panting like an animal. Dominique unclasped herself from him, and with her usual grace was helped away by two women who cleaned her up. Her eyes lingered hungrily on William, their rough mating had inspired her as always and she would yearn for him until he was ready for her again.

The drumbeat changed, more insistent, and Leah was dragged back to the altar by two Negroes, who held the sagging girl up by her arms. William usually retired at this point of the ceremony, but decided to stay, had asked to be able to administer the first cup of poison to her.

As her weak body drooped between the two men he picked up the chalice of poison and put it to her lips. 'Drink, my dear wife. Rid me of your presence. Allow the magic to work its wonders on you.'

She blinked her eyes open, looked vacantly down at the chalice, and opened her mouth in order to drink.

But then a shot rang out of the cane field, making the chalice ricochet from his grip. A second shot ripped through William and he dropped to the ground, the life fast ebbing from him.

Dominique rushed to him immediately, screaming and sobbing hysterically, trying to breathe life into her inert love. As men ran from the cane field into the clearing the Negroes fled, and within seconds there was no one left but the dead body of William Penrose and the two women, his wife and mistress. Now even the persistent sound of the drums had ceased.

Gideon Tempest held the almost lifeless body of Leah in his arms, his countenance raw with pain for what she had suffered. 'Leah,' he said gently. 'Leah, speak to me.'

Her eyes fluttered open, and despite the drugs they'd given her she recognised him and her heart soared. 'Gideon,' she sighed softly. 'I had thought not to see you again.'

'We will never part again,' he vowed as he took her up in his arms, and with his crew in attendance strode off to the plantation house with her.

Her eyes fluttered open on a sigh, she had been having the most wonderful dream; Gideon had rescued her from William's devious hands. He had taken her in his arms and carried her back to the house and made sure she was cared for. Of course it was all fantasy; she was good at pretence, with her life she'd had to resort to dreams, for there was little else to keep her going.

Jane entered her bedchamber. 'Captain Tempest is asking to see you.'

198

'Gideon?' she gasped. 'Then I wasn't dreaming?'

Jane brushed her hair until it was gleaming, and though the drugs she'd been given to quieten her ready for the ceremony had left her with a headache, she forgot about it when Gideon entered.

He held her hand tightly as she related her tale of the grave and of William's plans for her, his mouth set in a grim line. 'I cannot bear to think of you in the hands of that scum,' he snarled.

'But now you are here and William is dead.' Her relief was like a huge weight lifted from her shoulders. 'And although I thank all that is holy for your intervention, I still do not understand how you happened to be at *Wildwinds*.'

'It's a long story,' he admitted. 'One I shall relate to you on the trip to Tortuga.'

Leah licked her dry lips. 'Tortuga? Is that not a pirate's lair?'

Gideon smiled. 'You could say that, but it is my home for the time being and will be for the foreseeable future.'

She smiled. 'Then it will be my home too.'

Chapter Fourteen

Spanish Bel lounged in an oversized hammock outside the hut she called home on Cayona Bay, on the island of Tortuga, sipping her favourite brew of rum fusion; a mix of beer, gin, sherry, rum and gunpowder. Her black luxuriant curls, usually tied up in a bright bandana, fanned out about her head. Her shirt was open to the waist, her firm breasts pouting eagerly in the sunshine. Her lower half was naked, her trim waist flaring out to slight hips and slim legs. Sharing the hammock with her was a swarthy buccaneer by the name of Jake Blood. His leg insinuated itself between Bel's thighs and he stuck a large weather-beaten toe in her cleft, stroking the damp channel lazily.

Bel sighed and played with her nipples, trying to keep her mind focused on the digit that played between her thighs, teasing her little bud out of its hood and making her wet. And although the sensations were sweet, part of her brain insisted on thinking of the Blade and his mission. He had decided to sail to Barbados to settle a debt with a planter, and she was anxious for him to return. She had dallied with many a buck on the island, but her heart was lost to the captain of the *Revenge*.

She would go down to the quay on the morrow, to watch for the billowing sails of the forty-gun vessel Blade had captured and worked on till it was fast and sleek and named *Revenge* to suit his purpose.

Her juices wept over Jake's toe, his answer was to circle the opening to her vagina, the sides of his mouth lifting when she sighed her pleasure. Bel wriggled contentedly, wondering how Blade fared. Although she had sailed with him when her own ship had been incapacitated, and shared his bed, she was unable to figure him out. He stood out among the rough buccaneers like a candle in the dark.

Jake inserted his toe into her slippery tunnel, fucked her with it, smiling wider when the dark-eyed beauty gasped and tensed her muscles before allowing her body to go with the flow.

Bel dropped her glass and it fell to the ground, hit a stone and shattered into a thousand pieces. But Bel didn't flinch; she tweaked her nipples harder, her body writhing sinuously beneath Jake's ministrations. She liked Jake, but as always she imagined it was Blade, the scourge of the Spanish Main, making sweet music between her thighs, imagined it was his suntanned hands tormenting her nipples into splendour.

She knew part of his charm was that he remained a complete enigma. He could be a dangerous enemy, as many knew to their detriment. And he was driven to search out the Spaniard scum who had killed his crew, had sworn to twist his knife in his gut, but he was usually against bloodshed. He treated his prisoners well, ransoming them off to their families in Spain. And she knew that many of the black-eyed wenches he captured were eager to lift their petticoats for him before being returned to their husbands, for he was irresistible.

Jake's toe found the tender spot of her vagina and circled it knowingly, and within seconds Bel's body rippled with delight as she reached her congress. Jake crawled up her tanned limbs and fed his cock inside her, sinking home with gusto, and the slim girl beneath him was soon lost in the dance of possession as she imagined the tall Captain Tempest riding her to fruition.

Spanish Bel stood on the quay watching anxiously for sight of the billowing sails of the *Revenge*, and gave a hugely relieved smile when she eventually spotted her. Blade was safe and she would make sure that she welcomed him so well he would spend that night in her arms.

She glanced around at Cayona Bay. She loved the atmosphere, loved everything about this buccaneer kingdom that was protected by an imposing stone mountain fort, its guns pointing menacingly seaward. The harbour was a forest of ships, their spars seeming to touch the perfect blue of the sky. The quay was thriving with humanity. There was a busy market in progress; traders from all over the Caribbean flocked to Tortuga to buy the goods the buccaneers brought to port.

Spanish Bel lent negligently against a large cask, hands deep in the pockets of her breeches. Blade had arrived back in time to attend the captains' meeting that afternoon. The buccaneer captains always discussed everything before they put to sea and their plunder was always split fairly with the crew. The Brethren had a strict code of behaviour.

Her eyes sparkled with pleasure when she saw the tall, broad form picking his way along the sunny quay a while later. But who did he have with him? Her eyes narrowed. A tall woman and a dainty blonde girl. As they came nearer Bel gripped the hilt of her sword, muttering angrily beneath her breath. 'Dios, the blonde is indeed beautiful.'

It became worse as buccaneers, whores and traders alike stopped in their tracks and ogled the pretty piece. She was extremely striking in a gown as blue as the sky, with lavender petticoats beneath. The low décolletage showed off her divine bosom, and she had the most glorious hair that flowed down her back in a golden cascade. She supposed her ringlets had been washed away in a rain shower, for these English maids went in for such things.

Bel stepped in front of the group when it reached her, her black eyes flashing fire. 'Blade, what has been washed aboard the *Revenge* this day?'

'Bel,' Gideon said absently, his eyes skimming over Leah with adoration. 'This is Leah, and her maid Jane.'

He gave no excuse for their being on his ship and Bel's hand still fingered the hilt of her sword, but with more purpose now. So, the Blade was in love! What did this milk and water girl have that she did not? She should slit that pretty white throat, and then there would be nothing to stand in her way. She would soon teach him to love her. After all, whose bed did he search out when he needed warm arms to hold him in the night? She had been halfway to making him hers, she knew it. Now it was all wasted.

She stared after Leah as Gideon handed her into a carriage, her eyes like knives in the blue-gowned back.

Completely unaware of the enemy she had inadvertently made, Leah chattered happily as the carriage wound its way through the crooked streets of the seaport, gasping in excitement when it stopped outside a large house done in white stucco, with intricately carved balconies on the upper storeys. The windows and doors were stoutly protected by grilles and there was a guard at the front door.

It was even more captivating on the inside. Exotic, jewel-coloured rugs hugged the floors, expensive paintings lined the white walls and the furniture was exquisite. Ebony cabinets and tables, inlaid with glorious fan-tailed peacocks, adorned the large sitting room. The surfaces of the tables were dotted with precious jade ornaments, bowls and boxes inlaid with rubies and emeralds. Deep cushioned sofas were arranged at intervals and Leah was lost for words.

Gideon showed them the map room that led off it, with its dark oak table covered with charts. It was a man's domain and Leah knew she would not spend much time there.

Gideon introduced them to the housekeeper. Dinah was a middle-aged, jolly woman, who immediately set about feeding them. She and Jane seemed to be kindred spirits and found out straightaway that they already had one love in common – Muffy, Gideon's first mate, a huge bear of a man with a black beard and a merry countenance.

'He's a dear man,' Dinah sighed, and Jane reciprocated.

Gideon took Leah's hand and led her out to a spectacular garden with blooms of every hue. 'I have things to do soon,' he said. 'But when I go I will leave some of my men to guard you.'

Leah viewed him innocently. 'What can harm us here?'

'Cayona contains some of the worst cutthroats in the world, and you are a beautiful young woman, Leah. Many would risk death to have you.'

Leah shrugged. 'I was in far more danger with my own husband. I don't think there is anything quite so bad in this lovely place.'

Gideon sighed. 'Let me have my way on this. I know better than you the dangers of Cayona.'

When he left, Jane, Dinah and Muffy were playing a game of cards in the kitchen, and she wandered to the bedchamber she'd been allotted and watched as he marched away, his sword glinting in the sunshine, his even strides fast eating up the curving path.

They had left *Wildwinds* in the capable hands of Silas Webster's cousin, Ralph, who after not having news of him for a goodly time, had come to the island in search of him. Gideon made him promise to free the slaves and pay them proper wages. Dominique had confessed her part in Silas

Webster's downfall and been sent out to work in the fields for her trouble.

Ralph Webster was intending to send for his family, and Leah was content knowing that *Wildwinds* would finally have a heart.

She had been in Gideon's home but a few days, sat beneath the shade of the pimento tree inhaling the fragrance of the tropical garden, when he announced that he had to set sail on the morning tide. She looked up at him with pleading eyes.

'So soon.' They had made passionate love for the last three nights and she was loath to see him go.

'It is unfortunate, but it has to be this way, my love. This is how I do a service to my country, by destroying the fleet of the Spanish who would deny the West Indies the rights of other countries.' His eyes clouded momentarily. 'And when I find the cur who put paid to my ship and killed my men I shall rest easy, but not until then.'

He had told her what happened to the *Pride* and she let him go with a prayer on her lips, her heart heavy. She saw him off on the quay the next morning, tears threatening. And although Muffy was obliged to sail with him, he left four trusty men to guard her, but she was fast becoming bored and just wanted some fun.

When she wanted to go out she was escorted by two buccaneers, who glowered at everyone who came near, though she was allowed to converse with the pastor of the little church on the island. Because of the dangerous trade the freebooters dealt in there were many doctors and surgeons in Tortuga, and these were also deemed respectable enough for her to keep company with, and she entertained these men and their ladies and was entertained in return.

One day she was on her way to the busy market when she saw two buccaneers tossing coins outside a tavern. A pretty dark girl watched them anxiously. Leah was curious and asked Thomas, one of the buccaneer's who accompanied her, what was going on.

Thomas shrugged and grinned. 'They both like the woman and she cannot make up her mind between them, so they are tossing coins for her.'

Leah giggled. 'No wonder she looks anxious. What happens then?'

'The one who loses the toss marries her; the other is allowed to share her bed when the husband is away. It is an old custom known as matelotage.'

'It sounds very reasonable to me,' she said, secretly envying the girl. At least she would always have someone to warm her in the dark nights, to wrap his arms around her and tend to her urges; all she had were her memories.

That was when she made her mind up to go looking for some excitement to alleviate her boredom. She loved Gideon dearly, but she was finding his protection of her increasingly smothering. The streets and taverns were full of life, and she hankered after some freedom, some time without Gideon's guards making her feel like a prisoner in his house. The two problems would be evading them, and disguising herself. It would not do for Gideon to find out about her little adventure.

Excitement churned in her stomach as she opened one of the chests Gideon had taken from the Spanish, and peered inside. There was much gold and jewellery, and some black gowns of a heavy material that looked extremely scratchy. Then, to her abject delight, she found a dark wig and her plan took wings. She would make her face up like the wenches of the taverns. Wearing heavy make-up and the black wig no one would suspect that she was Blade's woman.

She settled on one of her own simple day dresses, from which she left off the pretty scarf that hid most of her bosom. Instead her breasts were naked almost to the nipples, and she added some ceruse to the pearly globes and some perfume in the valley between.

Slipping out onto her balcony she peered over the edge.

The two buccaneers guarding the front of the house were stationed to her right, deep in conversation. If she could manage to climb down the vine that clung to the balcony she could evade them by using the shrubbery around the house as her shield.

The men were conversing in low tones, boasting about their conquests. One leered lecherously. ''Twas a night like no other. Maisie was sucking me cock and Rosie was playing with me balls. In front of me Jenny was busy taking off her clothes, licking her lips and feeling her tits. Big 'uns they was, just like cannonballs, with nipples I swear were the colour of the hibiscus that blooms over yonder.'

His mate nodded and sucked harder on his clay pipe. 'What did ye do, Robbie?'

'Why, I watched her diddle herself till she fell on the bed all done in. Then I pushed the others away and fucked her good and hard, I did. Then I fucked the rest,' he boasted. 'I can tell ye, I needed a drop o' rum after that.'

The other was now giving an account of his adventures in low tones, and she prayed they would not hear her descent. She climbed over the balustrade, and pushing her skirts out of the way, clung to the vine and made her way down, wishing the moon were not so bright, for if they chanced to look up she would be in full view.

Just when she thought she was going to make it some of the vine broke loose and fell to the ground, almost taking her with it, but luckily she found the firmer support of a thicker vine just in time and flattened herself against the wall, hardly daring to breathe. Alerted by the noise the buccaneers moved towards the bushes, but just then a cat ran screeching from its hiding place, obviously frightened by the fallen creeper.

'Damn ye, ye four-legged devil!' cried one in obvious relief, while the other laughed loudly though shakily into the darkness.

'We'd best keep our eyes open,' said Robbie. 'The Blade'll skin us if anything happens to his lady.'

They rested a few yards away from where she hung precariously on the vine, and she cursed quietly. Her hands were becoming numb and she didn't think she could hold on for much longer, when the sound of raucous singing interrupted her train of thought. Some drunken buccaneers were coming up the street. The guards moved away from the shrubbery, their hands near their cutlasses.

It was a chance in a million; Leah climbed hurriedly down to the ground and stayed in the cover of the bushes. The guards, learning that the revellers were friends, began exchanging banter and Leah made gratefully away.

She walked swiftly down the crooked streets to the taverns without being stopped once, although some merry seafarers whistled and called after her, adding to her excitement. Some loud grunts from a doorway alerted her to a couple who'd been taken with lust in the street and had pounced on one another in the shadows. Leah stopped as their cries of passion rose to join in with the sound of the music in a nearby tavern, the flares from its doorway illuminating the scene, and she watched in astonishment as they tore aside their clothes, eager to meet flesh to flesh. The woman's legs wound around the man's middle and he thrust into her with great precision. So taken up with each other were they, they did not bat an eyelid when another drunken buccaneer joined them, so thrilled at the sight of the naked pair he began licking the girl's arse.

Leah knew she should move on, but she was so excited by the scene she could do nothing but watch. As the two rutted like animals, so the man pushed his tongue further up the woman's arse until he was fucking her with it. She moaned and the stranger began feeling the other buccaneer's balls, the first buccaneer quite happy with the situation, making a satisfied groan in his throat.

So shamefully turned on was Leah she lifted her skirts, and leaning in the shadows against a wall nearby slid a finger into her cleft and began to rub her nubbin. A single drunken buccaneer almost fell out of the tavern, but he was not so drunk he could not see what was going on. He glanced over at the threesome with interest, but when he spotted the dainty wench diddling herself, her belly and legs on delightful display, he soon sobered.

'Come, my pretty,' he drooled, lest he frighten her, 'don't waste this night by frigging yourself. Let Raoul pleasure you. My cock is bursting for some sport.'

Leah felt little fear or embarrassment, she was far too taken with chasing her crisis, and when the buccaneer lifted her and hauled her legs up around his waist she felt strangely unable to resist. His cock nudged against her tummy, but he soon managed to adjust his stance and buried it inside her, and was rewarded with a cry as she thrust with him, her bottom jogging up and down in his calloused hands.

The threesome in the doorway changed positions. The girl was now on all fours on the ground while the second buccaneer stabbed his cock into her from behind, as the first began fucking his fellow freebooter's arse.

Leah watched them in delight, getting so much excitement from their debauched liaison, right there in the street, her juices running freely over her own partner's cock.

'You're a sexy wench,' he growled. 'I can't recall the last time I had one so hot.'

Leah barely heard him; his cock was driving her to distraction and she reached her zenith with loud sobs of satisfaction.

The buccaneer let her down when he reached his own congress, and after giving her a kiss on the cheek rolled off down the street.

Leah gazed up at the moon, shocked and confused by her own behaviour and emotions, and then moved on unsteadily, leaving the copulating threesome still hard at it, not seeing the Spanish woman who'd been watching Gideon's house for such a stroke of luck, and who followed her stealthily until she stopped her but a street away and held a knife to her throat.

208

'I have you now, blonde one,' Bel growled triumphantly as she stole the wig from her head and shook it out with a cynical hoot of laughter. 'So you grow weary of your own company in Blade's absence. Your cunny tingles for the feel of a man's cock, while your titties need to feel the hardness of weather-beaten fingers. Well, I think I can help us both. Now let us see what is so special about you.' With the sharp edge of the knife she sliced Leah's gown and chemise from her shoulders, leaving the ragged ends drooping so that her breasts were completely exposed. Bel caressed the bare flesh roughly. 'So these are the titties Blade feels when his lust is up.' She pulled on the nipples so hard Leah cried out in pain. 'I can't blame him for that. You are a comely wench. Mayhap we can share you. 'Twould not be the first time we've shared a woman before fucking each other.'

Bel leered over her and Leah tried to drag herself out of her grasp. 'Don't touch me!'

Bel hooted with glee. 'Be quiet! 'Tis time you danced to Bel's tune, my lovely.'

Leah's hands were swiftly bound, and she was bundled down to the softly lapping water's edge and thrown into the bottom of a rowing boat. She was amazed at Bel's brute strength, for the woman was slim and her appearance denied the whipcord musculature honed by her rough life.

Leah was rowed across the calm harbour, the oars rattling in the rowlocks and their blades softly splashing as they sculled through the water. Bel's mouth was set in a grim line. People had thought it strange at first that she, a Spanish woman, should attack the ships of her own country, but Bel had no love for her own kind. She was the product of a Spanish don and a serving wench from Santo Domingo, Hispaniola. From birth she was ridiculed and despised. She felt she fit in nowhere, and at the first opportunity she stowed away on a ship hoping to get as far away as possible from her lowly beginnings.

The ship had been taken by buccaneers, but Bel felt no fear and stared undaunted at the big, brash, blond captain, thrilled to his touch, happy to be the ship's whore. Eric Danvers had been struck by her courage and soon learned her story, and how she longed to hurt the people who had hurt her.

Fascinated by this enigma of a woman, Eric taught her everything he knew. Bel was a willing and adept pupil and soon they were plundering the Spanish West Indies together.

When Eric was caught by an unlucky cannonball and died he left her his ship, and she gladly became captain of her own vessel. She had little trouble from the other buccaneers, for she had long proved herself to them and gained their respect.

They were soon at the side of the *Caribbean Queen*. Bel untied Leah, and switching the knife for a pistol from her belt, ordered her to climb the rope ladder to the decks of the ship. Leah longed to tell the Spanish woman what to do with her ship, but with a pistol staring her in the face there was nothing she could do but follow orders.

The man on watch lifted an eyebrow in surprise as the half naked girl climbed onto the decks under the gaze of the shapely Bel. But he wasn't overcome with curiosity; Bel had a raging craving for sex and she often brought wenches aboard to share with the men. Many an orgy had taken place on the *Queen* and Wilf' rubbed his hands in glee. If he was lucky a merry time would soon be had.

Bel tied Leah to the main mast, and going below called for the cabin boy. 'Send for the crew on the morrow. Tell them I have a tasty morsel to share with them.' That said she mixed her favourite brew of rumfusion and lay down on her bunk with a happy sigh, trailing her fingers in her cleft, rubbing herself to fruition. Then with her belly full of booze and her loins eased she fell into a deep sleep, her loud snores filling the cabin.

Leah strained at her bonds, fearful of the Spanish woman's plans for her. Bel had left her with a sly glint in her dark eyes and a hearty promise. 'Come the morning you will feel the sweet kiss of Bel's lash. Blade did not think me

210

fit to share his woman, and you will be punished for that. I have called for my crew to join us. I think they might enjoy the sight of your pretty back being whipped, and mayhap they will enjoy fucking Blade's whore when I have done.'

Leah refused to let her tears fall, though they stung the corners of her eyes. Let Bel do her worst, she would spit in her face and when Gideon returned he would punish the Spanish woman so hard she'd be sorry she was ever born.

Gideon, quite unaware of the drama being played out aboard the *Caribbean Queen*, was still with some of the buccaneer fleet. They had sighted a ship while en route off Eastern Hispaniola, that was outbound from Puerto Rico to Mexico, and gone in pursuit and finally captured her.

She was found to be carrying a wealthy cargo of cocoa, jewellery and gold. The men rejoiced at their good fortune, each silently totting up what his personal share of the plunder would be. The richly loaded ship was sent to Tortuga, where she was unloaded and sent back with a cargo of provisions to the island of Savona, where the expedition had awaited her return.

They decided to go on to plunder Maracaibo. But Gideon would not agree to this, his war was with the ships of Spain and no one else.

Francis L'Olonnois, unused to having his orders questioned, wheeled on his favourite. 'Then I suggest, Monsieur Blade, that you consider yourself no longer part of this venture.'

Gideon's dark eyes blazed. While he had no love for Spaniard's and would fight to the last in a fair battle, he would not stay and be party to L'Olonnois' whimsy for gain at any price. However, there was nothing he could do to prevent it either, for although the full fleet numbered seven hundred men, this was a goodly part of it and, though he was well respected, they had come on the mission for booty and none would go against L'Olonnois.

'If I cannot persuade you to change your mind I will not

stay to take part in any of it.' So saying he gathered up his crew, and boarding the *Revenge* set sail with much complaining from the men. But those dissatisfied with Gideon's decision made sure not to grouse in their captain's hearing, for it would not bode them well.

Gideon was determined not to return to Tortuga until he found a prize, and no one argued on that score. One fine morning, with the wind fresh and the sea the colour of the turquoise gown Leah had worn to see him off at the quay, Gideon heard the cry go up that a sail was sighted. He was still seething with anger over L'Olonnois, but this soon turned to excitement. The vessel was the *Santa Maria*, the ship that had captured the *Pride* on the fateful day that would be etched in Gideon's memory forever.

The Spanish captain mistook the *Revenge* for a large merchant ship and happily gave the order to pursue. It was, Captain Juarez assumed, a routine capture of a worthy prize, and his greed was such it could not be ignored.

At this point Gideon pulled a cunning trick; he turned *Revenge* away and the *Santa Maria* pressed after him. Gideon kept out to sea, running before the wind, but he allowed the Spaniard to gain on him slowly.

At ten-thirty the ships were within range, and Captain Juarez ordered his men to battle stations. By eleven the Santa Maria was within musket shot of the *Revenge*, so with great speed and precision Gideon turned her to starboard and let fly a devastating broadside.

This turn of events momentarily stunned the Spanish captain and *Revenge's* guns once more found their mark. There was a distinct smell of burning as smoke billowed from the Spanish ship. The main mast and rigging were shattered and came crashing down to the deck.

Captain Juarez collected his wits, but was stung into action too late and well before the smoke had cleared his vessel was crawling with buccaneers.

Gideon fought his way fiercely through the Spanish, intent on making a path to his arch enemy. When he reached his target the recognition on Juarez's face was instant. Gideon laughed dryly. 'Ah, so you know me, Spanish dog!'

'I only know that you are as good as dead, senior,' Juarez replied defiantly.

Gideon perceived the sly shift in his black eyes and sidestepped just in time to miss a Spanish sword slicing into his back. His knife found its way into the seaman's heart, but Gideon found himself facing the captain's pistol. As it fired he flung himself aside, but was wounded in his left shoulder, his rage so great he hardly felt the pain, grateful only that his sword arm was unharmed.

He circled Juarez, eyes glinting with revenge. Juarez glanced around helplessly, wishing he had paid more attention to his orders. He carried a valuable cargo and had been warned not to make any diversions, but his thirst for blood was too great to ignore and the *Revenge* had seemed an easy target.

Seeing his indecision, Gideon laughed. 'You cannot escape me, captain. I shall kill you and the ghosts of my murdered crew will taunt your embittered soul until it descends to hell!'

The vision Gideon presented brought beads of sweat to Juarez's forehead. He drew his sword and the two captains clashed on the small forecastle deck of *Santa Maria*, a fight Gideon had pictured over and over in his imagination since the *Pride* was taken.

Blood was oozing rapidly from his wound, but Gideon was ready to fight to the death, and Juarez, sensing his determination decided to make a quick end to the English pig, just as he had seen off his crew.

But he underestimated Gideon's prowess. He was not called the Blade in jest, and when his sword sliced into the Spaniard's heart, Juarez's eyes opened wide in shocked amazement before he slumped to the deck.

Gideon wiped the Spaniard's blood from his sword, sparing one last glance at the face that had borne his hatred these past years. There was no glow of triumph, no sense of exhilaration, but a feeling of peace swept over him, and turning to the sea he lifted his sword in a final salute to the crew of the *Pride*.

The ship's doctor soon patched him up; it was not a deep wound and would soon heal. The good news was that the *Santa Maria* carried much gold and many jewels – the greatest jewel of all the daughter of a Spanish Ambassador who had been to see some of her family in Hispaniola and was now travelling back home. Muffy brought the Spanish girl to Gideon's quarters, and he surveyed her with interest.

'You are beautiful,' he said, in the Spanish he'd learned from the many prisoners taken along the Main. She wore a white mantilla and a gown of white also; she looked like an exquisite bride on the way to her wedding, though he knew that Spanish women dressed mainly in black or white.

The senorita was just as taken with Gideon, but knew it would not do to appear too eager to romance the handsome English captain. She was quite unafraid of him and felt little pity for the overbearing Captain Juarez. 'Thank you, captain,' she said, fluttering her long eyelashes at him. 'My name is Catalina Menendez.'

Gideon offered her some Madeira and she moved around the cabin, curiously touching his maps and all the paraphernalia a captain needed to run his ship. 'You do not seem fazed by what has happened,' he averred in surprise.

The minx shook her head. 'My duenna was slightly injured in the attack and now lies in the bunk of your kind doctor. This is the first bit of adventure I have known. I am not usually allowed so close to handsome men, captain. I am expected to remain a virgin until I marry. My husband has already been chosen and he is a doddery old man who will expect me to share his bed until he cannot fuck any more.'

Gideon reeled with shock. 'I had not thought you cognisant of such language.'

The senorita giggled. 'The servants are sometimes careless with their words.' Casting all modesty aside she lent against him, plucking at his jerkin, her legs rubbing against

214

the leathern breeches that clad his long limbs. 'Take me in your strong arms, captain,' she urged. 'Let me lose my virginity to a young and handsome man before it is too late.'

Gideon was all man and could not resist this offer. His heart was with Leah, but it did not mean he could ignore his bodily urges. The young Spanish girl's perfume set his senses aglow, her soft body all curves beneath the white of her gown.

'Senorita,' he sighed as she pressed closer and his cock grew hard in his breeches, 'you are giving me little choice in the matter.'

'That is good,' she purred. 'Then take me, captain, for I am all yours.'

Her eyes were the eyes of a siren, and he knew that some girls were born with the knowledge of sensuality; it surged in their blood like the tide. He supposed it was the tide of life, for where would they be without that secret knowledge, without the clamour of feelings that made a woman want a man and a man want a woman?

He lifted her from her feet and laid her in his bunk, slowly stripping her of each piece of clothing until she lay before him in all her virgin glory, her small but perfect breasts rising and falling temptingly as she breathed. Gideon enfolded each one tenderly, the silk of her thighs beneath his making him throb with want.

She gasped and shuddered involuntarily. 'I have never felt such a wonderful thing before,' she admitted, 'as the touch of your hands on my flesh.'

'And your flesh is like the most expensive satin,' he returned, sketching his fingers down over her flat belly to the black curls that covered her femininity. His fingers lingered for a while, caressed the area above her pelvic bone, and she kissed him as passionately as any sexually aware woman ever could.

He slid his hands into her wet core and plunged a finger deep inside. She moaned softly and he swiftly followed with his penis. It thrust into her like a sword and she cried out at the pain. But when he soothed her and began to move inside her, building to a crescendo that swept them both away to the height of ecstasy, she knew how heavenly the mating of a man and woman could be.

Spanish Bel moved lithely around her prisoner, her whip periodically snapping against her thigh. 'You still look beautiful,' she intoned lazily, running a hand over one naked breast.

Leah cringed, she was tired, she had been hanging from the mast all night, and apart from some water her stomach was empty. Not that she was hungry, the thought of food made her want to retch. Bel's men had arrived on deck first thing, delighted at the sight of the lovely captive. They had grabbed her breasts, her bottom, some even insinuated fingers in her cleft. They took bets on who would have her first, after Bel punished her. Even now their faces leered at her and she closed her eyes in order to shut them out. Why hadn't she listened to Gideon? Why had her head been overruled by her quest for excitement? Tears squeezed from her eyelids when she thought of the way she blatantly watched the buccaneers and the girl in the doorway the previous evening, of the way she had allowed a stranger to have sex with her out there in the streets of Cayona Bay. She would never live down the shame.

Bel walked round her for the umpteenth time, and she trembled. The woman was obviously enjoying parading her in front of her men. 'Do it,' Leah demanded. 'Get it over with.'

Bel's lips lifted into a smile. 'See how eager she is to feel the caress of Bel's whip. How lovely her face is in her fear. I wonder if Blade's groin aches every time he sees her looking so radiant.'

Without further preamble Bel snapped the whip across Leah's back; it was but a tickle, she knew. The woman was leaving the worst until last. A second and a third snap took away the remnants of her gown and the crew threw their fists in the air and cheered upon sight of the naked girl hanging from the mast of their ship.

'Her cunny's pretty,' jeered one.

'Her sex is just ripe for sucking,' said another, and many voices agreed with him.

Bel lashed harder with the whip and Leah screamed. But Bel had no mercy and continued with one stroke after another until Leah hung limp from her bindings, barely aware of anything any more. Bel directed someone to douse her with a bucket of water, and laughed when the girl came round with a start as the icy water drenched her.

'Your back is crisscrossed with the marks of Bel's whip,' she stated with pride. 'But you bore it well. As a reward you will be tended with a healing cream that will take away the pain and make you feel better.'

Bel was true to her word, and the ship's doctor tended Leah gently. But when done she was retied to the mast, facing forward this time, and as the crew lined up for her, Leah bit her lip fearfully. She was being treated far worse than the lowest whore in Tortuga's taverns; at least they got to pick the man they slept with.

She glowered at Bel. 'You'll pay for this,' she warned weakly, but her persecutor's answer was a hearty laugh and a nod to the buccaneer who had drawn lots with the others and won the right to have her first. The man was a ruggedly handsome seafarer with blond tresses tied back from his face. He touched her hesitantly at first, but when the others jeered at him to hurry he took his meat out of his breeches and plunged into her.

One buccaneer after the other vied for the pleasure of taking Blade's lady, smoothing her golden curls and kissing the ruby lips that tasted even better than expected. Leah's fear was replaced with a dawning realisation that none of these men wished her harm – not serious harm, anyway. They were merely taking advantage of the chance to have a beautiful young woman. With this knowledge she began to relax a little, kissing the lusty buccaneers back when they kissed her, moving her hips with them when they fucked her, finding a kind of paradise inside her body.

After the last man had his way with her Bel cut her down, and had someone sluice water over her. She ordered that she be carried to her cabin, where she was laid in her bunk and Bel patted her dry herself. 'You did well,' she said, smoothing a soft towel over the reddened skin of her back, softly towelling her breasts, her stomach, and when she dipped into the cleft beneath the blonde curls her fingers were even gentler. 'You would make a worthy buccaneer.'

Leah looked into the dark eyes that viewed her with admiration, and smiled wearily. This was indeed a great compliment.

Bel mirrored her smile. 'You must know that I love the Blade,' she admitted. 'I was jealous of you.'

Leah gasped as the woman paid special attention to her clit. 'Does... does he feel the same?' she asked nervously, for she thought she would die if he did.

'He does not love me,' Bel said sadly. 'But he likes me very much and we please each other from time to time.' Bel laid aside the towel, and giving up all pretence, began to stroke her clit. 'You understand?'

Leah nodded, her body still aching from Bel's punishment and the men's cocks, and yet still receptive to the pleasure of her fingers on her sensitive nub. 'I think so.'

Bel smiled. 'But I do not feel the jealousy any more, because I find you very attractive.' One hand reached out and stroked Leah's neck and shoulders. 'In fact,' she said with a small sigh, 'I want you for myself.'

Leah's body was reacting shamefully to Bel's caresses as the pain she'd suffered made her enjoy the woman's attentions all the more. 'You... you do?'

Bel nodded. 'I can give you as much pleasure as Blade,' she boasted. 'I am as tough as any of the men on this ship. And although I don't have a cock I can please you in other ways.'

She stroked Leah's breasts, licking her pink aureoles

218

before paying special attention to her nipples, and when Leah was sighing with pleasure she brought out what looked like a hairbrush from underneath the bunk. Upon closer inspection, it was obviously not for grooming. For one thing it was much longer than a hairbrush, with one end fashioned like a man's phallus. The other end sported a few stiff bristles, but Bel's smile told her it was not made to use on hair.

'Take it,' she purred. 'Use it on your little pleasure nub.'

Leah shook her head. 'I would prefer it if you would show me how.'

Her green eyes were now sparkling with desire and Bel giggled. 'Does Blade know what a hot little trollop you are?'

Leah sighed. 'You whipped the devil into me, Bel, and I am lost.'

'No, querida, you will never be lost when Bel is around.' She moved the dildo, and using the spiky side circled it over Leah's clit, who cooed like a dove as her dew seeped and covered the love toy.

'Oh, how lovely,' she gasped. 'I shall come in seconds with you doing that to me.'

Bel's only answer was to smile smugly as she lowered her dark head and took one of Leah's nipples into her mouth.

Leah stretched out on the bunk, glassy-eyed, her mouth slightly open as the woman made love to her. And she was correct in her assumption; within seconds the toy had brought her to a convulsive orgasm.

Bel disrobed and lay on top of her, smoothing her body sinuously over the girl's flesh. Their pubes met and separated, their nipples kissed, broke away just as quickly only to meet again, as the knowing Bel rubbed herself all over her. It was only when Leah was completely incoherent with lust that Bel inserted the dildo and fucked her ferociously. When Leah's juices were flowing freely Bel began to lick her channel, lapping and sucking until Leah came again.

Leah snuggled up to her afterwards, her body aching with

a pain that only made her satisfaction all the more real, made it sing with a wonderful fulfilment. 'You love as well as any man, except Gideon,' she whispered as they lay together, their legs entwined, while Bel guided Leah's fingers to her clit.

'Then I am happy.'

Leah gave her a loving glance. 'But I can make you even happier.' With feline grace she moved between Bel's thighs and began licking her clit, and at the same time she finger-fucked her.

'Ah, chica,' Bel purred. 'You play me like a violin. But when I am done I want to see what it is like in Blade's fine bed.'

Leah paused momentarily, Bel's dew coating her lips. 'We shall have a sleep, and then go to Gideon's house where we shall fuck all night long.'

Gideon nodded to the guard outside his front door. The man nodded back. 'All is well, captain.'

Gideon had but one thought on his mind; he needed to reach his bed where his love would be waiting for him. She would wrap her arms around him and they would dance the divine dance she did so well.

But when he climbed the stairs he heard voices and the sound of a woman crying in ecstasy. With his hand on the head of his basket-hilted sword he swung the door of the bedchamber open, to see his Leah being serviced by Spanish Bel. The woman was lying over her, and Leah had her face in the pillow, her delightful bottom bobbing in the air while Bel wielded a dildo in her arse.

'What is this?' he snapped, and both stopped and turned to him.

'Gideon!' Leah cried. 'I did not expect you.'

'That couldn't be more obvious.'

Bel eyed him warily. They had shared women before, but this particular one was different, she was his love. 'We were overcome,' she excused.

Gideon regarded the naked pair silently, his face a livid mask of anger. Then relieving himself of his baldric, he removed the pistols from his belt and, sitting on the bed, pulled Leah over his lap in one swift movement. He surveyed her back. 'You've been whipped,' he drawled.

Bel licked her lips nervously. She might die this night, but at least she would die with the taste of the sweet Leah on her tongue. 'I punished her.'

'And?'

'She took it with great courage.'

'Did the crew fuck you?' he asked Leah, fully aware of what Bel got up to on her ship.

'Y-yes, Gideon.'

'And did she enjoy it?' he asked of Bel.

'She did,' she confirmed. 'As did every man aboard.'

He viewed Leah gravely. 'Then this time I shall punish you.'

He raised his large hand and brought it down on her left cheek. Then he spanked her right cheek, and Leah had barely felt anything so good; Gideon's hand firm and heavy, spanking her well, the marks from his palm soon added to those Bel had given her, making her almost senseless with need as the most wonderful climax overtook her.

Gideon viewed the blotchy marks on her bottom with satisfaction. 'I'll be the one to say who you shall and shall not sleep with,' he ground out angrily, tipping her off his lap. 'Bel may wear breeches but I am the master here. Is that clear?'

He glowered down at her as she lay on the floor where he'd tipped her. 'Yes, Gideon,' she said submissively, loving this side of him even more.

'Bel,' he snorted, 'over my knee. You have a lot of making up to do before our friendship returns to the old footing.'

Bel, head bent, crawled over his lap. 'Yes, captain, you are right. I have been very bad.'

Her bottom rode the slaps well, and when he finished she

221

was thrown onto the bed along with Leah, where the two lay side by side looking up at the tall buccaneer removing his breeches.

His erection seemed even larger than usual, and Leah's eyes widened. 'Open your legs, wench,' he growled. 'I'm going to fuck you until you can't walk.' He looked at Bel. 'Then when I've rested it will be your turn. And mark me well; if I have to I shall rip the skin off your arses to teach you that I am master in my own house.'

Leah opened her thighs, readying herself for the rigid cock that threatened from between his legs. 'You shall always be master,' she said softly, knowing she had found her niche in the world. Rose was right in her predictions; there had been the objectionable Percy and the foul William, but now she was with Gideon, and he was the only master she wanted.

For a copy of our free title newsletter please write to

Chimera Publishing Ltd
Readers' Services
PO Box 152
Waterlooville
Hants
PO8 9FS

or email us at
info@chimera-online.co.uk

or purchase from our range of superbly erotic titles at
www.chimera-online.co.uk

The full range of our titles are also available as
downloadable ebooks at our website

www.chimera-online.co.uk

***

www.chimerabooks.co.uk
www.chimerasextoys.co.uk
www.chimeralingerie.co.uk

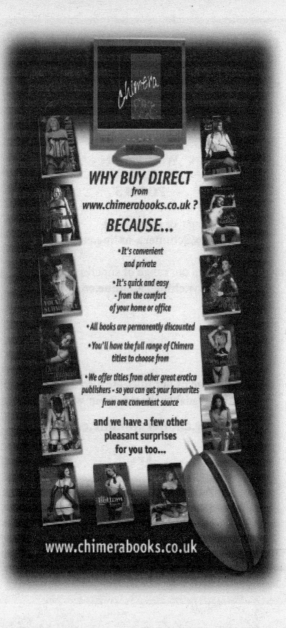